To Aar

May all your flying dreams come true!

Mahina Rises

John Blossom

Aloha,
John Blossom
Dec. 13, 2025

Published by J.T. Blossom, 2024.

This is a work of fiction. Similarities to real people, places, or events are entirely coincidental.

MAHINA RISES

First edition. October 1, 2024.

Written by John Blossom.

Mahina Rises

By John Blossom

Prologue

"MAHINA, DAUGHTER, LISTEN carefully. Come to me and learn to fly! Here's how you do it: Leave doubt and fear outside, even when things seem hopeless. Break down the wall that is blocking your portal and enter the lava tube. Walk until you feel our family's power.

"When the time is right, stand as straight as you can with your eyes closed. Tighten all your muscles. Crinkle your brow. Concentrate harder than you have ever done before. Dig deeply, believe, and think, 'Up, up, up!'

"When you feel yourself rising, trust yourself. Bend your knees and raise your heels to the back of your legs. Settle comfortably onto the cool damp air and lean forward. Open your eyes. Drift ahead and float deep into the tunnel.

"When a luminous cavern opens in front of you, look up and ascend through the bright opening in the roof toward the sun. Flying is our next power, your power. You will be the first to breathe the cool and pure high air carried by the winds, to zoom over hills, mountains, and trees, and to play tag with the birds. Clouds and rainbows will shimmer their grateful welcome for you to enjoy.

"You may have doubts and think about falling. Acknowledge these and let them go, but if the rainbows disappear, and the clouds get dark

and stormy, descend and know that the earth is suffering and expressing its confusion and anger. The Moemoea Family does not give up. Just hike back to the entrance and start over.

"Flying is the final expression of our family's healing mana. Embrace it. Pass it on. Inside every human is a better world waiting to be discovered, and the planet's storms will go away if everyone concentrates very hard. *Oh, daughter, you are the next leader in a long line of powerful leaders! Revel in our cavern mana until every doubt disappears, and the earth and all living creatures breathe freely again. The time is now. You are needed. Don't delay. Learn to fly, my daughter! Come to me and rise into your purpose and light!"*

Chapter One

Mahina Moemoea lay under the covers with a frown on her face, remembering the thunder and lightning that accompanied the urgent but loving words in her dream. Was it really the voice of her mother who spoke to her from the cave every night? Yes, she felt it really was, but she had no way of knowing for sure because her mom and dad had died when she was too little to remember them.

She had only Olina to comfort her in the morning when she woke from her dreams. She reached across her pillow to pet the cat's soft black and white fur. "I love you, Olina. You're my beautiful girl," she whispered.

It was windy out, and she could hear her tutu downstairs making breakfast with the radio on, but the busy clattering of pans on the stove was nearly drowned out by the fierce gusts hitting the house.

In the dim light, Mahina looked sleepily out her second-story window and longed to be able to fly in reality as she flew most nights in her dreams. Even in this wind, she could imagine soaring over the pastures of her ohana's thousand-acre homestead with her long black hair streaming behind her. She smiled. Every day the utter beauty of her nightly flying made her heart flutter with excitement, but this morning's dream settled with a different feeling. Her smile faded, and she rubbed her eyes.

The house shuddered again. The wind was really very strong. Her frown deepened when she noticed the eucalyptus trees along the pasture fence bending wildly in the growing dawn. Yikes, the hurricane!

She rolled out of bed, sending Olina flying, and scurried to the bathroom remembering the scary weather reports on the radio last night. Scary, especially because her parents had perished in the last hurricane, a category two that blew in shortly after she was born thirteen years ago. She wished she knew more about how they died, but it was a family tragedy that Tutu never liked talking about.

She splashed water on her face. This hurricane, Byron, was even bigger, the radio had said, like so many around the world these days. It was a category five hurricane, one that had never hit the Island of Hawaii before. Most storms skirted to the south, she learned, and Tutu had said everyone was counting on that. But hurricanes were tracking farther north now due to the warming oceans, and being so big and strong, Byron had a worrying chance of hitting them. The weather announcer said it measured four hundred miles wide and was located only a few hundred miles east when Tutu turned the radio off with shaky fingers and told her to go to bed.

"Tutu! What's happening? Is this the hurricane?" Mahina said, descending the stairs to the bright kitchen. The power was still on.

"No, Granddaughter," said Tutu, reaching her rough and wrinkled hand over the stove to turn down the radio. "Not yet. It's still over the ocean, moving slowly."

"Any news?"

"Other than it will probably hurt the ones least responsible for it, our people, rather than the mainlanders who caused it? No. They are still saying it will likely veer south."

"No one called from school?" Out the kitchen window, she saw that the wind had died down for the moment, but it was starting to rain hard.

"The rich people's school? They don't care about storms and the ʻāina's problems. It's more important to them to teach the next generation to be as destructive as the last one, right?"

"Oh, Tutu. Poʻokela is not like that at all. I love it there, and it's not just because they let me be a freshman. The teachers love Hawaii, and they care deeply about the environment, especially Ms.

Reynolds. No one makes fun of me there. They like smart kids no matter how young they are."

"Hmph," said Tutu. "Well, you've got to go somewhere, unfortunately, and they did let you skip a grade and give you a full scholarship. Still, it'd be mo' better if you could just stay on the ranch with me every day. You have the Moemoea Ohana's size and strength, and I could use more of your help around here. But that's against the law nowadays, even though it would be the best thing for you." Tutu sighed. "Go get started on your chores so you won't be late for the bus. Wear your raincoat and boots. I'll have your breakfast and lunch made for you when you're pau."

Chapter Two

"My parents almost kept me home today. They should have," shouted Mahina's friend Koa as they sprinted through the rain across the Po'okela Academy campus to Ms. Reynold's English class. The winds were as strong in town as they were on the ranch. She loved to talk story with Koa, and lately she didn't mind that people she didn't know probably gossiped that they were going together.

Her friends knew that because Koa and she were the same age and the best students in the class, they naturally liked to hang out together to chat and do homework. They didn't go for boyfriend and girlfriend stuff like holding hands or anything, although she wouldn't mind if they did.

Koa Kahale was dark and handsome, a little smaller than Mahina, but just as strong and the best wave-thrasher in the school. He was thirteen and had also skipped a grade at Po'okela before enrolling. They had a lot in common, but she mostly loved that he enjoyed using his imagination. The best part about classes so far was debating with him in English, but she also loved talking with him about books and making up stories and games at lunch and between periods.

Disheveled, they reached the steps to the classroom lanai, and she looked up at the dark, swirling clouds. She knew that today Koa wasn't making up a story about the wisdom of staying home. The sky was as ominous in reality as it had been in her dream last night. She thought about the dangerous monster lurking and swirling just off shore over the ocean.

"Right? What are we *doing* here, anyway?" she shouted to him as they crossed the lanai to the classroom door. "The bus was really getting tossed around, but the radio said the best prediction is that the hurricane will swing to the south. There goes Hilo, I guess."

"I hope not," said Koa using both hands to hold the wind-blown door open for her. "My mom says Mauna Kea and Mauna Loa are tall enough to stop any storm dead in its tracks, but my dad disagrees with her because this storm is so big. The mountains should slow it down, though, I think. I hope so, anyway."

They slipped into the classroom and let the door slam behind them.

Their English teacher, Ms. Reynolds, was dressed in heavy-duty rain gear today instead of her signature wrap-around skirts.

"Hi, Ms. Reynolds!" Mahina said.

"Good morning, Mahina. Hi, Koa. I hope you brought your umbrellas today!"

"No one uses umbrellas on this island, Ms. Reynolds. This isn't New York!" she said, smiling at her. She knew Ms. Reynolds' previous job was teaching at NYU.

Ms. Reynolds laughed. "Yes, I realized why, when the winds popped mine inside out this morning! Let's hope the weather doesn't get any worse."

"My dad says it might," Koa said. "This storm—what are they calling it? Byron?—could go any number of ways, including right over Waimea."

"Well, let's hope not!" said Ms. Reynolds. "But if it did, I wouldn't be surprised. Online it says that hurricanes are more likely to hit Hawaii now. The Pacific Ocean is in turmoil, and climate change has made everything so different and unpredictable." She shook her head.

The rest of the students in their class blew in like a hurricane themselves and took seats in the circle of desks, chatting about the storm. Before they even had their books out, the skies opened up with a waterfall of rain that pelted the roof and rattled the windows of the classroom that once was an old farm cottage. She thought about Tutu in her own cottage at home.

"This storm seems worse here than they said it would be," she called out to Ms. Reynolds over the pounding. "Don't you think we should go home?!"

As if to answer her, an announcement came beeping over the phone on Ms. Reynold's desk. "This is a notice that school is canceled for today. Parents have been contacted to come pick up students. If you can't get a ride at this time, please come to the office, and a bus will take you home. Do not walk home, even if you live close by. I repeat, *do not walk*. Come to the office, and a bus will take you home."

"That can only mean one thing," said Koa. "My dad was right. The storm didn't veer south! It's headed right for us! Come on, Mahina. You don't have to wait for the bus. My dad and I can take you home."

The class bustled out merrily, everyone excited to get the day off of school.

"So long, Ms. Reynolds!" they shouted over their shoulders.

"Stay safe!"

"Enjoy the hurricane!"

Ms. Reynolds frowned and shouted at the door slamming behind them, "Seriously now, there is nothing *enjoyable* about a hurricane. This shouldn't be happening! I will be listening to the radio for updates and praying for all of you to stay safe."

Mahina nodded and raised her eyebrows to show Ms. Reynolds that she agreed with her that hurricanes were no joking matter, then said, "I had a weird dream last night with thunder and lightning in it. Not sure yet what it means, except maybe that things are not right with the world right now. Anyway, take care, Ms. Reynolds! Will you please call the office and tell them that Mr. Kahale is giving me a ride home? Thanks!"

She followed Koa out the door into the driving rain with her backpack over her head. It just took a moment for them to locate his dad's truck on the street in front of the school flashing its lights at them. They piled in.

"Hi, Mahina," said Koa's dad, a spitting image of Koa except for the heavy three-days' growth on his face and a smile as wide as the ocean. "Does your tutu know that we're taking you home?"

"The office knows, in case she calls. Thanks for driving me. Wow, what a storm!" She clicked into her seat belt and wiped her eyes as Koa's dad steered his way around soaked and anxious parents standing outside their idling vehicles.

"And it's going to get a lot worse," he replied. "You got everything you need out there at the ranch?"

"I think so," she said. "Tutu is on it, usually."

"Well, if you need help with anything, just call us."

"If your old landlines are working, that is," Koa pointed out, looking at the telephone wires whipping around by the side of the road.

"We'll be fine, I'm sure," she said, but she wasn't sure. She wished Tutu would break down and buy cell phones. The urgent feeling from her dream revisited her, like she was somehow responsible, or that it was happening because she forgot to do something. Should she maybe stay with the Kahales? The buildings on her ranch were even older than the ones at school. No, she needed to get back to Tutu.

There was so much wind and noise from the rain hitting the roof of the truck that conversation was impossible, other than shouting "goodbye" and "good luck," when Koa's dad boated through the puddles in her driveway and dropped her off. When she stepped out of the truck into the mud, the wind felt like the strong hands of a bullying thief trying to steal the backpack off her back. She gripped the straps hard and leaned into the rain to walk up the steps of the front lanai. Just like at school, it took both arms to open the door and then a knee to prevent it from slamming behind her.

"Well, I'm certainly glad you are home," said Tutu, filling jugs of water at the sink. "Stupid school, insisting you come in today. Ridiculous."

"Mr. Kahale gave me a ride. Are the animals inside?" she asked, taking off her wet school shoes and happy to see Olina in the living room peering out from under the couch. The wind was so loud it felt like it was blowing inside the kitchen itself.

"I took care of it. Gave them extra food and locked them in. They won't want to venture out until this blows over anyway, and neither should we. The radio says the hurricane is still a category five and headed toward Hilo. We'll definitely feel it. I figure the eye of the storm will pass over the island in four or five hours if it doesn't weaken."

Mahina put her unused lunch bag in the fridge. "Are we safe, Tutu?"

"About as safe as anybody, I suppose. Your great-grandfather built this house. It's not fancy to look at, but he used ohia wood for the roof beams and the foundation. There's not a stronger wood around. It will hold up. Come on. Let's have a big lunch and pray the storm doesn't wipe out those among our people who don't have houses as strong as ours. The farmers down in Waipio must be terrified of the wind and storm surge."

Tutu often talked this way about the struggles of other Hawaiians who lived in various places on the island, yet she almost never left the ranch. Mahina couldn't remember the last time they had driven the treacherous road down to Waipio Valley with its lush vegetation and beautiful black sand beach. Tutu apparently knew all the taro farmers down there, but Mahina was too young to remember any of them.

Tutu fiddled with the volume dial on the radio and then set out sliced sweet buns for pulled pork sandwiches. Mahina steeped a pot of mamaki tea. They sat at the kitchen table with candles ready, eating coleslaw and sandwiches and listening to the rain punish the side of the house. Lightning, unusual for Hawaii, flashed outside the windows, and thunder shook the posts holding up the house, making her doubt the faith Tutu had in her great-grandfather's workmanship. She thought about last night again and wondered if this real storm was what had brought the storm clouds into her dream and put the urgent edge into her mother's voice. Why couldn't she let it go?

She looked at Tutu, who also seemed worried and tired. Maybe she should have called her on Ms. Reynold's classroom phone before coming home with Mr. Kahale. Had Tutu been concerned about being out here all alone without her nearby? After all, hurricanes had already devastated their ohana once. "Do you really think we'll be okay?" she asked her.

Mahina jumped when Tutu shouted, "No, we'll *not* be okay! No one is going to be okay! This shouldn't be happening. They've ruined everything with their pollution and disrespect of the ʻāina! They've ruined Waipio Valley. They've ruined Pololu. They've even ruined the beaches, and they spend millions of dollars every year to come sit on them! You'd think they would care at least about the beaches! So much garbage!"

Mahina got up to put her arm around Tutu. "I'm sorry, Tutu. I know, it's terrible."

"And the beaches aren't even the best part about the ʻāina!"

"I know, the garden is."

"Right, the soil! The land! Hands in the ʻāina to massage the heart of the earth, oh our poor earth!"

Mahina remembered with fondness the many times Tutu had taught her to feel the special tingling mana in the soil of their huge garden. It was a moving and beautiful experience, but over time it became lonely to feel it with only Tutu. When she dug in the soil these days, the chicken skin sensation on her body and in her heart made her want to fly into town like a hawk to share it with Koa.

"I know, Tutu. I know. I agree with you. The world's gotten too far away from that."

Tutu straightened up in her chair and patted Mahina's hand. "Thank you, my dear. I'm sorry. I didn't mean to yell. It's just that so much of our home is getting ruined. The world isn't the way it used to be anymore, the way it's supposed to be." She wiped her eyes with a napkin and took a sip of tea. "The storms. I don't deal well with storms, you know, ever since Hana and Kiawe died."

An extra strong gust of wind jolted the house and startled them both. Tutu ran to the window and looked out. "We're losing part of the barn roof!" she said. Mahina joined her at the window. Through the sheets of rain, they could see some of the metal was peeling back on the top of the barn and flapping around.

"I hope Ikaika and Costco are doing okay," said Mahina.

"They're scared, I'm sure, but they're in their stalls. They'll be okay, I think, if the barn holds up. The chickens and the pigs are in more danger on the backside. At least *you're* not outside, lost in this." She looked at the barn roof and shook her head. She shut the curtain and sat back down at the kitchen table.

Mahina hesitated. She didn't want Tutu to get mad again, but maybe this was the chance she was waiting for to ask about the death of her parents. Tutu herself had brought the subject up, and there was nothing they could do at the moment but sit in the kitchen with the radio on and wait. All Mahina knew about how she had become an orphan was that her mom's body was found in one of the many lava tubes that criss-crossed their thousand-acre property. Her dad's body was never found. Mahina took a deep breath and took a chance. "Was there a warning, you know, before Mom and Dad died?"

"Not knowing where they were should have been my warning," Tutu said, raising her eyebrows. "The last thing Hana said to me was that she was driving into town with Kiawe so they could get more batteries for the flashlights. The wind and rain were so strong, and I was so busy with the animals behind the barn that I didn't notice that their truck had never left. That day, everyone felt the whole island would be destroyed. Hana was in a panic."

"I heard her voice, I think, again in my dream last night," said Mahina as softly as she could and still be heard over the wind. Dreaming was another subject Tutu never liked to talk about, especially when Mahina described that dreams felt like reality and being awake sometimes felt like a dream. Only when she mentioned her dreams to the Kealohas up the road, did she learn that Tutu's mother was very unusual, that she had special visions, ones that could tell the future. When Tutu chanted with Mahina and placed her hands in the garden's soil to feel what she called "the healing mana of the ʻāina," the feeling was the same for her as when she dreamed of flying. Did Tutu's mother experience the same thing?

"I told you to ignore your dreams!" said Tutu loudly, startling her again.

"I know you did, Tutu, and I *try*. But it's really hard. They happen every night now. Last night, I dreamed of a storm, and Mom was urging me to fly."

Tutu stared at her for a moment. "If *I* can ignore them, you can too."

"But why do we *have* to? Flying dreams are beautiful." A flash of lightning and a simultaneous boom of thunder rattled the house.

"That was close," said Tutu, looking upward. Then she looked at Mahina and shook her head slowly. "I suppose I can tell you this much. The dreams started with me. I'd hoped you would be spared, but clearly, you've got them now like Hana did. The Moemoea dreams." Tutu sighed. "There's a long history, and when *my* tutu was alive, the dreams were mostly just intuitions, beautiful and right, like our earth. But now, dreaming is not a good thing anymore. Things have changed. They are a curse. Your mother had the curse, and I'm certain that her dreams were what led her and Kiawe to their deaths."

"Oh," said Mahina.

Tutu's expression went from fear to sadness. She brought a napkin up to her eye.

"I miss Hana dearly. You've always looked so much like her that watching you grow up is like watching your mother grow up all over again, only you are way less stubborn, thank goodness. Most of the time, that is." She smiled through her tears, and Mahina smiled back at her. Olina walked in and brushed herself against Tutu's and Mahina's legs, but a crack of thunder sent her scurrying back under the living room couch.

"The power of intuition is what brought my own tutu to this beautiful island in the first place," Tutu went on. "Everyone on Oahu was tempted by the free land available for ranching and farming over here, but no one except my tutu, your great-great-grandmother, actually came. And she was a little late, as fate would have it, which is how we ended up here. No one wanted this parcel, you see, even though it was three times as large as any of the others set aside by the Queen. It was the last one available, and local kupuna warned her that it was cursed because of all the spirits and strange whistling sounds wafting from the lava tubes everywhere. Tutu said those things were tests to weed out those too weak to handle the power."

Mahina thought about the amazing labyrinth of caves and lava tubes running everywhere under their ranch. You really had to know where you were placing your feet to walk safely in the pastures or to ride a horse. There were dozens of holes covered with long strands of grass that could swallow you up in an instant with one errant step. She knew where all of them were, or most of them anyway. The caves themselves were amazing, and even though Tutu forbade her from going inside them, she often couldn't resist climbing down into their cool, dark beauty. Dangerous or not, they were perfect places to escape the midday heat.

Tutu shook her head. "This ranch wasn't cursed and full of evil spirits, of course, just the opposite, but superstitions were taken seriously back then. Only the wisest and most perceptive spirit seekers could overlook the stories of the kupuna and see our ranch of lava tubes for what it truly was—the island's richest depository of mystery and good.

"Your great-great-grandmother was one of those visionaries, even though she too had lost her parents at a young age. She understood this land with her entire mind and soul, and the ranch loved her back with the passion of a massive living being desperately in need of being understood. Tutu always said, 'The earth is our mother and begs for us to know her,' and even though her aunts and uncles pleaded with Tutu not to leave Oahu, one breath of this place told her that her destiny lay here on Hawaii Island, and sure enough, because of her deep love of this ranch, she became one of the most powerful leaders Waimea has ever known."

"She was a chief?" Mahina asked. She poured some more tea into her tutu's mug. The lights flickered and then died, along with the whine of the refrigerator compressor. Tutu lit candles as she went on, making her face glow eerily as strong draughts played with the flames.

"Mercy, no, a wahine couldn't be a chief! That didn't mean, though, that she didn't run things in her own powerful manner. She was a leader because she was the visionary, the spirit seeker. Even though she didn't go out of her way to tell people what to do unless they asked, boy did they ask! She aligned them with what the earth wanted from their existence. And her advice was like gold to them. In a very short time, everyone around here owed their livelihoods to her guidance.

"It was really something to see the way they came from all over the island to line up every morning at the end of our driveway to talk to her. Because of her wisdom, the community gave us everything we needed, and when Tutu passed away, the people continued to come and support my mother because Mama was a seer, too, even more powerful. They were both big, big people."

"I know that. The Kealohas mentioned it to me."

Tutu nodded. "The Kealohas got into cattle-raising because of Tutu. For years, people from all over the island brought us fish from the ocean and meat from the land in exchange for advice and guidance in matters of love and work. Our pantry was never empty because of that, and we grew vegetables, amazing vegetables, and eventually raised our own beef, pork, and chicken. Grew our own taro, too, just like we do now. The land, riddled with dangerous caves and holes, was not a curse for us back then because we honored it for what it was and worked hard to take care of it. Now, of course, the mainland has ruined everything, all around the globe. It's different. The earth is angry and dangerous now, filled with holes of a different type."

"Did *you* ever provide visions, Tutu?"

"Oh, no, no. I didn't need to with Mama and Tutu around, and it was a good thing too. My mama, your great-tutu, lived a long life, but now times have changed. Back then, she was better at dreaming and seeing things than me. Plus being an only child, I had my hands full working on the ranch. I was the first to have special dreams, mind you, not just strong intuitions. But I was too busy to pay attention to them and too afraid to learn how to use their power.

Tutu paused, and Mahina thought that would be the end of the conversation. It was difficult to hear her over the wind and occasional crack of thunder, but to her surprise, Tutu went on. "Not that I didn't have Moemoea powers like Mama. I did, and Mama tried her hardest to get me interested in talking about them and to go for spirit walks with her around the fields here and inside the caves. She said the dreams and the walks were like being born into a higher plane of consciousness. They were important for helping people and the plants and animals of the earth. But I was too frightened. Even then, I could sense things changing in the world, getting ruined. I was afraid of the earth's anger. I didn't want to explore the inside of that mighty anger and expose myself that way. Mama scared me too, to tell you the truth—her power scared me, her intuitive connections, her deep knowledge of earth's purposes, all the complicated people she chanted with and connected to every day. No, that was not for me. So, I tried to find my path alone by helping in other ways."

Mahina couldn't imagine Tutu being afraid of anything, other than maybe a hurricane. She was old and a little creaky, but she was big and strong and could still ride horses and wrangle cattle as well as any of the neighbors, including the Kealohas. Mahina took a sip of tea and remained quietly thinking about how Tutu seldom visited the Kealohas or any of the other neighbors anymore. It might have been different if her parents were here, and maybe some brothers and sisters, but it made Mahina feel lonely just doing work on the ranch with Tutu and nobody else. She wanted to tell Tutu that's why she loved school so much. It was like an extended ohana, instead of her real one on Oahu. But over the howling wind, Tutu was finally opening up, and she didn't want to say something that might make her stop.

"The dreams were too real and too horrifying," Tutu went on after another long sip. "So I ignored them, swallowed their power away like I'm swallowing this tea, and tried to forget about them. And it mostly worked. Eventually, the dreams became infrequent. I didn't mind. I preferred the smaller things, like working the garden, feeding the livestock, and going to market—but mostly working the garden—and doing the chores that had to be done around here to stay fed. The world was just too hamajang to try to deal with it as Mama and Tutu had done in their day.

"When your mom started dreaming the kind of dreams I had, though, I was afraid for her. There is a price to be paid for wisdom, and I told Hana it was best to ignore her dreams as I had. But she didn't listen to me."

"Did you dream of flying, Tutu?" Mahina asked after a long silence.

Tutu's eyes drooped almost shut. "No. Moemoea powers come from our desires and what the earth has in mind for us. Flying was not my desire. My desire was to know the truths, but the truths I was shown were too painful for me." Then Tutu sat up straight like she was coming back to reality and said sharply, "I told you, dreaming is a curse, Mahina. The pain is real. So much *danger* now, in the weather, in the earth's mana. Moemoea dreams always reflect the spirit of the earth, so I'm warning you. They will tempt you into their underground world of truths too big to handle and then spit you out like the blood-red water that flows in our streams!"

Mahina shuddered at that image, but Tutu wiped the side of her mouth with the back of her hand and went on. "Your mother dreamed about marrying Kiawe, and so she did, just like Mama did with her husband, and I did with mine. It was my one dream that wasn't painful because when it comes to marriage, Moemoea dreams are always one hundred percent reliable. Maybe Kiawe encouraged Hana to ignore my warnings about dreams because Hana's dreams were what brought them together. I don't know. Kiawe was a good man. As I said, the people Moemoea women dream of marrying are always good, so maybe Hana figured that everything else she dreamed about had to be good as well. She was wrong about that, dead wrong. But he was a handsome man, your father, and a good worker—but stubborn, like your mother.

"I knew Hana and Kiawe were ignoring me, so I tried to get them to move away from this place, away from the power of this ranch, to somewhere less dangerous. Maybe back to Oahu so they could rejoin our ohana over there. But no, they wouldn't listen. No one in their generation listened to their parents, the fools! They had a saying not to trust anyone over forty. Unbelievable! Not like my generation. We *respected* our kupuna, at least most of the time. So Hana and Kiawe ignored my warnings and stayed here." Tutu shook her head. "I should have insisted harder."

The house jolted with a sharp crack, and Tutu's hands gripped the kitchen table as she looked toward the window. "Mama predicted the hurricanes long ago, while I was still a child. She called them the Great Unbalance, and blamed Captain Cook for being the first one. Talk about a hurricane coming! A category five, that guy was! Later, after Mama passed and Hana came along, I could feel the storms coming when I slept too, although I didn't admit to it. And I certainly never upset Hana by telling her about the horrible things I saw the storms do to this island in my dreams.

"There was nothing I could do to stop the Great Unbalance. The colonizers had taken over. I thought I could make the feeling of impending disaster go away if I just worked harder to ignore my dreams. I often woke up with the feeling that the first horrible storms were coming soon, but I didn't know exactly when. That's why I was so unnerved when I could sense Hana and Kiawe were lying about ignoring Hana's dreams. I should have known she dreamed about the storms too and why she was so upset by them."

The wind was howling so loudly now outside that Mahina could barely hear what Tutu was saying. Mahina scooted her chair closer to Tutu.

Tutu took another deep sip from her mug. "I don't know if Hana dreamed of the Great Unbalance like Mama did, but I like to think she and Kiawe would not have been anywhere near the caves if Hana had known a storm was coming that day. Whatever she was thinking, your mom didn't tell anybody where they were going or what they were going to do in the cave, and they didn't leave a note. They were deep inside the earth when the storm caught them by surprise. They probably didn't hear the rain pounding above them, and they had no chance to escape the flood waters rushing through the lava tubes. I had a dream that morning about her getting trapped and drowning. I should have warned her."

Mahina remained silent as Tutu lowered her head and cried. Eventually, she wiped her swelling eyes with her napkin again and went on.

"I know more about your dreams and their dangers than I let on, Mahina. I never told Hana why I wanted her to ignore them. Maybe I felt telling her why would have made them more attractive to her somehow and given her more fuel for her rebellion against me. It was just so hard to know how to raise her!

"But times have changed, and I'm not going to make the same mistake with you. I was hoping you would be spared the Moemoea curse, but unfortunately, it seems you inherited the dreams, so now, whether you like it or not, you have a responsibility to me and to yourself. I've learned many lessons about the curse of our dreaming, and I know that what I am going to say to you is absolutely true, so you need to trust me. Will you?"

"I will, Tutu." Mahina's heart was beating fast. She leaned in farther to hear better and waited.

"All dreams seem real, but most of the dreams you had before were not like the ones you are having now. It was the same with me. Before I was a teenager, my dreams were like little mixed-up snippets of movies all running between and over each other, and mostly based upon recent experiences and memories. Now that you are older and your brain is becoming aware of our family power, your dreams are like edited full-length movies shown to you from somewhere outside your mind. They don't jump around anymore, and they are frighteningly easy to remember."

Mahina nodded her head vigorously and opened her mouth to speak. Tutu raised her hand to stop her. "I know, just listen."

"You like the dreams, but the power is not in the dreams. It is in *you*. If you let the dreams take over your life, their reality will get stronger the more attention you pay to them. If you use your power to pay attention to the dreams, you will want to live that dream reality more and more. It will become like a drug. You will merge with your dreams, and your dreams will merge with the earth, and the earth is not safe right now.

"The intuition of the women in our family is special, and it becomes stronger with each generation. It's thrilling to fly, to predict the future, and to fulfill all the other desires that our dreams might allow you to fulfill. But in the damaged world of today, where things are becoming not what they should be, the Moemoea dreams are only a pathway to pain, suffering, and death.

"Your mother did not listen to me, but you *must*, Mahina. Your true power, like mine, comes from *ignoring* dreams. They are only empty temptations and very dangerous. I can't tell you exactly where your power can be expressed just enough in reality to give you peace. You'll discover that safe expression in time. Perhaps it is in studying, or in gardening and ranching as it is for me, or maybe it can stay forever hidden in your heart somewhere. But I do know that our power of goddess dreaming is dangerous now, like this hurricane. You must promise to fight it. Put the dreams out of your mind and let them fade back into the caves where they belong!"

Mahina felt guilty remembering how much she enjoyed focusing her mind and flying as her mother instructed in her dreams. It was like being a god. She wondered if it was too late to heed Tutu's warning, or if she even could. She opened her mouth to promise, but instead, she asked, "The cave where Mom and Dad died, it's the one at the base of the hill, that way, all sealed up with cement blocks, right?"

Tutu looked through her tears at where Mahina was pointing and nodded. "I asked the sheriff to seal it off."

Mahina stared at Tutu and thought about their conversation. She was glad Tutu finally told her about these things. Even if Tutu didn't know everything about her parents' death, at least Mahina was closer to finally learning exactly where they had drowned. And now she better understood Tutu's fear of dreaming and could share Tutu's grief more intimately. Her eyes watered with gratitude that Tutu was treating her like an adult who could handle secrets and the truth.

Her silent tears overwhelmed the many questions she still wanted to ask: What had her mother and father tried to do in the cave that was now sealed by concrete blocks? Was the changing world the only painful truth Tutu wanted to avoid? Was the world really too broken to be trusted anymore? What did all this mean for her and the flying dreams she had almost every night? Could she try hard enough to stop them like Tutu wanted her to? If so, how?

Another time, another pot of mamaki tea, she decided. Right now, Tutu had turned to her and was waiting for an answer. She tore her mind away from the image of the flowing grass hiding the concrete wall blocking the entrance to her parents' cave. She took Tutu's hand in hers, and whispered over the wind, "I promise, Tutu. Thank you."

They moved to the living room and sat on the couch without talking for a while, staring at the candle and listening to the radio. The wind and rain intensified furiously and then settled back into being merely very strong.

"Well, there's nothing more we can do tonight. I'm headed up to bed," said Tutu after the battery-operated radio informed them that

Byron had diverted south of Hilo and was headed out to sea, but that damaging winds were still possible. The weather reporter said they expected Byron to keep heading southwest, so it would eventually become a threat only to the fishermen who decided to ride out its fury on the ocean instead of leaving their boats moored at the harbors.

The worst may have passed, but the wind was still screaming, and the rain was unbelievable.

"What's the record for inches of rain to fall in a few hours?" Mahina asked Tutu, after giving Olina her supper under the couch.

Tutu just shrugged and looked up. "Whatever it is, we must have broken it. If the roof hasn't washed away yet, it isn't going to." She took a candle from the table and handed the other to Mahina. "Might as well get some rest before assessing the damage in the morning. Good night, Mahina." Mahina followed her upstairs.

Deluge, that's the only word for this, Mahina thought as she blew out her candle and climbed into bed after one last fearful look out the rattling window. The yard surrounding the house was a lake, and she could hear the little stream that ran outside her parents' cave in the distance roaring like a giant river. The unrelenting lightning revealed destruction everywhere she looked, enough to convince her that she wouldn't be going back to school anytime soon.

The power might be out for days, and the cleanup was going to be huge. She had already seen that the tool shed had blown over, and there were pieces of the barn roof hanging off the edge like broken pterodactyl wings. She hoped the roof over the chickens and pigs on the other side of the barn was okay.

She crawled deep under her covers and pulled the quilt that her great-grandmother had made especially for this bed snug under her chin. She thought about her conversation with Tutu and her promise. If the Moemoea powers were real, did it mean that she could actually fly? Could Tutu dream the truth about things still if she wanted to? What was her mom's special power, her desire?

Then she remembered she needed to not think about those things anymore. She sighed. Tutu was right about one thing—things are pretty confusing in the world right now.

She loved Tutu, but she felt lonely in her bed, as she almost always did on this vast ranch. She hoped Olina would be okay in her sanctuary downstairs under the couch. Olina was usually a very calm cat and almost always slept with Mahina, but with the thunder, there would probably be no meditative purring in her ear tonight. With Olina missing from her bed, Mahina wondered if sleep would come at all for her tonight with the waves of wind and rain still slamming into the house.

But she must have been more tired than she thought because two thunderclaps later she was out cold.

When the rain suddenly reduced itself to a light patter on the roof hours before dawn, she awoke in a panic. "Olina?" she said out loud. She reached out and felt the warm fur of her companion in her usual snuggling place by her pillow. Relieved, she cuddled closer to Olina and drifted back to sleep. And then she dreamed ...

Chapter Three

The hill looms in front of them. Olina's long claws are out, and her back is against the huge boulder that is blocking the entrance to the cave. She is guarding it with all of her might, hissing and snarling.

The familiar and urgent voice of my mother shouts from behind the boulder. "Mahina, you cannot hold onto doubt and faith at the same time and get to where you want to go, where *I* need you to go, where the *world* needs you to go. Only *you* can move the boulder. Don't you know that yet? An animal can't stop you from doing that, even one you love. No one can stop you! *You*, my daughter, *only you* have the power.

"Yes," I say. "Move out of the way, Olina! You can't stop me. I will do it! I must!" I grab Olina gently by the shoulders, but she swipes her claws at me and scratches furiously at my hands and face.

"Stop it! Stop it!" I yell, stepping back, raising my elbows to protect my eyes. But Olina doesn't stop. She burrows her body between my arms and looks me dead in the eye. Her mouth opens wide, revealing fangs. I peer deep into the cavern of her throat and hear the desperate voice of Tutu buried in Olina's gut, screaming, "No, child, it is not your time! Don't you know that? Not your time! Not now. Not *ever*!" Then the voice bubbles and fades as if drowning underwater. Olina, her warning delivered, closes her mouth. Her claws retract. She wriggles from my arms and leaps hissing into the sky.

"It *is* your time, Daughter!" Hana's voice from the cave repeats pleadingly. "The world needs you, even if it's dangerous and unpredictable!"

There is a rumble, an earthquake. The boulder lurches, and suddenly blood-red water gushes around its edges and spills over my feet knocking me over. The crimson deluge surrounds me and sweeps me into its current heading toward the ocean. I bounce against rocks and tree trunks. I can't take a breath. I need to escape in order not to drown, but the swirling water holds me relentlessly in its grip like a shark.

Chapter Four

Tutu was already outside in the morning sunshine when Mahina, in a daze, stumbled downstairs to the kitchen. Her head hurt from her nightmare, which had repeated itself over and over until she awoke. She couldn't believe the horrible view out the front window. Was it real, or was she still dreaming? Puddles and blown debris were everywhere, and chickens and pigs were wandering about freely like they had no cares at all in the new, interestingly disordered world. She pulled on her boots and stepped outside to see the destruction.

She really needed her morning cup of Kona coffee for the destructive changes to seem real. All around her were tree branches and pieces of roofing from their property. There were even roof tiles she recognized from the Kealoha's ranch house half a mile away. All the usually tall grass on the hillsides was flattened, especially where rivers and streams had flowed through places where they never had flowed before. Everything was soaked. Even where there weren't deep puddles, the earth felt soggy, like walking on giant sponges overfilled with mud and water.

"Lucky I had the foresight to move some tools inside," said Tutu when Mahina caught up with her behind the barn. "Help me get these hinges screwed back in so we can move these hoggies back to where they belong."

Mahina commanded her arms to work and held the pig door in place while Tutu used the battery-operated screwdriver to reattach it to the leaning barn wall.

"We can winch the side of the barn back up later. This'll hold 'em for now." Tutu drove another screw from her mouth. "I can round up the pigs. There's still dry feed in the bins. Go use some to get the chickens back into the outside pen. It needs repair first, though. Use some wire and the cutters I left on the porch. We can repair the coop after I lure back these pigs. I haven't counted, but it looks like we might have lost a few. We'll have to check the pastures to see if any got stuck or drowned. If so, we can salvage them, provided they didn't get swept away."

"Okay, Tutu. Looks like there's some roof damage up there." She pointed at the roof of the barn.

"Not too bad. The barn stood strong. We can tarp it if necessary. Now get going. We don't want those chickens laying eggs everywhere this morning!"

Mahina tiptoed back through all the junk in the driveway to the porch and grabbed the wire and cutters. The coop looked like it had been run over by a wild bull, but the chicken yard only needed a few holes patched in the fencing. She laced the repair wire through the jumbled fence where it was sagging and rehung the gate that had also been blown askew. The result wasn't pretty, but it would have to do.

She went into the barn and scrounged a bucket of semi-dry chicken food. Then she called to the chickens from inside the pen and scattered the feed on the soggy ground. Chickens were easier to entice than pigs, but Tutu had a magic way with the big animals, and they both finished their rescue tasks at about the same time.

"Okay," said Tutu. "The horses did okay in the barn last night, just a little spooked as far as I can tell, and I'm glad the power came back on, miracle of miracles. I'm going to saddle up Ikaika and ride the perimeter to check the cattle. Can you do a walking survey close in for any stray or dead pigs? Then we'll see about breakfast."

"Sure, Tutu. I don't think we'll have school today."

"You think? You and your schooling!" Tutu shook her head and disappeared into the barn.

Mahina looked out at the dampness of the land and thought about her headache and her dream. She was supposed to teach herself to ignore her dreams, but how was she supposed to ignore them when they featured her very own cat attacking her face? And the voices. And getting swept away in a flash flood! Everything was so real. But feeling the pain in her temples, she thought maybe the dreams *were* evil, and she should try and do as Tutu says.

Yet the first place she found herself walking toward was the forbidden cave with the cinder blocks.

A half-hour later, she had discovered no dead pigs, but there was a small new streambed emerging from the bottom of the cinder block wall covering the cave. Many of the cinder blocks at the base had shifted into the bed, and some were even missing along the left side, washed away by a torrent of cave water that had rushed to cross the ranch and descend toward the ocean.

She stomped through the leftover mud and poked her head inside the jagged hole. Her head fit, but the opening was too small for anyone to safely climb through. I should tell Tutu about this in case she wants to repair it, she thought, but she hesitated because the discovery of the broken wall felt like a secret gift meant just for her.

As she pulled her head out and slogged her way back around the other hills near the farmhouse, she decided it was okay not to tell Tutu about the damage to the cave barrier just yet.

"She probably will never see it," she said out loud. Tutu would have to investigate the cave as closely as Mahina had just done to even notice that there was a new opening.

Mahina wondered if it was a form of lying not to tell her about the damaged barrier. But she thought about the barn repairs and the junk lying all over the ranch and decided that telling her later if necessary would be just fine. As guilty as she might feel about keeping the information to herself, it certainly wasn't evil not to give Tutu another thing to worry about right now.

Chapter Five

Mahina was tired and Tutu had to stop often to stretch her stiff joints, but by the time hunger finally drove them back into the ranch house for a very late breakfast, the chicken coop was back up, and most of the blown junk had been collected in a giant pile in the middle of the front yard. They found many of the hand tools from the shed scattered about in the muck, but the structure itself was unsalvageable. Fortunately, they had stored the saddles and bridles off the ground in the barn, so they were spared from the foot of water that had swept through. But about half the chicken and pig feed had been washed away.

"We can afford more feed, but that roof is going to be the thing," said Tutu, shaking her head and cracking eggs into the frying pan. "Get a package of pulled pork from the freezer and put it in some boiling water. It'll be good with these eggs."

Mahina put down her glass of cool water and went into the pantry to do as Tutu asked. Just then, the phone rang.

"Moemoea's," she heard Tutu say. "That's me." There was a long pause. Mahina dug out the package from the freezer and reentered the kitchen.

"Oh, I'm sorry to hear that," said Tutu as she put the water on to boil. "So, how long does she get to stay home?" There was another pause. "Okay, thank you very much." Another pause. "No, not too bad. Nothing like that, just some roof damage as far as we can tell right now, but there's always lots of work to do." Pause. "Well, thank you." Pause. "I'll tell her. Okay then, good luck, and mahalo for letting us know."

Tutu calmly picked up her spatula and flipped the eggs. "Looks like no school for you for a while," she said. "That wahine told me the hurricane destroyed the classroom building. I guess the winds in town must have been worse than out here."

"Oh no, that's horrible!" Mahina said. "Was anybody hurt?"

"Wahine didn't say, but I'm glad you weren't still there like they wanted you to be." Tutu shook her head but kept her eyes on the frying pan.

Mahina shook her head back at her. "They didn't *want* us to be there, Tutu. They just wanted school to happen. Then the forecast changed, and they sent us home."

"They should have known better. But it doesn't matter now. They're closed down."

"You're *happy*, aren't you?!" Mahina said.

Tutu turned to look at her. "No, dear. I'm not *happy*. It was a tragedy, but it also means we can catch up on some things here. These days you take what nature gives you. Your school will have to cope, just like we'll have to cope, and everybody in town and our neighbors out here will have to cope."

A lump formed in her throat. Mahina thought about Ms. Reynolds and the great classes she'd had with her. She thought about Koa and her other new friends at Po'okela Academy and how much they meant to her. No more school? That couldn't be possible! She looked at Tutu who seemed unconcerned emptying the bag of pork into the frying pan. Certainly, there was more they could do than just say that people had to cope. But first, she needed to see things for herself.

After their late brunch, Tutu hauled a big blue tarp onto the lanai from the attic to nail it over the missing part of the roof on the barn. Mahina's job was to hold the ladder, but first, she told Tutu she had to call Koa.

"Okay," Tutu said, "but don't be long."

"I won't be, Tutu. I'll help you. Just a few minutes." She waited until Tutu carried the tarp inside the barn then dialed Koa's number. His dad answered.

"Hi, Mr. Kahale. It's Mahina. Thanks for taking me home yesterday. Did you guys survive the storm okay?"

"A tree fell on my boat. Other than that and a few shattered nerves, we're fine," said Mr. Kahale. "How about you? Did you get flooded out?"

"Not too bad. A few damaged roofs and some missing sheds. Not as bad as the school, I guess. Have you seen it? Is Koa there?"

"He's right here, Mahina. I haven't seen the school yet, but I hear the whole town is in pretty bad shape from the flooding and the wind. I'll put Koa on now."

"Hey," said Koa.

"Hey," she said. "Are you okay?"

"Oh yeah, no problem. Want to go surfing? The waves are epic right now!"

"What?! Can't. Got to fix the barn roof. You're kidding, right? Are you really going *surfing* right now?"

"I want to. The waves are epic, but Dad says we should stick around and help folks who need it in town."

"Check on Ms. Reynolds, will you? I'm worried about her."

"Okay, good idea, if we can get there. Lots of power lines are down. Any other requests?"

"Yes," she said. "Can you come pick me up tomorrow morning so I can look at the school? I don't feel safe riding my bike yet. Too muddy."

"Okay, I'll ask Dad."

"Thanks," she said.

"Hey," said Koa. "Maybe after we look at the school, will you go surfing with me?"

"That would be great, but I doubt it," Mahina said. "I still need to help Tutu with the repairs."

Chapter Six

Mahina stood with Koa and his dad on the sidewalk in front of what was left of Po'okela Academy discussing the hurricane's aftermath. Mr. Kahale said that since Waimea was built on a hilly plateau between Kohala Mountain and Mauna Kea it was used to getting heavy rain, so while some houses had flooded, the water drained quickly and revealed more wind damage than anything else.

They saw that the old theater that served as an auditorium was still standing, but all the classrooms and the rambling old farmhouse that branched off from the theater were flattened.

"Oh, my gosh!" she said. "It looks like a fallen house of cards."

"Pretty much totaled," said Mr. Kahale, shaking his head.

"Hey, you folks can look, but stay on the sidewalk!" yelled a police officer in a fluorescent yellow vest. "We're still checking for live wires."

"Sure thing," said Mr. Kahale, stepping back even though he was already on the sidewalk.

"Here comes Ms. Reynolds," said Koa. Ms. Reynolds was riding her old Sears three-speed bike and pulled up next to them. Her tires were caked with red mud.

"Hi guys," she said, putting down her kickstand. "School has been canceled indefinitely, you know."

"We know, Ms. Reynolds," she said. "But I needed to see it for myself."

"It's just horrible," Ms. Reynolds said, shaking her head.

"Do you know what they're going to do?" asked Koa.

"Well, right now, the head of school and the board are trying to figure that out. The governor and the mayor have declared this part of the island a disaster area, so there might be low-interest loans available eventually, but there's a rumor that the school might not be able to afford even that."

"They've got to figure it out!" Mahina said. "What about our classes?"

"Well, I'm sure they're working on it as best they can, but if the school can't reopen, they'll have to refund tuition, and that would bankrupt them," said Ms. Reynolds.

"That's the risk of being a private school, I guess," said Mr. Kahale, looking sad and putting his arm around Koa.

"There's got to be something we can do!" Mahina said.

Koa laughed. "It's climate change. What do you have in mind, Mahina? A bake sale? It's going to cost a million dollars just to rebuild this place. Then it could all just happen again."

She looked at him being comforted by his dad and a lump formed in her throat. She didn't let herself get upset with Koa for the bake sale comment or with Mr. Kahale for telling the truth. She knew that Koa was as frustrated about climate change as she was and that he especially hated that so many reef and fish species were dying in the ocean. She just didn't think Koa had figured out yet that their favorite teacher would probably have to go back to New York if the school couldn't somehow raise enough money to rebuild. She gave him a look, and he moved out from under his dad's arm.

"We're going to miss you, Ms. Reynolds," she said, turning to her. Koa bit the fingernail on his thumb.

"Oh, dear, that's sweet of you, but I'm not going anywhere. Not yet, anyway. There's no insurance for the building—no one can get hurricane insurance anymore—but they do have a policy to cover salaries for a while, I think. The school will figure out something to keep going, even if we have to teach in tents."

"Tents might be okay for the moment, but without permanent buildings, the school will lose its students to the public schools," said Mr. Kahale. "Po'okela Academy has to survive as a business as well as a school, you know."

"Well, one step at a time," said Ms. Reynolds. "In this universe, things have a way of working out, even when they look dire. Like you guys coming to check on me and helping my landlord fix the broken windows so quickly. Thank you again for that. I had no idea what I was going to do."

"Hey, no problem, Ms. Reynolds," said Mr. Kahale. "Being a contractor, I always have spare windows hanging around. And speaking of fixing things, we better get you back to your ranch, Mahina. Your tutu didn't look very happy about you coming to town this morning."

"You're right, Mr. Kahale," Mahina replied. "There's lots of extra work for everyone now. I just wish there was a way to snap my fingers and bring the school back the way it was before."

"I know, dear," said Mr. Kahale. "We all love Po'okela Academy, but sometimes there are things that happen that just can't be fixed that easily."

Through the tears forming in her eyes she saw Koa looking at her. "That might be true, but Mahina can still dream about it, can't she?" he said.

She smiled at him. She was upset and sad but forgave him for laughing at her earlier.

"Of course, she can," said Ms. Reynolds, looking compassionately at her and also smiling at Koa. "Nothing wrong with that at all. If there's one thing I've learned in my short life, there is nothing more powerful in this world than a worthwhile dream!"

Chapter Seven

That night, with Olina curled up on her pillow, Mahina remembered Koa wanted to go surfing and felt her exhausted mind slip once again into a dream. She was on the water with him at the harbor ...

"THIS WAS KING KAMEHAMEHA'S favorite thrashing spot," Koa yelled at me from the curl of a wave. The sky was clear, and the sun was shining brilliantly on the water.

"You think I don't know that?" I yelled back at him, leaving him in my wake. The sun was brilliant on the water. "Follow me! Do what I do. Can you keep up?"

"Hold on, I'm looking at the algae in this wave. Do you see? They're giving themselves to the urchins. And the urchins are giving themselves to the crabs. The crabs are giving themselves to the fish. The fish are giving themselves to the fishermen. The fishermen are giving themselves to the village. The village is giving itself to the whole world. The chain of life. Everyone is important. Everyone giving a little more of themselves than they get."

"I see it. Cool! Okay, now follow me!"

"No, not yet! Listen to these lyrics!

Taking more, giving less
Is what got us in this mess.
Taking less, giving more
Is what rebuilds the world before.

"Wow! Look deep into the water, Mahina. Use your ears. Music is playing in the sand on the ocean floor. It's a concert. Can you hear it?"

"Yes!" I say. "The chain of life, the chain of giving! Very cool! Thank you! Are you ready now? Are you ready to fly?"

I mount my surfboard. The wave crests and launches me toward the rocky seawall that separates the surf from the harbor. I concentrate and bend my knees. *Up, up,* I think. No doubts. No fear. The wave-lapped boulders loom ahead. I pull my board powerfully beneath me. I fly over the wall and then up over the bobbing sailboats in the calm harbor. I zoom toward the volcanic flank of Kohala Mountain looming over the coastline.

"You see? Flying is easy!" I yell over my shoulder at Koa, but I don't hear his answer. I turn to laugh and shout it again, but he is just a tiny figure far behind me bobbing on his board in the breaking waves and holding onto my surfboard as well. What?! I look down at my bent knees and at the winding riverbed zipping by far beneath me.

"*That's right, Mahina,*" says the familiar voice. *"It's just you flying as you do. But soon you won't be alone. You'll see."*

"Mom?" I ask looking up, the wind buffeting my hair.

"You're doing great, my dear. Keep going. Follow the river of pain backward with open eyes, and you will see."

I see the town up ahead; people are sad.

I see my school destroyed by nature; the earth is angry.

I see my classmates clinging to the spokes of Ms. Reynold's bicycle; they are confused.

I see new riverbeds slicing through the hillsides of my ranch.

I see the blocked entrance to the lava tube where you died.

I see my iron hand reaching for the concrete blocks.

"*Grab them,*" shouts the voice. "*You're strong! Bust the blocks away, Mahina! Make it big enough. Your time has come. There is so much for us to do. I need you.*"

"I will! I *am* strong. I'm already flying, aren't I?" Hovering in the air, I toss the blocks aside like they're made of Styrofoam and will myself forward.

"*Strong. Yes, yes you are! You have made your opening, and you have proven worthy to fly inside. I'm so proud of you, Mahina. So talented and capable! You are destined to be here. Look around. You already know the way through the cave. Feel it! Pull yourself forward. The cavern of light is ahead. Fly with me, my child. You must be reborn from the cavern as I was. Death awaits everyone if you don't, and the world desperately needs you!*"

"Yes, dying. The world is dying. Needs my birth! Needs me!" I shout. "The world before! Yes! Build life! Build living! Save the world! It's my time! I can *do* something to make it better! The world is not yet broken! I *will* do something! I *can* ..."

The cave fills with rushing water. "*You can't do anything in here, Grandchild!*" says Olina who wraps her giant claws around my leg and, with the strength of Tutu, and pulls me out the way I came. "*It's an evil trap. The earth is broken. You will* die!"

"No!" I scream, but I'm plunged into the blood-red current raging toward the ocean. My head scrapes painfully against the rocks, and I feel again in my heart that there is no escape.

Chapter Eight

"What? Why are you grinding me so hard?" Mahina mumbled as her eyes flew open. She pushed Olina away from her head on the pillow. Then she realized that the scraping sound of Olina's freakishly rough tongue on her ear was what woke her from her nightmare.

"Ouch," she moaned, rubbing her head, and Olina, as if she understood that her task was done, shifted to licking her paw and rubbing it over her own ears instead.

"Thanks, but you're a total weirdo, you know that?" she mumbled, still in a daze from her dream. "And why are you always attacking me?" She rolled over to dry her ear on the sheet and thought about the horrible river of pain that Olina threw her into. Then she smiled remembering Koa appearing in her dream for the first time, and the amazing flying, the encouraging voice of her mother.

"No!" she said out loud when she realized what she was doing. It was impossible to ignore her dreams while she was having them, but she could at least follow Tutu's advice when she woke up. She pushed the dream out of her cobwebbed mind and climbed out of bed. She couldn't believe how groggy she felt. Maybe if she could make the dreams go away, she would wake up more refreshed? Or maybe that's just the way it was being thirteen and having to get up early to do chores on a farm, dreams or no dreams.

Drink a cup of coffee, feed the animals, eat breakfast—the daily routine never varied. The only thing missing today was getting on the bus to go to school. Because of the hurricane, today's agenda was more repairs and replanting the vegetables that had gotten washed away. She stood next to Tutu in the yard and looked up. The blue tarp looked tacky but secure on the roof of the barn.

"It'll have to do for now," said Tutu.

But it turns out that it didn't. The Kealohas up the road called and soon pulled into the driveway with a truckload of metal roofing. They told Mahina and Tutu it was from extra supplies they had been saving for an emergency. They said they saw their roof damage from the road and decided to help fix it. Two hours of hammering later, the roof was as good as new. After they left, Mahina and Tutu spent the rest of the day putting together a return gift for them of frozen pork and garden root vegetables from the pantry.

"It's the way it's always been," said Tutu that night after supper. She was washing the dishes, and Mahina was drying and putting them away. "People help other people out here, everyone in the ahupua'a. Mauka people help out makai people, and makai people help out mauka people. We have good neighbors." Mahina remembered that the ahupua'a was the ancient way of dividing the island into triangular slices so that all villages contained people who lived in the mountains and along the shoreline. It always made her want to eat a slice of pizza whenever kupuna talked story about it.

"If only the neighbors could help us rebuild the school," she said.

"That school's too fancy," said Tutu. "The ancient ways don't work for something all fancy and book learning like that."

This was an old refrain for Tutu. No matter how much Mahina tried to convince her that books, writing, and intellectual scientific discussion were the key to the future, Tutu just came back to the argument that nothing is more intelligent than nature.

"The ability of a taro plant to take nutrients from the soil and give humans sustenance. What could be smarter than that?" she said.

One time when she wanted to talk to Tutu about a book, *To Kill a Mockingbird*, Tutu cut her off and said, "You want to learn how people should get along with each other better? Just watch goats.

They are wiser about how to live a life in a community than those fancy teachers of yours, that you can count on!"

Mahina dried the last dish quietly and then went to her room to read. She knew Tutu was impossible at times, and she was willing to give her the benefit of the doubt about dreaming, but she didn't have a clue about the value of education. Po'okela Academy was as much their neighbor as anyone else. Sure, it was a predominantly haole school, and most of the families there were richer and had not been on the island as long as the Moemoea Family had, but the school was good. Using your mind was interesting, and there was a lot to learn about the wider world by going there. Way more than at her previous school, that was for sure.

"Geez," she thought, plopping down on her thrift-store bean bag chair. "How many kids have the problem of a Tutu who *doesn't* want them to get an education?" She shook her head and tried not to be angry. Olina meandered into her room. "I can be as stubborn as Tutu is," she growled at the cat, but Olina's beauty and loving presence was enough to quickly dissipate her anger. "Even if I really love Ms. Reynolds and the school, I guess Tutu has the right to feel the way she feels, just as I have a right to feel the way I do." She gave Olina a long pet down her back.

Suddenly her mind brightened with inspiration. "I'm going to figure out how to raise enough money to rebuild the school!" she said out loud. Olina leaped onto her lap and meowed her apparent approval. Mahina scratched her gently on the top of the head and laughed.

Olina leaned in and got a full body scratch. Then Mahina decided she better get some homework done, so she grabbed her literature book and climbed into bed. Olina followed, but Mahina was too distracted by her inspiration to read, so she put the heavy book aside and let her mind drift, petting Olina's soft fur again. She thought about the neighbors and how kind they were to fix the roof. Despite her resolve, she thought about her last dream and how Koa made her stare deeply into the ocean. And then, as she was almost asleep, she felt heat in her chest and the brainstorm hit her.

She knew how to rebuild the school!

She bounced out of bed, startling the cat, and reached for her school computer. "Sorry, Olina," she said. She opened Google, squinting at the screen's brightness, and tapped the keys. She couldn't find any fundraisers structured exactly as her brainstorm imagined, but searching "cumulative bartering" and "pay it forward" gave her enough information to convince her that her crazy idea might just work.

Chapter Nine

The next morning, Mahina raced through her chores and rode her bike vigorously to Koa's house to share her inspiration with him. She found him waxing his surfboard by the garage and spilled her idea scarcely taking a breath.

"Taking less and giving more is what builds the school before," repeated Koa out loud. "Catchy. Where'd you get that from?"

"You, believe it or not. It's a song lyric that you told me about in my dream last night," she said. "We were surfing, and you were talking about the food chain. We don't necessarily need to use that as the slogan, but I think it's cool, don't you? We have to find really rich people to do the donating. It's like everyone gives something and gets something a little better in return, except the last gift in the chain is a new school building."

"Wild!" said Koa. "Cool dream, and for sure, it's a cool idea. It's like a rich people's feel-good giving game. Everyone wants to contribute because everyone gets something back almost as good as what they give away, and then the gifts grow bigger until someone gets something almost as valuable as a new school, so giving a new school doesn't seem like such a big sacrifice. I get it. It's a snowball, a Hawaiian snowball!"

"Exactly! Well, maybe the first person to give something might feel a little left out since they start the giving without getting anything first," she said. "But even that shouldn't be a problem because everyone always has something they don't need that someone else would appreciate. It's like a well-meaning Ponzi scheme!"

"True. Plus, they'll have the excitement of being the first in the chain that saves the school!"

"Right!" she said.

"Okay, let's do it! Let's get this snowball rolling!" He frowned. "But how?"

"I don't know. You're the first person I've told about it."

Koa carried his surfboard back into the garage. "Let's go find my dad and see what he thinks."

They found Mr. Kahale in his workshop painting some two-by-fours. "Sounds like an interesting idea to me," he said after they told him about it, "but there aren't that many truly rich families at the school. You'd need help from the public, and I don't know how you could get enough people to come to it without using advertising. Would they care enough about it? Maybe you should talk to someone at the school? Like maybe the development director?"

"Or Ms. Reynolds!" Mahina said. "She always has great ideas, and she told us she organized a bunch of climate change protests in Berkeley before she taught in New York. She'll know what to do!"

"If you can wait a few minutes, I can give you a lift to her house," said Mr. Kahale. "These boards are for a house right next door to her."

"That's okay, Dad," said Koa. "Mahina is on her bike, so we'll just ride over there."

"Call her first, though, son. It's polite." Koa had his own smartphone, something Mahina tried not to be jealous about.

"Sure. I'll send her a text. No one *calls* anymore, Dad." Koa rolled his eyes, and Mr. Kahale just laughed and waved them on their way.

On the bike ride to Ms. Reynolds' place, she saw that most of the debris had been cleaned off the roads, but there were still crews working on the power lines, and many houses had flood and roof damage. They rode their bikes on the back roads behind the school until they came to a colorful two-story house with fresh new windows and a pile of torn-out debris in the yard. Ms. Reynolds waved to them from her downstairs lanai. An older lady, maybe the landlord, was on a ladder with a bucket of paint. Ms. Reynolds was holding the ladder steady for her.

"Hey, Ms. Reynolds," said Koa. "Those windows look great!"

"Thanks to your dad! We're getting there. Just the painting left. How's your ranch, Mahina?"

"We're okay. Our neighbors helped us put a new roof on the barn yesterday."

"I love this little town," said Ms. Reynolds. "If only the whole world was as generous as the people of Waimea!"

"That's kind of what we came to talk to you about," said Koa.

The other lady climbed down the ladder, smiled at them, thanked Ms. Reynolds, and left to put the paint away in a shed across the lawn. She and Koa pulled up rocking chairs on Ms. Reynold's lanai and explained her nighttime inspiration for raising money for a new school building.

When they finished, Ms. Reynolds laughed and said, "You must have taken me literally about the power of dreaming, Mahina! Good for you. It's a great idea, but if it's going to work, it has to appear to be totally your idea. High school students with a clever idea to raise money for a new school building, especially for a private school, will get a lot more publicity than teachers or parents trying to do the same thing.

"But I can give you some advice," she went on. "Getting people to help you with a cause requires two big things. First, you have to be organized. Then, you have to deliver your message in a way that is memorable, like when I got arrested in college for tossing spaghetti at a Van Gogh in the art museum. You need to make your pitch truly newsworthy so that TV, radio, and newspaper reporters will pay attention to you. Now, any ideas?"

"Can't you just tell us how to do it? *Legally*, that is," said Koa. "I'm too young to go to jail!"

"Considering what I just said, I'm clearly not qualified. Obviously, I'm not kidding that it is way better if the energy and the idea come from you. You guys thought of it, after all. In fact, you probably shouldn't tell people we even had this discussion, and not just because of the Van Gogh thing. You don't want anyone to think *I* gave you the chain idea. I'll certainly step in and help you any way I can once the giving starts happening, but getting the whole thing up and running should be entirely up to you."

Mahina rocked and smiled. "We can do this, Koa. Let's brainstorm. We need something to bring a lot of rich people to the school to see the damage and make them want to help."

"Like throw a party?" said Koa.

"Yeah, maybe. A party where people listen to our snowball giving idea and sign up to participate."

"How can we get them to come to a party? People are depressed right now and busy cleaning up their own places," said Koa.

That was true, thought Mahina, but then something in her stomach prodded her not to give up. "Not people *here*. People who can fly here on private jets. People with lots of money. I mean, everyone can come, of course, but we need celebrities from the mainland and people who can participate in the chain at ridiculously high levels."

"I don't know," said Koa. "Did I say anything about that in your dream?"

Again the heat in her gut, and Mahina remembered. "Oh my gosh, *you* did! That's it! You said there was a *concert* in the sand!"

"A concert! Great idea! I'm imagining a free 'Save Our School' lawn concert at the park followed by the fundraiser."

"That's exactly what I was secretly thinking," said Ms. Reynolds, unable to hold back her excitement. "Music is a great idea! And you came up with it all on your own!"

Mahina leaped to her feet, and Koa said, "We can even get some snow from the top of Mauna Kea and have a snowball fight! You're the best, Ms. Reynolds, and don't worry; I think we can figure out the rest of this. My dad knows a lot of slack key guitar players with gigs at the resorts along the coast, and it doesn't take a rocket scientist to find the phone numbers of TV and radio stations."

"What I *can* do for you, though," said Ms. Reynolds, smiling, "is call the head of school and the development director and tell them you want to meet with them about an interesting idea. I'm sure they'll love it, and they can help you set the date for the concert, maybe even send out some announcements about it."

"Wow, Ms. Reynolds! Thank you!" said Koa, following her onto the lawn.

"Call them now!" Mahina said.

In a flash, they were off on their bikes again.

Chapter Ten

Over the next couple of days, Mahina was very busy in town, and she was nervous about telling Tutu why. In the mornings after chores, she would make excuses for having to leave the ranch, saying she was helping Koa and his dad with projects, which was technically correct since Koa's dad was helping them book musicians for the concert.

The way Tutu shook her head and looked at Mahina when she got on her bike to leave told her everything she needed to know about how she would react when she did hear about the fundraising project. Clearly, Tutu was disappointed she wasn't viewing this time off from school as a golden opportunity to do more projects at home, even though she made it a point to work extra hard and cheerfully on her chores before she disappeared.

But, of course, as soon as word spread like magic across the islands about the upcoming concert, and KWAH TV in Oahu ran an interview with her standing arm in arm with Koa next to the destroyed school building, there was no keeping the secret from Tutu any longer. It took less than a week for her to find out.

The cat slipped out of the bag when Mahina came in from chores around breakfast time to feed Olina and found Tutu spitting with anger into the phone.

"No, I told you. You may not come out here!" she shouted. "I absolutely am *not* interested in giving an interview about my granddaughter! Yes, I know she's amazing. Don't you think *I* know that? You heard my answer, now, goodbye!" She hung up the wall phone and turned to Mahina, who focused intensely on taking off her boots.

"Mahina! What have you done? That was a *TV reporter* who said your *interview* made national news, and the KWAH editor wants her to film an interview *with me* about what it was like to raise you! They said you created some kind of special fundraising concert for the school. How come *I* didn't know anything about this?!"

"It's just an idea the school liked that Koa and I are working on to rebuild the classrooms, that's all," she said, putting her boots away. "I didn't think it would happen so fast. KWAH was filming the hurricane recovery in town when they found out about it. They said they had to interview me this morning while they were on the island. I planned to tell you about it right now, as a matter of fact. Ms. Reynolds is helping us, and Koa's dad is putting together a free concert to get it started. People are going to give each other things in a cumulative sort of way until the last person, we hope, donates a new building. It's kind of like how we got help with our roof, you know? The Kealohas helped us, and then someday we'll help them even more because they did that for us."

She sat down at the table as calmly as she could, keenly aware of Tutu's eyes boring into her.

"Yes, I know. That's the way we do things around here. We support each other *quietly*. Whose idea was this, Koa's or yours?" Tutu continued to stand by the phone with her hands on her hips.

"It was mine, Tutu. Koa and his dad are helping me because they liked it."

"And your teacher too, apparently. Did Ms. Reynolds encourage you to make a big fuss about this? Call the television stations? Don't answer that, of course she did. I heard about her rabble-rousing past on the mainland. *Your* idea, huh? And how exactly did you come up with it?"

"I told you. It's like our getting the new roof for the barn."

Was Tutu really trying to make her feel bad about this? Why?

"Do you think the Kealohas want TV reporters hanging around documenting how generous they were? My goodness, child! What has gotten into your head?"

"I don't know, why not?" Mahina snapped, fed up. "It'd be more than we've ever done for them, or for any of our neighbors! We never go anywhere. We just stay here and do the same things just for ourselves over and over."

For a moment, she thought Tutu might explode, but then Tutu's expression changed, and she shook her head wearily and took her hand off the phone. "Oh, why do I even ask this question? You're a Moemoea. Of course you would notice I haven't been supporting the neighbors as much these days." Tutu sighed and sat down with her at the kitchen table. "When is this concert, anyway?"

She smiled at Tutu. "This Saturday morning, before the afternoon rains roll in. I hope you'll come! Please come, Tutu!"

Tutu gave her a resigned look and stretched her fingers. "You are always asking me to tell you more about your mother. Well, right now, you're acting just like her, child, wanting to help others. But you're also like her wanting to make a big splash and coming up with giant ideas to save the world. I told Hana, and I'll tell you. The world doesn't need saving with giant ideas. It just needs love, just a simple sweet-smelling garden pie of love, with everybody humbly enjoying their own slice of what's left of it." Tutu's eyes turned upward, pleading. "Please don't let this be happening to me again. The next thing you're going to tell me is that this idea came to you in a *dream*."

Mahina swallowed hard and watched Tutu bring her fearful eyes back to her again. What could she say? It was true that the idea had come directly from her thoughts about the dream, a dream she hadn't ignored. But what did it really matter if it came from a dream, anyway? And who can really shut dreams out completely? They're in your head! Besides, it's just a fundraiser. The worst that could happen is people will enjoy music and donate money to the school!

Mahina put on her most serious expression. "Don't worry, Tutu. I'm *not* trying to be a big shot. I just want my classes back, and I don't need dreaming to help with that. School right now *is* my little slice of life to love—along with you and the ranch, of course."

"You've got the giant eyes growing in you, Mahina. I can feel it," said Tutu warningly. "Like your mother. Just remember that your eyes, no matter how big, can't always see what's going on behind your head."

Tutu was lecturing her, but the tone of her voice had softened, so Mahina decided not to argue with her this time. "I'll remember that, Tutu. Can we have breakfast now?"

"So you can go off to school again?"

"Well, I'm hungry, and I want to go help out. But I won't leave you if you don't want me to."

Tutu sighed and walked to the fridge. "I don't know who's stronger, you or that hurricane we just had. But I do know one thing. I don't need a stormy girl on the ranch today, so go to your rich people's school and get it done. And *yes*, I'll come to your neighborly concert."

Mahina's heart leaped. "I love you, Tutu!"

Chapter Eleven

Mahina couldn't believe how quickly everything came together for the big event. To say that the inspiration for a concert to kick off the fundraising campaign was a good one turned out to be a Big-Island-sized understatement. Everyone she talked to was absolutely *hungry* to do something, and it turned out that music lovers on the mainland for whatever reason also wanted to help rebuild the iconic "Hawaiian paradise" school in the center of their little town.

Thanks to social media, the slack key guitar concert somehow got national attention and packed the town park next to Po'okela Academy with people from California, Alaska, Nevada, Tennessee, and even New York. Maybe she underestimated the connections local musicians had with celebrities on the mainland, especially in Nashville and Las Vegas, but once Slide Pickens decided that rebuilding a little paniolo school in rural Hawaii was worth a quick flight to play some great country music, the whole thing went viral under the hashtag @HawaiianSnowballAloha.

After the music, when Ms. Reynolds called Mahina and Koa to the stage to open the fundraising, the giving became like a race, and Slide Pickens, who was once friends with the original owner of the biggest ranch on the island, kicked it all off by donating a priceless keyboard he used for his earliest concerts. He then playfully threw an "aloha" snowball into the crowd and started a whole new thread by donating a guitar given to him by Jimmie Rodgers.

Mahina watched from the stage with Koa as the unexpected double thread of bidding indeed became a huge snowball of donations that rolled its way between more songs through unused yachts, vacation homes, and even whole small businesses in Nashville until everything came together at the end with a disguised heavy-hitter pledging four million dollars cash to rebuild the school.

Their crazy idea was a success! It made her heart zing with happiness.

"Hawaiian Snowball Warns Climate Change to Cool It!" said the memes. "Aloha Snowball Fight in 'Cowboy' Hawaii Heats Up Education After Byron."

"You did it!" cried Ms. Reynolds, hugging them both when they came off the stage that, only that morning, Mr. Kahale had hastily created from his stash of plywood. "New school, here we come!"

"Yes, and I guess we're actually celebrities now," Mahina mumbled, looking once again in disbelief at the national television crews covering the concert and the paparazzi following Slide around and lining up to do interviews, including one with her and Koa. Along with the instant fame, it occurred to her that her idea had probably raised more money for the school in one afternoon than all the school's fundraising efforts put together in the past ten years.

"I can't believe how your dream really caught the mood of the country," exclaimed Ms. Reynolds. "So many people want to do something about the climate crisis, and the true country celebrities most of all!" Mahina could barely hear her, but she could tell the boisterous crowd was making her teacher feel like she was back at Berkeley again marching for the earth.

Mahina thought about what she'd said for a moment then shouted, "It's not *really* doing anything about the climate crisis, Ms. Reynolds. I wish we really could dream up something about *that*. But I get what you mean."

It looked like an army of cameras was marching backstage to meet them. Mahina tried to look beyond them at the lingering audience. She knew Tutu had been sitting with the Kealohas on beach chairs in the outfield for the whole thing. Mahina strained her neck to see if she was still there, but she'd probably already left for home. Crowds of strangers were definitely not Tutu's thing. But Mahina was grateful she had made the effort to come with the neighbors. Usually, Tutu only came into town alone.

"The universe is abundant," shouted Ms. Reynolds back at her. "All good things are flowing toward us. We just have to open our eyes to them. I learned that when I gave up being too angry about things and went into teaching."

"So you think the hurricane was a *good* thing?" shouted Koa, overhearing.

Ms. Reynolds smiled. "We can't stop the one that already came, but we might be able to stop the next one, and that would be a good thing, yes."

"It's great, what we did tonight," Mahina shouted back, "but maybe you're overestimating the power of mantras and manifestations right now. I'm thrilled we saved the school, but I think saving the planet is a little beyond our powers!"

Ms. Reynolds looked like she might have argued with that, but the wave of reporters had finally surrounded them, and it was too noisy to continue the conversation. Then it was posing for pictures with Slide Pickens and his friends, and reporters interviewing all of them until Koa's phone vibrated with a call from his dad. A few minutes later, Mr. Kahale drove his truck through the crowd right up to the stage and rescued them with takeout pizza and a ride home to their welcoming beds.

Chapter Twelve

That night, even with Olina cuddled close to her and the lingering music of "Ridin' Man" in her ears, the excitement of the long and surprisingly successful week prevented Mahina from closing her eyes. If she slept, she couldn't remember doing so. It was the only night in recent memory when she didn't dream of flying or trying to fly. But the whole day before had been like a dream, she thought, a dream come true. She let herself drift in bed, smiling into her pillow and replaying the memories.

The sun was just lightening the eastern sky when she heard a quiet car's tires popping the gravel in their driveway. She looked out the window. It was Ms. Reynolds in her beat-up old Prius. Mahina rushed to put on her clothes before she heard the gentle knock downstairs, but Tutu beat her to the front door.

"Oh, hello, Mrs. Moemoea. Hi, Mahina. I'm sorry to disturb you so early. I'm Ms. Reynolds."

"I know who you are," said Tutu. "Not still on the stage? It's a little early for rabble-rousing, don't you think? You out here to unionize the pigs and chickens?"

In spite of the dim light, she saw her teacher's face drop. "I, uh, no, I'm ... Look, I didn't get much sleep last night. I don't think anybody did. It was kind of an amazing night. But I got up early to give you and Mahina a heads-up about the reporters on their way out here this morning. I thought you might want to know, Mrs. Moemoea, that they are excited to meet you and to see the ranch where Mahina grew up."

Tutu scoffed. "I'll bet they are. Mahina, put your boots on right now and go lock the gate. Don't worry, we'll let you out in a minute, Ms. Reynolds, but not before you and I have a little chat."

Mahina put her boots on. She knew better than to argue with Tutu when she started ordering people around, especially so early in the morning.

Her head was still groggy when she got back from the gate. She was worried about what might happen, but she was glad to see that Tutu had at least invited her teacher inside to sit at the kitchen table.

"No, I didn't tell them how to get out here," Ms. Reynolds was explaining, "but there isn't anyone in town who doesn't know where you live, so ..."

"This is a peaceful little ranch, Ms. Reynolds. Sacred, in case my granddaughter didn't tell you. We don't want lookie-loo reporters traipsing to our door at all hours of the day for no good reason. Don't they have other people to bother? Other places to go that have already been ruined? Haven't reporters ruined enough of the island without having to ruin my place too?"

"I don't understand, and I want to," said Ms. Reynolds gently. "Reporters coming here are going to ruin this place? How? Can you explain it to me, please?"

"Geez, for a high-falutin college graduate, you sure don't get it, do you? Been to Waipio lately? Pololu? Those canyons used to be the wildest and most beautiful places on the island, and what are they now? Nothing but tourist traps full of mainlanders sucking the spirit out of the land and leaving their trash behind when they leave. And don't get me started about Mauna Kea!"

"Tutu, we're not like those valleys. We have a *gate*," Mahina said. "It's private land. We live off the food we raise here. You have said many times that everyone needs to get back to living off the land. Sure, we could just lock them out, but what's wrong with showing them how we do it?"

"Because, Granddaughter, they're not interested in knowing how we do it, that's why. You came from *this* world, our ranch, and you made a splash in *their* world, the rich school, and now they just want to use your story to make themselves famous too. Hotshot city reporters, they don't care about how we live out here, any more than tourists who fly here care about the spirit of our people that was literally born in the canyons of Waipio and Pololu."

Ms. Reynolds looked thoughtful. "Mahina has written in class about her life with you, Mrs. Moemoea, and I have to say, it's pretty incredible what you've done out here. With the earth changing so much these days, I think people really are ready to get back to a lifestyle like yours. Maybe the attention Mahina has gotten for saving the school is just a start toward something better?"

"Maybe for you in your protected little world, but if you knew better, you wouldn't be so naive. I spend a lot of time out here on the ranch, but that doesn't mean I don't see what's going on outside. They might say so, but people are *not* looking for a simpler life, even if the weather is starting to go lolo. What they're really looking for are more thrills or for the next expensive car or gadget to make them happier than their neighbors, and they'll step on and destroy anything that gets between them and what they want."

Mahina had quietly put out three small glasses with ice and poured some leftover coffee into each of them, followed by a splash of fresh milk. Tutu pushed hers away, but Ms. Reynolds nodded her gratitude and graciously took a silent gulp.

"It's amazing what Mahina has done for the school, you know," said Ms. Reynolds gently once she had swallowed.

A horn sounded out by the road, making Tutu jump. "You know, I'm getting sick of you people assuming I don't know anything about my granddaughter! Of *course* it's amazing. Good for the school. She's amazing. We're amazing. We're big and powerful people, it's true. Our ranch is amazing. Our *lives* are amazing, and I want them to stay that way, and that means *enough is enough*. Now here's what you are going to do, Berkeley girl. Mahina is going to let you and your car out the gate, and once it closes, you are going to park in front of it and explain to those nosy reporters out there that we're not open for exploitation. Then, when every one of them is gone, you can go back to the shiny new schoolhouse my daughter gave you and *never come back here again!*"

Mahina couldn't believe what she was hearing, but Tutu kept her stern eyes laser-focused on her teacher until they got up to do as she said. Neither she nor Ms. Reynolds dared to speak a word until they stepped outside.

"I'm sorry, Mahina," said Ms. Reynolds. They got into her Prius and shut the doors.

"No, *I'm* sorry. She has no right to say those things to you. I don't know what her problem is, but Koa and I could never have pulled off the fundraiser without you, and you don't deserve to get yelled at for it." Ms. Reynolds started the car without saying anything and headed back out the driveway.

There were three media vans parked at the gate, so there was some jostling required before they could get the Prius out and the gate closed again behind them.

"Mahina Moemoea! Are you amazed at what happened last night?" a reporter with a trim beard who was the last to move his van shouted at her.

"Yes, it was beyond my wildest dreams, but I can't talk with you right now because I have to feed the pigs and chickens, and then I need a little rest. Thanks for covering the event, though. My teacher, Ms. Reynolds here, is available to answer any of your questions. Aloha!" She waved at them and smiled.

She mouthed her thanks to Ms. Reynolds, let herself back through the gate, and walked slowly back to the ranch house, thinking about Tutu. She found her still in the kitchen looking sad.

"Tutu, *why* did you do that? Ms. Reynolds is my teacher!"

"Are they gone yet?" Tutu said, staring at the two empty cups of cold coffee on the table.

"No, but they will be soon. Ms. Reynolds is talking to them. I don't understand you. Are you mad at me for saving the school?" She sat down across from her.

"The chickens need to be fed and so do the pigs. You can take a nap after chores if you need to recover from your big night."

"It *was* a big night, Tutu. The biggest of my life. We raised *four million dollars*!"

"I know that dear. It was amazing, *unusually* amazing. That's what worries me. Not only did your eyes get bigger, but now, so is your head. It's a dangerous path you are treading on. *Very* dangerous."

"Really, Tutu? I have the feeling that if I told you I somehow won back Hawaii for the Hawaiians last night, you'd say I sold myself to the devil. My soul is clean and completely mine! What are you afraid of? You believe in Pele and nature and all that, not fear-based myths about red-horned angels making deals for human souls! What happened last night at the concert was a *great thing* for the school. It was a lucky idea that worked out perfectly, that's all. Those reporters just want more people to feel good about it because good news is rare these days and getting rarer."

"Lucky idea, huh? Was it really? Tell me the truth, Mahina! *Was* it just luck?"

The dream. Her first impulse was to blurt out an answer that wouldn't upset Tutu, but Olina curled herself around her leg, meowed, and trotted toward her breakfast bowl. Mahina bit her tongue and got up to feed her, but then anger overtook her, and she changed her mind.

She swung around to face Tutu. "Okay, Tutu, you win. I got the idea from a *dream*, okay? Ooh, a horrible, dangerous, and scary *dream* that I can't even believe I *survived* because it was *so* dangerous."

She saw Tutu inhale sharply and put her hand over her mouth.

But she went on. "You know what, Tutu? I'm kidding you. It *wasn't* horrible and dangerous. It was a dream, just a very nice simple dream that taught me something useful, and you're just wrong, Tutu! The dreams we have are *not* evil. They're my friends. They're like hands in the ʻāina. I can't believe you believe in the power of the garden and not in the very same feelings that come from the dreams! I *like* my dreams, and if another idea comes to me in them, guess what? I'm going to pay attention to it because this one worked out *pretty darn well!*"

Tutu stood up. "You're just a child, Mahina! You don't know what you're talking about! You're getting pulled in. The caves are wrapping their claws around you. You're going to end up lost inside them, naked and powerless. When I was your age, I myself could barely resist them, and I was *strong* and my special power was *truth*! Your weakness is bringing dreams back into this house again, not just for you, but for me too. I was not strong enough then to face their kind of truths, and I'm sure not strong enough now. None of us are. The garden is enough! It's not my mama's and my tutu's time anymore. It's the time of the Great Unbalance. It's pain, Mahina. Remember that. Do you know what killed your mother, what put her in pain? Her fears, the earth's fears, and her big head. You're treading down the same path, child. Stop. It will *not* work out 'pretty darn well'!"

Mahina watched the blood coursing through Tutu's face as Tutu left the kitchen without saying another word. She heard her stomp up the stairs crying and slam the door to her bedroom. Olina meowed impatiently and looked up at Mahina. She sighed, went into the pantry to fill Olina's bowl with kibble, and pulled on her boots to go outside to do her chores.

Chapter Thirteen

Even though it would be months before the new building would be completed, Mahina was thrilled that the school was able to rent enough temporary classroom trailers and a big tent so that classes and assemblies could meet again right away. That was great, but she couldn't focus on schoolwork yet with the continuing media coverage and all the people around the country wanting to consult with her and Koa about student-initiated fundraising.

Luckily, when emails and the outside demands overwhelmed her, Koa was always happy to step in and talk to anybody who called or stopped by. She loved the excitement, and she was jealous of how much support Koa got from his father about their accomplishment and their new celebrity status.

Meanwhile at the ranch, even after Tutu finally stopped sulking, Mahina had to avoid any talk of school and dreams to keep the peace. Even with the annoying tension, however, she couldn't help feeling that leaving Tutu alone at the ranch every day was a betrayal.

To deal with the emails, Koa started a blog about their lives at school, and this turned into a mini-consulting service for students in other schools in need of better classes and funding. Their social studies teacher even gave them credit for the blog in place of a research paper.

In art, Mahina painted a watercolor of her school with the slogan, "Taking Less and Giving More Is What Rebuilds the World Before," and Koa's dad had it printed on a bunch of t-shirts for them to sell online. "It's never too late for you guys to save for college," he said, but Mahina insisted any money they made from her designs should go to the school instead, and Koa agreed.

Getting closer to Koa was the other reason school was going so well, despite the temporary nuisance of the poorly ventilated trailers and way-too-hot Dakine Porta-Johns. His smarts and hard work tempered with good humor and an easygoing surfer attitude just made everything more fun. He could debate fiercely with her in English class about a controversial passage one minute, then laugh and hug her the next with no hard feelings. She loved how he held his nose like a goof when he walked across the schoolyard to use a stinky Porta-Potty. He seemed to believe that things would always work out if you had patience and an easy sense of humor. She only wished Tutu could learn that from him.

The more she appreciated Koa's good qualities, the more she valued him as someone more than just a partner in their enterprises. She especially loved their daily lunch on the red picnic tables outside the classroom trailers in the bright sun and cool breezes. They talked freely and openly about things, even with the usual throng of people sitting with them. Often, even the teachers liked to join the crowd and talk story over Spam musubi and poke bowls from the nearby convenience store.

As the weeks went on, and the framing went up on the foundation for the new building, Mahina felt there was one big part of her life that she and Koa hadn't talked much about—her cave dreams, which had started up again with intensity. Unable to turn to Tutu for advice without freaking her out, and not wanting to bore Koa or anybody else every day about her nightly adventures, she was forced to digest them all by herself.

As before, the dreams were predictably the same: sometimes she went through the lava tube and flew with no problems, and sometimes she got stuck trying over and over to enter the portal. She would hear the instructions from her mother's voice about how to fly, almost get in, and then get thrown into the raging stream by Olina, who shouted at her with the voice of Tutu. Sometimes she would ride the stream of pain all the way to the floor of Waipio Valley and out into the vast expanse of the glittering ocean.

Finally, one Friday at lunch, she couldn't stand keeping it to herself anymore. She asked Koa to move away from the picnic table to a private spot under the giant leaning Norwegian pine tree that towered over the front of the school.

Game as always, Koa said, "So, you want to discuss all the great places we're going to sneak off to together to go surfing this weekend, right?"

"Don't I wish. But we both know there is no real way to sneak off until one of us gets a license and a car, and we're both too young for that," she said as they walked toward the tree. "I do think a little ocean time would be a great idea, though." They both found a comfortable spot to lean against the trunk and opened their lunch totes.

"But there's still a lot of work to do at the ranch, I know," said Koa, fishing out a sandwich.

"Maybe I can get away. Tutu's not exactly the greatest company these days."

"I'm sorry, is she still upset with you for some reason? I don't get it."

"I don't either—or maybe I do, actually. That's what I want to talk to you about." She unwrapped her egg salad sandwich and turned to face him. "You remember when I told you about my recurring dreams?"

"Right, the ones about flying, I do. So cool! Are you still having them?"

"Yes, but there's something bothering me about them, something important."

"Okay ...?" She got lost for a moment in his eyes.

"Look, I don't understand everything about this, but I have a deep feeling this may be part of something bigger than just dreams." She put down her sandwich and took his arm gently. "This is a secret, even from your dad, okay?"

Koa nodded and put his sandwich down to give her his full attention. His serious and sincere expression gave her the courage to go on. She loved how he could cut the goofiness and be one hundred percent there for her when she needed him to be. How many high school guys were like that?

"Okay, here's what I haven't told you before about my family. Every woman on my mama's side has been unusual like me. My mama, Tutu, my great-*tutu*, and everyone before her. Way back when, my relatives used their visions to make predictions about the future for people, predictions—and I'm not kidding, Koa—that were *accurate*. They made their *living* out of doing this."

"Whoa," said Koa. "Can *you*, um ...?"

"Predict the future? No, that stopped with Great-Tutu, from what I can gather. Tutu had weird dreams too, but she didn't want to use them for predicting the future or for anything else. She told me she ignored them on purpose until they sort of went away for her. You know how she's so big and strong, especially for her age? Somehow she says she got that from her dreams. But I'm not sure because she doesn't want to talk about our family dreams, other than to warn me not to pay attention to them. She thinks they're what killed my mom and dad."

"Oh, wow. That's heavy. She's afraid of them, then?"

"Right, and she thinks that they reveal scary truths. She wants me to be afraid of them too. But you know what, Koa? She won't really tell me *why*, besides that the earth is so hamajang right now. Frankly, *I'm* not afraid of them. Sure, there are a lot of unanswered questions, and they maybe were bad for my mom and dad. But honestly, I *want* the dreams in my life. I *like* flying every night, although recently it's been harder to get there."

She watched Koa think about this and nod slowly. "So, these are just dreams, right? Hmm, I'm on *your* side on this. I don't see what the problem is. I say just keep dreaming if you want to. Enjoy them! Tutu doesn't have to know, does she?" Koa picked up his sandwich and took a bite.

"Oh, she'll know. But there's more to this that you don't yet understand. More to the dreams than just dreaming. I mean, things *I* have already experienced."

"Okay," said Koa, chewing. "What?"

"Look, I'm not a hundred percent sure, but you know how I told you how my idea for the fundraiser came from a dream?"

"Right, I was in it. Then Ms. Reynolds picked up on the idea of the concert to kick it off, I remember, of course."

"Well ..." She looked around to make doubly sure no one was within earshot and then whispered, "I'm pretty sure the dream helped me on purpose. In fact, I *am* sure about that. I just don't want to talk about it a lot because ..."

Koa laughed. "Because it sounds woo-woo?"

"Exactly! Like I'm some kind of woo-woo, tarot-reading, crystal-sucking hippy!" Mahina looked around to see if she had said this too loudly.

"Which you're obviously not," Koa said, now serious again.

"Right, which I'm obviously not. But Koa, what if I really *am*?"

"Crystal-sucking! I don't think so."

"Not *that*, what if I really *do* have a family power? Like Tutu's strength? Or Great-Tutu and Great-Great-Tutu's ability to predict things? What if that idea came to me not by chance, but by something within my dreams that I just don't understand yet? A power Tutu understands and fears?"

"Interesting. You feel this way because your dreams are so consistent, vivid, and unusual."

"Yes, *that* exactly. I know what regular dreams are like, Koa. I used to have them, and I'm telling you the ones I'm having now are *not* like those at all. These are ... I don't know, something bigger, something expansive, something monumental that feels like, I don't know ..."

"Destiny?"

"Yes, destiny! Like the dreams have chosen *me* somehow. Sounds weird for a thirteen-year-old to say, right? What am I, some kind of psychically disturbed, fame-seeking egomaniac?" She glanced around the tree again to make sure they were still alone.

"Okay, listen to me. You're not a psychically disturbed, fame-seeking egomaniac, even if you are freakishly smart and mature for your age, like me." He smiled. "So, maybe the dreams are hinting at a destiny for you, or one for *them* perhaps? We don't know. We don't know where they are coming from, other than maybe your genes or your imagination, and we don't know what they want, if anything. Your mom had them, and your tutu thinks they might have somehow killed her. Now you're having them. You could ask your tutu more about them, but she seems unwilling, right?"

"She insists I ignore them because they're dangerous, in her opinion. But they're *flying* dreams, and they have my sweet *kitty* in them doing horrible things! Who's capable of ignoring *that*?

"But Koa, here's the thing I'm wondering about. Just exactly how powerful are these dreams? I didn't ask them to help me with the fundraiser, yet they must have known I was worried about how to save the school after the hurricane. The dream sent an idea unbidden to me that worked out great, like *magic*. It worked out *better* than great, Koa. Honestly, and it wasn't even all that amazing of an idea. Po'okela is a tiny little independent school. It wasn't even a *public school,* yet the national media covered it."

She paused to let this sink in. "I can't help thinking about this. What do you think would have happened if I had *asked* the dreams for help to save the school? Would it have worked out even better than it did, or would it have crossed some sort of line?"

"You're wondering if the dreams are on your side and would always help, and maybe also wondering if there's a price to be paid for their help if you ask?" said Koa, munching again.

Mahina fished her sandwich back out of her lunch box and took a bite too. She wasn't in the mood for chewing anymore, but people were looking over at them now from the picnic table, and she didn't want anyone to think their conversation was serious enough to skip eating.

"Basically. I keep having the same dream about the cave over and over with little variations here and there, but lately, I haven't been able to fly like before. Instead I get carried away by a river. I keep thinking there's something I need to do or change in myself if I'm going to get the flying dreams back all the time again. And I want them back so much! They're part of me. But Tutu insists I ignore them. She seems to think this is somehow a deal with the devil—or at least a deal with some kind of Hawaiian spirit, I don't know.

"It's not obvious, the deal? If there is one, I mean, inside your dreams?"

"Not at all. I don't even know if it's a deal. If it is, it's not a conscious one. *Nothing* about this is obvious, awake or asleep. That's what's driving me crazy."

"Well, look. It's almost time to go to our last class before the weekend. Let's finish eating, think about it, and talk more at the harbor tomorrow. I'm sorry this is plaguing you. Honestly, the whole thing does seem very mysterious and powerful. Does it help if you remember that your dreams are not the only way in which you, Mahina Moemoea, are unusually powerful? And I don't mean how big and strong you are physically, like your tutu. You're the smartest person

I know, not to mention the kindest and most generous. The dreams may be part of the heritage of your family, but they are also part of *you*, and as far as I can figure, there's no one I know who is more powerful than you are. You'll figure this out, I'm sure."

She packed up her lunch. "Thanks, Koa. You're sweet. But powerful or not, I think that if I'm going to figure this out, I'll need some help."

"You can count on me. Goes without saying, my friend. There's the bell. Come on, we can hone our detective skills first on easier problems, in math!"

Chapter Fourteen

When Mahina asked Tutu that night if she could go surfing with Koa and Mr. Kahale the next day, she begrudgingly gave permission, but only after Mahina promised to get her chores done early and help Tutu catch an injured hog that needed to be slaughtered. Somehow, the poor thing had hurt its leg during the hurricane, and it was only getting worse despite a very expensive visit by the vet. Fortunately, the Kealohas were happy to come over and pick it up and cook it overnight in an imu.

They cornered the pig in the barn using a piece of plywood with handles. It was a noisy process, but there would be lots of delicious meat for everyone's freezer by the end of the weekend.

Mr. Kahale loved to surf as much as Koa did, but Mahina saw only one surfboard in the back of his pickup when they swung by in the middle of the action to pick her up.

"Hey, Mahina," said Mr. Kahale. "Aloha, Mrs. Moemoea. How are things going?"

"Busy. You know how it is. Keep her safe and have her back by supper, is all I ask, and say a blessing for our aumakua in the bay before you begin." Tutu wiped her brow as she helped Mr. Kealoha and his daughters expertly drag the limping animal up the ramp and into their truck. Mahina smiled at Koa and put her surfboard into the back of the pickup.

"Sure will," said Mr. Kahale. "You ready, Mahina? Where's your swimsuit?"

"I got it on underneath. Bye, Tutu!"

"Aloha, Mrs. Moemoea!" said Koa. Tutu gave him a distracted and grudging nod.

They piled in the front and rumbled out the driveway.

"Where's your board, Mr. Kahale?" Mahina asked.

"I've got to come back and work today. Too much to do since the hurricane hit. But you two can manage without me. Surf's up, so there'll be a lot of people around. Plus, Koa has a waterproof belt pouch for his cell phone."

"Do you mind stopping by Pelekane Bay? I promised Tutu I'd visit our aumakua."

"Not at all. I'll just drop you off there, and you can paddle from there to the steps."

"What about the lunch bag?" asked Koa.

"It's waterproof. I'll pick you up at the steps when you call—and hey, no later than 4:30 guys. I guess you have a feast of pork to come back to!"

"Maybe, but it usually takes overnight to roast a pig that large," Mahina said.

"Hey, pork and eggs for breakfast! Sounds good to me!" said Koa.

"Me too!" said Mahina and Mr. Kahale at the same time.

The sun was shining through the back window of the pickup as they made their way down the winding road. They could see the breaking waves painting fluffy white lines along the shoreline below.

"Looks like the surf is perfect," said Koa eagerly. "Thanks, Dad, for driving us."

"No problem. I wouldn't do it if I didn't know you were both good surfers. Just be careful out there."

"We will, Dad," said Koa.

After descending Kawaihai Rd. to the coast, they took a left into the industrial area of the harbor where barges came every day to deliver shipping containers full of supplies for the island. She could never see the harbor without thinking about Tutu saying that most of the stuff shipped to the island was unnecessary junk full of plastic packaging that clogged the landfill. Tutu hated the harbor, mostly because it interrupted the natural flow of currents by the shoreline and created places where run-off got trapped and polluted the waters horribly. Pelekane Bay was one of those, and Mahina was sad to see the ugly, murky water when they parked next to it and unloaded.

"Hey, look, sharks!" said Koa, pointing to the middle of the small bay surrounded by kiawe and coconut trees. Sure enough, Mahina could see six or seven fins dancing above the brown water.

"White tips," said Mr. Kahale. "That's right where the shark heiau used to be."

"Still is," Mahina said. "Only it's all covered in muck."

"At least Pu'ukoholā still looks good," Koa said, looking up at the giant pile of rocks in the shape of a wedge high on the hillside above him.

"Yep," said Mr. Kahale. "King Kamehameha's warning. Well, those sharks won't bother you. Just stick to this shoreline until you get beyond the breakwall. Your cell phone is full, right, son?"

"It's good, Dad. Thanks! See you later!"

"I'm jealous. Happy surfing!" said Mr. Kahale.

As she promised, Mahina walked to the shoreline and tossed some green grass from the ranch into the waters while thinking about her ancestors. She didn't know the specifics of her lineage as far back as when King Kamehameha united the islands, but Tutu loved the story of him ordering thousands of rocks to be carried from Pololu Canyon, over twenty miles away, just to build Pu'ukohola, a sacrificial altar gigantic enough to strike fear in any other island chieftain who had visions of overthrowing him. She looked at it towering above her on the hillside. Did Pu'ukohola affect the environment as much as all the rocks dumped by bulldozers into the ocean to create the harbor? She didn't think so, but the impulse to alter the world in massive ways for human purposes did seem to her as true for her ancestors as for everyone else.

"Come on. Let's get a few rides in while it's not crowded," she said to Koa, who was waiting patiently and watching the sharks. She stuffed her overalls and work shirt into her backpack and slipped her surfboard into the murky water. Soon they left the pollution of the bay behind and were paddling in the fresh currents that had been diverted oceanside of the long sea walls enclosing the harbor. They stopped at the small set of steps leading down from a parking lot, and Koa hauled their packs to a shady spot under a kiawe tree to hang them away from the ants.

She bobbed on her board waiting for him to return. She loved the feeling of catching waves, especially in this favorite surfing spot of King Kamehameha's where there were no hidden reefs or big rocks to worry about. Koa ran back down the steps, and they took off paddling into the waves toward the line-up for a full morning of fun.

At the end of each ride, she thought of her dream when she rose into the air and flew over the harbor, leaving Koa behind. This morning, of course, she simply turned around and paddled out with him for another run, but surfing with him was almost as thrilling to her as a flying dream.

Almost. Even enjoying herself as much as she was out in the sun and the waves, she couldn't stop thinking about her dreams and how they've become more ominous. After two dozen waves, she was ready for a break. More importantly, she was ready to talk. She hoped Koa hadn't forgotten.

As she watched Koa confidently carve the last swell by her side without a care in the world, she got an inspiration about what she should do next. But could she convince him to help her? She hoped so, but he might think the idea was crazy.

What she had in mind was too dangerous to attempt herself. It was also exactly the opposite of what Tutu wanted her to do. Suddenly, she was sure her idea was crazy, but maybe exploring the idea with him might at least help her come up with a better plan. She high-fived him, and they climbed out, dripping and laughing.

"Man, the waves are *great* today!" said Koa. "Did you see those dolphins?" He rested his board next to hers against the tree with their packs.

"Sure did. I thought they might join us for a ride, but they weren't in the mood, I guess."

Koa smiled. "I can't understand anyone not being in the mood for surfing." He checked his phone strapped to his waist for messages.

"Well, you don't get to spend your entire life in the water. Maybe if you did, you'd find other things to do that are just as cool." Mahina grabbed a towel from her pack and sat down on a rock. There was a nice stretch of grass between the ocean in front of them and the beach access parking area behind.

"Yeah, like eating fresh sushi all day long! Let's see what my mom packed us for lunch."

Koa opened his bag and pulled out a flexible cooler. In it were the same things he always ate at school—Spam musubi, a large container of poke, a big bag of One-Ton chips, and guava juice in a can. They dug in happily, passing the poke between them.

She was happy that Koa liked to surf with her. Her friends from her old school would go with her all the time, and she missed the easy pleasures of being with them. Being on the ocean, relaxing in nature, the beauty of the Kohala coastline, all of it felt to her as simple as a Spam musubi—a piece of seaweed, a slice of hot Spam, a fistful of rice, that's it, yet nothing tasted better.

The laughter, the friendship—she could understand why so many of her friends' older siblings would come back from trying to make a living on the mainland. They all said Las Vegas was exciting, but compared to this, too lonely and dangerously complicated.

She loved it here. Yet she knew that once the day of surfing ended, and she headed back up the road to her lonely ranch, her longing for something more adventurous would start again. It always did. "You're hopelessly confused about life," she said to herself.

"Did you say something?" said Koa, tearing open a bag of chips.

"Oh, nothing. I was just thinking about how surfing is so much like flying, you know?"

"Yeah, it's pretty amazing. Someday I want to try one of those foil boards with a wing. I heard they are *exactly* like flying."

"I suppose, but they're expensive, and there's never much wind here."

"I know. That's what my dad says. He says why bother spending so much money when surfing is just as good and almost free? Still ..."

"Maui is the place for foil boarding, I hear. Kahului side," she said, looking at Haleakala rising in the distance over the water.

"Maybe you could fly there in one of your dreams and tell me what it's like," said Koa with a smile.

Once again, she was impressed with Koa's gentle way of letting her bring up the subject at hand. "Yes, my dreams. I need to talk to you about them."

"I'm all ears," said Koa, offering her the bag of chips.

"Okay, the thing you don't know is about my parents. Dad, as far as I know, never had the dreams. They get passed down on the maternal side of my mother's family."

"Right, and the women in your family kept their surnames. You said your tutu had dreams, and she said your mom did too."

"Yes, and Tutu blames my mom's dreams for my parents' deaths."

"I don't understand how that could be," he said, shaking his head. Does Tutu think your mom's dreams told her to do something that got her killed, or did the dreams themselves kill her?"

"I've heard of people dying of a broken heart, and I suppose dreams *could* make you depressed, especially if they are nightmares that happen over and over again. But actually outright killing you? I doubt that's it. Tutu is sure Mom and Dad drowned, although they only found Mom's body after the storm."

Koa moved closer to her on the rock and looked at her intently. "Tell me more."

"It was shortly after I was born, literally days after, so I don't remember my mom at all. They went into one of the caves on our property, a big one pretty near our ranch house. It's closed up now with cement blocks. I should have figured that was the one where they died because it is the only one sealed up like that. Anyway, Tutu says they were deep inside the lava tube when rain from the hurricane hit. Mom's body was found inside the lava tube wrapped around a big boulder. Dad's body was never found. It probably washed down into the ocean."

Koa nodded his head. "And you think this might be the same cave you visit every night in your recurring dream?"

"I'm sure it is. At least, my dreaming mind thinks it is. I don't know how it could be any other one."

"Interesting. But why not? Why not any cave at all?"

"Your questions are amazing, Koa. I haven't even told you yet that I think it's the voice of my mother that calls me to that very cave every night."

"Oh, wow. That's pretty freaky."

"I know it is, especially since I've never heard her real voice, at least that I can remember. But the voice in my dreams talks to me like it loves me, and it sort of sounds like a grown-up version of my voice, only distorted a little bit."

"So you hear what you think is your mother's voice calling you to that one specific cave in your dreams, and the dreams happen every night, and they don't vary?"

"Same story, same setting, some variations, and almost every night, unless I'm really tired."

Koa scratched his chin. "And the dreams came up with the idea for the fundraiser."

"More or less. And that's not just a coincidence. My great-grandmother and her mother made a living predicting the future for people on this island. I'm telling you, this is a superpower in my family." She looked at Koa intensely.

"One your tutu wants you to ignore."

"Yes, *commands* me to ignore, and she won't tell me why, other than the earth is angry and the dreams killed my mom and dad."

"Wow. But despite your tutu's objections, your mom is somehow calling to you."

"That's what I think. No, I'm *sure* of it."

"And you don't know what to do because, first of all, your tutu doesn't know that a human can't ignore dreams, and second of all, this is your *mother* we're talking about. It doesn't matter if she's *actually* talking to you from the dead or if you're imagining her talking to you. Whichever is the case, you obviously can't ignore her, any more than I could ignore my mom when she wants me to stop playing video games!"

"You got it. Mom and Tutu are both telling me what to do as if my life depended on it, and it *sucks*." She picked up a loose lava rock and threw it into a wave breaking against the seawall below them. Koa just watched the splash and let the conversation pause while they both stopped to think.

"Surfing just now, I figured out what I want to do," Mahina finally said, "but I think I'm going to need some help, and it's taking a big risk because if Tutu found out, she'd really be mad at me."

"Hypnosis? Find a psychic?" asked Koa in all seriousness.

"No, I need to figure this out on my own. I need more information, but it might be dangerous, and I don't think I'm going to get any more from Tutu."

"What then? Whatever it is, I'm in. Let's get to the bottom of this! It's too important not to!"

Once again, she looked into Koa's eyes that were reflecting the light on the water. In them, she saw only openness, sincerity, and enthusiasm. She felt that in some important ways, he understood her better than Tutu did. He listened to her better, that's for sure. She could obey Tutu and try to ignore her mom's voice and never solve the mystery of her dreaming, or she could trust this friend to help her learn the truth about herself and her family's power. Doing that could turn out to be a regrettable mistake, but at least she would have a chance to get some answers, instead of being in the dark like she was now.

"Listen up, world. I'm never going to be able to ignore my dreams, and I've always wanted adventure," she shouted at the ocean. She took Koa's hands in hers. "Okay, here's my idea. How good are you at busting concrete blocks?"

Chapter Fifteen

The next Monday afternoon, Mahina and Koa stepped off the school bus together at the end of her long driveway. They had three hours before Mr. Kahale agreed to pick up Koa after their horseback ride.

"You've ridden before?" Tutu asked Koa in the barn, where they found her checking on a new litter of pigs that had just been born.

"Sure have, Ma'am. Here and in Colorado, where my uncle has a ranch with six hundred head."

"Okay, but Mahina, ride Costco and let this young man ride Ikaika. She's less jumpy. Koa, you should follow Mahina closely out there. It's great that you two want to check the perimeter fencing, but there are lots of holes you could fall into."

"That's what I heard," said Koa. "We'll be real careful. Also, Costco ...?"

"He was a gift from the neighbors," Mahina explained, "who named him that because every time he needed something, they spent more money on him than they should."

Koa laughed. "I get it."

"Turns out he had colic, that's all," Tutu said. "Good horse, but a very rough trot."

"We're just going to walk, Tutu," she said.

"I hope that's all you're going to do," said Tutu, giving Koa a look.

"I'm sorry about my tutu," Mahina said when they got to the horse stalls at the far end of the barn. "She can be annoyingly suspicious."

"Well, she kind of has a right to be, I guess, considering what we're up to."

"It'll be fine. We'll trot the perimeter quickly and tie up the horses on the other side of the hill. We should have plenty of time to do what we need to do."

They brushed and saddled the horses and closed the barn door behind them. They waved goodbye to Tutu and headed back out the driveway toward the fence line. The small, handheld sledgehammer weighed heavily in her backpack.

Feeling Tutu's eyes on her as they made their way around the perimeter, Mahina waited until they were out of sight of the barn before breaking into a trot. "There are actually no holes along the fence line. Most of the cave entrances are concentrated at the foot of the hillsides," she said, her voice shaking a bit from the bouncing.

"Wow, it's sure beautiful out here. Look at the sun!" said Koa, his voice steady despite Ikaika's gait. The sun was peeking behind patchy cumulus clouds halfway down the western sky. "It'll be a great sunset tonight, that's for sure."

"Hopefully we'll be done and out by the time it happens," she said.

"We better be, or my dad will kill me."

She led the way on cattle trails through the tall grass, sometimes scaring off part of the herd, but mostly just trotting with Koa in the vast expanse of the hills and pastures. Birds were everywhere. A colorful pheasant took off in front of them at the back of the property, and francolins were making a racket in the distance with their loud calls. A half-hour later they completed the loop, except for the last section that would take them back to the barn. Threading her way through a maze of mounded hills, she approached the back side of the largest one that contained the walled-off cave.

"We can tie them up here and go the rest of the way by foot," she said. "We're about a mile away from the house. If we stay low when we get to the entrance, Tutu won't be able to see us over the grass, even if she's looking right toward the cave."

Koa checked his cell phone. "We've got about an hour and a half, leaving a half hour to leisurely ride back," he said.

"Come on. Let's go before I chicken out," she replied. There weren't any trees or bushes to tie the horses to, so they wrapped the reins around a couple of big boulders. "They'll be okay with all these fresh weeds to munch."

When they got to the cave entrance, she could see that the previously flattened grass from the flood had straightened back up, and new sprouts were now covering every square inch of exposed dirt. She hefted the hammer out of her backpack. They scrambled a few feet up the side of the walled-off entrance to where the flood had washed away a few of the cinder blocks.

"Wow, feel that cool breeze coming out of there!" said Koa. He grabbed one of the loose cinder blocks and tugged. It came away easily in his hands, and he tossed it behind him.

"It's like a cold blast from a fridge. Is that hole big enough to get in?" Mahina asked.

"Maybe, but let's try to remove a few more of these first." He held out a hand toward her. "Sledge?"

The next block came out as easily as the first, but it took a few blows of the hammer to remove three more blocks and create an entrance that was big enough to get through, yet still hidden by the grass.

"Perfect," she said, admiring his work. "You ready for the plunge?"

"Are you?"

"No strange feelings yet," she said. "Let's do it."

"Lead the way," said Koa, laying down the hammer and taking out his flashlight.

They didn't need their flashlights at first as they stepped down a little bit from the entrance onto the floor of the lava tube, but as they started following it farther into the hillside, the damp darkness descended.

"I've got goosebumps, it's so cold in here!" Mahina said.

"Yeah, it is. I'm surprised your family didn't use one of these as a root cellar."

Before the first curve of the lava tube, Mahina looked back at the bright light of the entrance disappearing behind them.

"It looks like a wound," she whispered, but Koa didn't hear her. Why was she whispering? She walked slowly, afraid to leave behind the light from the entrance. The cave wouldn't collapse, but she couldn't help imagining that it might. She shuddered, remembering Tutu's face and her warning about getting lost in the labyrinth of lava tubes, naked and powerless.

She took a deep breath. Koa was with her. If she wasn't scared in an unfamiliar cave, she wasn't human. *Leave doubt and fear behind*, she remembered from her dream.

She gripped the flashlight harder and followed its illumination around the curve and deeper into the tunnel. Koa's beam jittered along the rocks behind her at her feet. Was he scared too? She didn't ask him. If he admitted he was, they might decide to go back without accomplishing their goal.

But what exactly *was* their goal? She couldn't decide. Did she think that her mother's ghost would be sitting there on a rock, asking her what took her so long? Or that there was a hidden cosmic tape recorder that broadcasted dreams to her over and over? She didn't know. She kept trudging onward.

"This reminds me of biology class," said Koa, after a few more twists and turns. "A giant intestine. You know, like the colonoscopy video we saw before the hurricane. Look, there's a polyp now!" He pointed his headlamp at a boulder hanging down from the ceiling.

It was shaped like that punching-bag-looking flap of skin in the back of your throat. Mahina had to laugh because that's exactly what it looked like, only a lot rougher.

Ten minutes later, the lava tube split into two equal-sized directions. After some discussion, she took the left-hand one that led slightly upward. Then that one split again.

"Good strategy. Be consistent," said Koa as she chose the left-hand turn again that headed slightly upward. Going up seemed better to her than going down if they wanted to find a cavern with a hole in it, provided it even existed.

"I feel like Egyptian tomb robbers heading for the treasure room hidden high in the eye of the pyramid!" Koa said.

After so much work to get there, she hoped something would reveal itself, but even after a few tricky maneuvers around boulders that had fallen from the top of the tunnels, there was nothing, especially not in her mind. No whispers in her ear from mysterious voices. No dreamlike sense whatsoever that she could bend her legs to float upward and fly through the lava tube. No wide-open cavern with an escape hole to the beckoning sky. It was just a plain old lava tube, not much different than a dank prison, and she was getting cold and discouraged.

Koa checked his cell phone. "We better go back, but hey, we can for sure come back again and look around some more," he said.

"Yeah, I guess so," Mahina said, but she was starting to think that this approach to learning more about her dreams was a literal dead end. She sighed deeply.

She let Koa lead the way back to the entrance and tried once more to conjure up the feeling from her dreams. Nothing. Was she just a deeply wounded soul trying to compensate for the tragic loss of her parents through a twisted and misguided imagination? No, that couldn't be it. The tingling feelings she got with Tutu in the garden were real, and there surely must be a reason Tutu was so afraid of this place.

She looked at Koa ahead of her and felt bad for dragging him into this mess. He said he was willing to try again, but was he really? How could he not think she was crazy? Heck, *she* even thought she might be crazy. By the time they were back at the entrance and had crawled with relief back into the warm air of the late afternoon sun, she felt completely drained and not a little bit foolish.

"Wow, that was a cool place!" said Koa, clicking off his flashlight and stuffing it and the sledgehammer into his pack. "I'd for sure come back sometime!"

She looked at him carefully to see if he was being sarcastic, but again, she realized that Koa didn't have an insincere bone in his body. "Thanks," she replied, "for coming with me in there. It was stupid, I guess." Dejected, she headed back around the hill to where they had left the horses.

"Not stupid at all. Information, Mahina! We know a lot more now than we did before, and I'm sorry for my enthusiasm just now. I forgot your parents passed away here."

"Yeah, that's okay. I forgot too. Maybe that's why ..."

"Hey, like I said, we can come back. There are a lot more tunnels in there to explore, and the more familiar we are with the landscape, the more you can focus on the supernatural."

"You're amazing, you know that? But you should probably dump me as a friend, I think."

"Why? You're the most interesting person I've ever met!"

She stopped and turned around to look at him. There was really no such thing as failure for him, and he was a faithful friend. Her heart started to beat faster. She reached out to hug him—but stopped when she heard a horse snorting frantically.

"Hey," Koa said, "something's wrong with the horses!"

Mahina whipped around and followed him running. Ikaika was still where they left them making a racket, but Costco was nowhere to be seen. Ikaika was shaking her head and pulling back on her reins, trying to free them from the boulder.

"Costco must have gotten loose and run back to the barn," Mahina said. "Come on, we've got to get back fast before Tutu has a heart attack!"

"Easy, Ikaika, easy!" She grabbed the quivering horse by the bridle and patted her on the neck. Ikaika calmed down just enough for her to untie the reins from the boulder and climb on.

"We should ride back together. Get on the rock," she said, the horse prancing. Koa scrambled onto the boulder and jumped behind her onto the saddle. Ikaika lurched, and Koa hung on tight to Mahina's belly as she fought the reins to prevent the revved-up horse from galloping back to the barn.

Fifteen cramped and painful minutes later, they dismounted at the gate to the yard. They led the still-shaking Ikaika around the back lanai of the house, toward the barn. There, they found Tutu trying to calm Costco, whose legs were flying up and down like the needle of a sewing machine.

Ikaika and Costco whinnied at each other. Tutu saw Mahina and Koa and yelled something with her hand up, but Mahina couldn't hear it over the neighing of the frantic horses. Tutu didn't look happy at all.

"Easy, Costco, easy! What happened? Are you two all right?" said Tutu when they finally got close enough to understand her. She patted the sweaty neck of the horse firmly in her grip, while the two reunited horses pressed their noses together and kept whinnying and dancing around as if they had just gone through the worst experience of their lives. Tutu's legs were like a sewing machine, too, as she tried to avoid being stepped on.

"It's okay, Ikaika. Calm down, whoa, whoa, whoa!" Mahina said, separating the two horses enough to make it safe to stand near them. "Costco got loose out there, that's all. We're fine." She looked at Koa, who nodded and helped her hold Ikaika steady.

"What, did you fall off or something?" asked Tutu.

"No, we tied the horses to a rock, and Costco got loose. He must have pulled back pretty hard when I wasn't looking."

"What could you possibly be doing that you had them tied to a stupid rock and not the fence or a tree? Is there a break in the fence out there?"

"Um, we were on the way back and we kind of had to go to the bathroom," she said, again looking at Koa, whose eyes were widening.

Tutu gave both of them a suspicious look then shook her head. "Well, I'm glad you are okay, and now you get to walk these guys around until they're cool. Don't let them drink too much water until then. At least I can count on you two to know that much. And don't forget to brush them out. Maybe you'll learn to bring a rope and a halter next time you go adventuring in the grass, instead of using expensive leather reins. Here you go, cowboy. Maybe you can keep control over this horse."

Tutu handed Koa Costco's reins, and without saying another word, walked upright across the yard and back into the house.

"Sorry, Tutu!" Mahina yelled after her.

"Whoa, she's mad at me," said Koa.

"Not at you, me," she said. "Or we just scared her. Can't blame her for feeling upset after seeing a horse come back without a rider."

"Or she doesn't like me hanging out with you."

She looked at him, concerned.

"Or you're right," he went on quickly. "Horses can be dangerous if you're not careful. We should have brought halter ropes. But, wow, that was quite an adventure!"

She put her head against Ikaika's sweaty mane and closed her eyes. "Yes, *all* of it was, I guess. Tutu will be okay. She can get really mad, but then she gets over it. Thanks for going into the cave with me, even though it was kind of a waste. Phew, I'm glad this day is over."

She couldn't believe how tired she was all of a sudden. Was it from lying to Tutu, she wondered? From the stumbly exploration of the lava tube? She didn't know. The ride was strenuous at the end, but it wasn't really that long or hard, not enough for her to have heavy eyelids and jelly legs like she did.

She looked at Koa, energetic and smiling as usual, and she was very grateful he was there to help her unsaddle the horses and walk them in the yard until they were calm and cool enough to put back in the barn.

Was today worth all that sneaking around? Did they learn anything, or was it just plain luck that her idea for the fundraiser was so bizarrely successful? It certainly didn't seem that any special knowledge of the future could have come from that cave, at least not from what they saw of it today.

But then why did her parents dare to go in there when they knew a hurricane was on the way? Why in her dream did her mom call for her from inside the cave, while Tutu and Olina wanted so desperately to keep her outside? She didn't know, and her mind was too burned out to come up with any theories. Right now all she knew is that she wanted to crawl into bed with Olina and sleep, and it wasn't even time for supper yet.

Chapter Sixteen

After Mr. Kahale came to pick up Koa, Mahina found a pot of Portuguese bean soup on the stove in the kitchen and a note from Tutu saying that she was going to do some paperwork upstairs for the evening.

Unhappy that Tutu was avoiding her, but grateful that she didn't have to lie further about the details of her ride with Koa, Mahina fed Olina and slurped a bowl of soup while watching her chomp on her kibble. Either Tutu was just tired from the scare about the horses, or she didn't believe her story about why Costco got away from them in the pasture and didn't want to confront her about it. Whichever was true, both scenarios made her feel bad.

Part of her wanted to come clean and tell Tutu what she had done, but then she would have to admit again that she wasn't obeying her about not paying any attention to her dreams.

"You're just really tired," she mumbled out loud to herself. She remembered what Koa said, that their investigation wasn't over yet, and she decided that he was right that it was too early to give up. "I don't want to spend my whole life not knowing!"

Olina finished her last kibble and looked up at her quizzically.

Monday nights were always heavy homework nights, but she knew she didn't have the brain power for it when she trudged upstairs trailed by Olina. *I'll do it on the bus tomorrow morning,* she thought. The light was on in Tutu's room, so she yelled, "Good night, Tutu!"

"See you in the morning, Mahina. Glad you're okay," came the muffled reply. Mahina sighed. She hoped things would get back to normal tomorrow. It wasn't that she just felt guilty. Lying to Tutu made her life feel even more lonely than it did before.

Mahina pulled on her pajamas and did a lazy job of brushing her teeth before climbing under her great-tutu's quilt. Olina was curled up on her pillow chomping on her front paws with her teeth.

"I wish you wouldn't do that in bed, Olina," Mahina said. "It's gross, and I have to clean up the bits of your claws that you spit out everywhere."

Olina just gave her a look like, "Yes, I know you love me," and went right back to her feline mani-pedi, only stopping her self-torturing session when Mahina couldn't stand it any longer and put her arm around her.

As often happened when she was exhausted, the dreams left her alone for most of the night. She noticed this with some relief when she got up to pee sometime after midnight with the full moon shining through the window. When she sleepwalked back from the bathroom and climbed into bed again, it looked like Olina had gotten much bigger all of a sudden.

She reached out to investigate. Weird, her bed seemed to be growing too. She touched Olina's warm fur, but Olina pulled away from her fingertips and sank deeply toward the floor creating a huge depression. The edge of the mattress snapped up like a wave and sent Mahina flying. She lost her grip on the sheets and tumbled downward on top of Olina ...

LETTING GO, I LET MYSELF fall across white clouds into the gigantic warmth of Olina's fur. It envelops me completely, and I swim with my arms and legs through its expanse. I breathe as easily and comfortably as a kitten cuddling against her mother's belly. My swimming hand reaches her neck, and Olina's head jerks up to look at me with fangs exposed.

"I'm sorry!" I mumble.

Olina's giant mouth opens to reveal an enormous pink tongue and a soft, cavernous throat. "*If you love me, you wouldn't be sorry. You would* obey*!*"

"But I do love you. Why won't you talk to me? Why won't you help me?"

"*Why won't you help* me? *You are living my deepest fears. You make them real again, so terribly real. I must stop you, or you will suffer and die!*"

"No!" I say, and push against her head. "I'm not afraid of your claws. Your fears are not mine. I *will* dream. Oh, Mother, let me hear your voice instead! Where are you?"

"*It is time, Daughter. You are our last hope. One more time, you must enter me. What you seek, the truth, awaits you.*"

"Enter *you*?" Then, in a blink, I am at the entrance of the cave. "I was here today already," I say to her voice.

Olina is gone, but Ikaika is kicking at the concrete blocks. She stares at me, shakes her head, and gallops away toward the barn.

"*Concentrate,*" the voice continues. "*There will be no resistance. You have taken the necessary steps. It is the Moemoea duty to the people and the earth for each generation to help teach the next one to be more powerful. See now what the cave is in reality! Walk within in fullness!*"

The night air is cool, but nothing like the damp, musty chill inside the lava tube as I duck down and squeeze inside. In the dark, I know what to do before being told. I keep my head down, concentrate, will my knees to bend and my ankles to rise. Confidence flows through my blood vessels like a spreading fire, setting my skin aglow and illuminating the very walls of the cavern that snake their way ahead of me.

"*Yes! Good! You understand more deeply now. Deeper! Come deeper!*"

I am a floating balloon. My mind guides me as I follow her voice and drift forward, sure of my power. I know this time I will not fall or scrape my knees or bump my head. My skin is glowing and so is the path. I know the way: I turn right, zoom ahead a long while, turn right again, float another long while.

I embrace the warmth and the luminous light in this voice that calls me. I fly ahead. My mind guides me perfectly. The passageway gets wet and narrows dramatically, and then I float into a huge, glorious cavern glowing with silver light shining from a hole above.

I am free here. I fly—oh my, how I fly! Around the walls of the cavern I go! Back and forth. The walls know when I approach them and make room for me. The cavern is alive and gives me infinite space and more energy than I will ever need. I fly, and my body vibrates with a hot pleasure that is as simple as it is strong. I can fly anywhere. I simply think where to go, and I go there.

"Remember this, Daughter. This is all you need to know. This feeling is life, *pure and simple.* This *is flying. Simple flying. Nothing is better. This is where life begins and where it ends. You must help them remember that the flight of living is enough. There is no better adventure once you know that, and flying is free to everyone who is alive. Show them the* feeling *is enough, my Daughter. Take on people, not nature. Nature will heal when people change. Show them that life alone is enough. I know because I so foolishly lost it."*

Yes, this feeling! The tingling feeling! Never has flying felt so good. Never has there been such freedom in just being alive, soaring and breathing!

The cavern is delicious and nourishing, but there's more for me to explore and learn. I head for the moonlight and fly past the grassy vines hanging around the opening and out into the clear night sky.

And now the feeling expands. I embrace the world in its amazing wholeness. I feel the heat at the center of the earth. I feel the snow on Mauna Kea, virginal in the moonlight. The ocean glitters beyond the hills of Waipio and Waimanu Valley. I understand everything. Everything is a part of the feeling of the cavern. I am enough! I am beautiful!

Tears stream from my eyes from the beauty, the amazing beauty, not just of the land, not just of the cavern, but of the cavern that I carry in *myself.*

Me, flying, exploring, loving! I soar toward the ranch house to share this with my family. Did Olina and Ikaika make it home? There is a light on in Tutu's upstairs window. Oh, there she is, my beautiful Tutu in bed with Olina by her side! Oh, Tutu, join me in this feeling! Join me in life! I've learned the lesson of life!

Tutu sits up in bed, terrified, and stares me in the eye. Her mouth opens and her monstrous voice rattles the foundations of the house. "You disobeyed me! You entered the sacred cavern without permission or guidance! You don't know what you've done! Oh, I've lost you, just like I lost your mother! Now you must see its dangers for yourself!"

Olina leaps out the window from Tutu's bed and flies toward me. She yowls and sinks her claws into my knees. With unimaginable strength, she drags me through the moonlight back toward the cavern.

No, Olina! Let me go! *Let me go!*

Chapter Seventeen

The darkness was silvery when her eyes snapped awake. Her body was shivering, and the ground was hard. Where was her bed? Her covers? The air smelled musty and damp. Cold moisture was seeping into her pajamas from where her mattress should be.

What the heck? She struggled to her feet.

Was she still dreaming? She touched her wet pajama bottoms. No, this was real, all right. But what had happened? Where was she? Obviously, she had been asleep, or had she blacked out? If so, doing what?

She looked up at the cavern in her dream!

How did she get here? In her pajamas? Had she walked here in her sleep?

"Hey, can anyone hear me?" she yelled.

No answer. Alone.

She looked up at the hole in the cavern and tried to move toward the shaft of moonlight that was striking the cave floor, but the lava rocks under her feet were sharp and painful. She stumbled to a stop. How did she get in here without shoes on? All the way from the ranch? She couldn't have! Her feet would be cut to the bone.

She shivered and looked down at her wet pajamas. They were torn to shreds around her legs. Was that blood? How did she get all scratched up? Then she remembered. Her dream and Tutu being angry with her.

"Olina, how could you do this to me?" she cried. My sweet kitty? No, it was just a dream. I must have somehow scratched myself getting in here.

She looked again at the hole in the ceiling of the cavern with a few distant stars visible high above. It was too far up to climb to. This was like one of those deadly sinkholes in the lava fields near Kiholo Bay that the poor goats stumble into, only larger and deeper. The thought of being trapped here made her shiver even harder. She sat down and wrapped her arms around her torso to warm up.

"No, I've got to move," she said. The walls of the cavern echoed her words. *But move where?* she thought. *And how?*

"Hey, Mom," she cried, "can you maybe let me fly again, so I can go home?" Her words echoed off the walls but no answer. She didn't figure she'd get one.

This was no longer a dream, unfortunately, although a dreamlike mood still lingered persuasively in her mind. Was tonight even the same night when she flew and saw Tutu through her bedroom window? It had to be, but she didn't know for sure because everything was distorted and strange since she awakened. Being awake in this cave felt more like a dream than her dream had felt. But, wasn't that proof that she was awake? You had to be awake to think about how weird your dreams were, right? And how *great* they were. She remembered the amazing feeling of flying up and out of the very same hole that hung there now so far out of her reach. How beautiful it had all been—until the end, when Tutu freaked out and screamed that she had lost her. Was Tutu using her own dreaming power to punish her? If so, might she be really lost, as Tutu warned?!

Was it possible that Olina, or some spirit in the form of Olina, had somehow dragged her back to this place in *reality*? Maybe right out of her *bed*? Was her dream world finally merging with her real world, as she so often joked that it might? Her cold and wet body sure made it seem that way.

But if her dream had been real enough to somehow bring her body here, then she should be able to find her way back to the entrance by retracing the way she got in here in her dream. Maybe Tutu didn't do anything to her. Maybe Tutu only *feared* she would get lost in here. Maybe she didn't have to be lost, if she could use her head and leave her own doubts and fears behind. She had to try!

She struggled stiffly to her feet and looked around at the walls behind her. There in the faint moonlight was the shadow of the narrow passageway that had rained on her in her dream before she floated into this cavern. She thought hard, retracing in her mind her journey to get here, the glow on the walls of the lava tubes, the twists and turns she had made. She was pretty sure that to go back, she needed to go through the narrow passageway, walk a long time, go left, walk another long distance, then take another left for a while, and she'd be out! But there had been light to see by when she floated here in her dream. No light now. She looked at the skin on her hands. No glowing skin and worse, no shoes. How was she possibly going to make it?

She took a deep breath. What would Koa do in this situation? She saw his smiling face in her mind. He would use the tools he had available. Hmm, what tools did she have?

Pajamas!

Weighing the alternative of keeping her pajamas on for a little bit of warmth and being unable to walk, or taking them off so she could at least have something to wrap around her feet, she chose the latter. Shivering, she used her top around one foot and the bottoms around the other, tying the flannel around her feet as securely as she could. *The caves are wrapping their claws around you. You're going to end up lost inside them, naked, powerless.* She wasn't going to pay attention to Tutu's fearful words. As weird as this situation was, she didn't feel powerless now having figured out her shoes. She felt like she was living in a romantic poem, one in which the images and words that made the least logical sense were closest to the truth, and that everything would be okay if she just had faith. It was her poem. She would figure it out!

Her new pajama shoes were bulky but effective, but she needed to move fast before she shivered to death. Fortunately, getting the wet pajamas off actually made her skin feel a bit warmer. She stepped carefully toward the narrow opening and ducked inside. The moonlight from above, already dim, faded quickly to nothing as she shuffled over the wet rocks away from the cavern. It wasn't long before she stubbed her toe on an exposed hunk of lava.

"Ow!" she cried. "This sucks!"

Ignoring the pain, she retied her pajama top over the wounded toe. Moving again, she stuck to the left side of the lava tube as it widened and went on. A walking spider, her hands gingerly felt their way along the wall's edge while her feet navigated around the uneven rocks.

It was slow going, and the movement did warm her up a bit, but not enough to get rid of the goosebumps all over her body.

"It sure was a lot easier to float through here!" she complained, but still there was no motherly voice answering her. Whatever magic got her in here, she was apparently on her own getting out.

She tried not to think about where she was. It was terrifying to maybe be lost underground, especially in such utter darkness. Was this what it was like to get buried alive like Edgar Allen Poe feared so much? She forced herself to not think about it. Instead, she thought of her dream and the beauty of the cavern when she was flying.

Step by step, she moved along the lava tube both in reality and backward on the map she held in her head. At the intersections of lava tubes, where in the dream she had floated right, she spider-walked left. The distances, she hoped, were the same, but it was frustratingly hard to calculate the number of uneven steps needed to equal a moment of floating.

Was she going too far? Not far enough? What if she misjudged and took a wrong turn that led her even farther from the entrance? She might never find her way out! And what if it started raining?

Again, she forced herself not to imagine what her mom and dad had gone through in this very cave.

Better, she thought, to keep channeling Koa's confidence and clear thinking. It was the dream version of him, after all, who had suggested the fundraiser and the concert. Yes, she remembered her dream journey into the cavern, and yes, she was smart enough to judge on foot the distances she floated. She had the resources. She would reach the end of the poem and she would be free. She just needed to be confident and concentrate hard on what she was doing.

Yes, her mom might not be answering her questions right now, but if the dream was real, then Hana could still be watching over her. What had her mother told her? That each generation's job was to make the next generation's power greater. Surely her mom hadn't encouraged her to come here just to let her die. But why wasn't she helping her? Maybe she couldn't help her because Tutu and Olina were the ones who brought her. What had Tutu said about family guidance? This certainly wasn't very good guidance! Not like her mother's, anyway.

After a while, there was a juncture with two choices, one on her left and one on her right. She could feel the two jagged openings with her hands, but she couldn't remember an intersection like this in her dream. Had she missed a turnoff? Gone too far? Was this the first right she had taken in her dream, and she just hadn't noticed the second one just beyond the boulder? Where she was emerging did seem a little lower than what she remembered, and it was hidden behind a boulder. Maybe she and Koa had overlooked it, and she was only discovering it now because she was feeling her way along with her hands?

She decided to ignore the opening on the right and take the left one beyond it. She could always come back if the turn she chose was wrong. But now she had to hold two maps in her mind: the original one she was following backward, and the new one that could lead her back to the three-way juncture if necessary. One was a visual dream map translated by necessity to the sense of touch, the other a tactile map dependent totally on the recent memory of her hands.

On she went, one careful arachnid step at a time, concentrating hard on where she was going and even harder on not panicking. It was exhausting. She was still very cold, and now getting thirsty. At least the cold in her legs and feet numbed out the pain from the cut on her toe and all the scratches on her legs. Would the entrance never come?

"Help me," she said out loud to no one in particular.

Then there it was, moonlight outlining the straight edges of the cement blocks that had been busted open by the water from the hurricane and then widened by Koa. Never had such an ugly slash of destruction been such a beautiful sight to her. Never had she felt so suddenly strong. She crawled her way out into the dry night air and fell sobbing to her knees in the soft grass.

"I made it! I'm alive!" she whispered. She inhaled with utter relief the deeply familiar green smell of the hills and pasture. "Thank you, thank you!"

Because of the grass on the cattle path, her feet were in far less pain as she walked than they had been in the cave. Although the night air was not as cold as the cave, the dew soaked the pajamas on her feet until they felt like blocks of ice when she finally crossed the barnyard to the lanai. No lights were on upstairs.

She sat on the steps and carefully unwound her feet. She shook out the bits of rocks and bundled the filthy material into a ball that she held in her shivering arms. As quietly as she could with her shaking hands, she let herself in the back door, crossed the living room and kitchen, and tiptoed painfully up the stairs.

Avoiding the squeaky floorboards, she moved past Tutu's door to the bathroom where she drank long and hard at the sink and then splashed water on her face. She took the towel and started to wipe the dirt and blood from her legs, but the shivering cold and exhaustion overtook her. It was all she could do to stumble to her bedroom and take the filthy towel with her so Tutu wouldn't see it.

She opened her door, and there was Olina halfway buried under the covers and sound asleep in the moonlight. She climbed into bed and wrapped herself like a heat-seeking vampire around her faithful cat. She was home. She was alive.

"Oh, Olina. No more dreams tonight, please!" she said, finally closing her eyes. "And thanks, Koa, for helping me get home."

Chapter Eighteen

The overhead light in her room came on abruptly, and Mahina woke up to Tutu standing by her bed. Olina jumped up and scurried from the room.

"Sweetheart, I'm sorry to wake you, but are you okay?" Tutu said. "There's *blood* all over the house and on the bathroom floor. Footprints in blood! What happened to you?"

"Uh, I don't know," she mumbled. It all came back to her in a flash: the cave, being lost, the long walk back in the dark with the pajamas wrapped around her feet. "Blood?" she said.

"Yes, everywhere. Did you cut yourself? How? Why didn't you wake me?" She sat up and rubbed her eyes. Tutu spotted the balled-up pajamas on the floor by her bed. She held them up. "What the hell happened to these?"

"I don't know, Tutu. I must have been sleeping."

"Check yourself. Were you sleepwalking? This is a lot of blood and ... mud? Were you *outside*?"

"I don't know, Tutu. I must have had a nightmare."

"Let me see you," said Tutu emphatically. Mahina swung her legs over the side of the bed, keeping the covers over her body.

"Oh my gosh, you are a mess!" said Tutu. "Your legs are cut everywhere! And what did you do to your toe? That might even need a stitch!" Mahina looked down at her blood-encrusted foot. The cut on her toe did look awful, but upon closer examination, it wasn't really that deep, and the scratches on her calves were numerous but not any worse than ones you might get from a hard skid on a playground.

Tutu went to the kitchen and returned with a basin of warm water, some hydrogen peroxide, and a clean towel.

"You don't remember anything?" said Tutu, washing her feet.

She remembered everything, but she was awake enough now to know she didn't want to tell Tutu anything about it.

"I vaguely remember walking around outside in the dark, I think," she said, "but I'm not sure. Do you really want me to try to remember?"

"No, no, I don't! Obviously, this happened in a dream, which means they are getting worse. I told you, you've got to fight this, Mahina!"

"I know, Tutu, I'm trying. Do you really think I want to go wandering about in my sleep with all the cave holes out there?"

"No, of course not. But why did you mention the cave holes? Oh, my. It was the same with your mother. She was obsessed with those things, too. It's the dreams, isn't it? The dreams again, the cursed dreams! I won't let you live here if this keeps happening. I'll send you to Oahu before I'll let you kill yourself like Hana did!"

She regretted her mistake in mentioning the holes. "Look, Tutu, let's just finish with the bandages, okay?" Maybe Tutu would calm down if she stayed busy with her hands. "It's time for me to do chores and get ready for school."

She was relieved that Tutu didn't seem to remember her flying outside her window or screaming at her last night in her dream. She certainly didn't want to bring it up. Tutu was already upset enough.

"You're not going to school today. You look exhausted." Tutu put her hands on her hips.

"Yes, I'm tired, but it was just a rough night. I'm young. I'm okay. I want to forget about it. There's stuff I have to do at school. I never think about my dreams when I'm busy at school, you know."

Tutu sighed and left for the bathroom. She returned with the first aid kit and put a butterfly bandage on Mahina's big toe and a few large Band-Aids on her calves. "You will wear your jeans today to keep the scrapes covered," she said firmly.

"Yes, I was going to anyway. The temporary classrooms can be cold this time of year, and I've had enough of being cold for a while."

"I can imagine. Whatever you did outside in your sleep with your pajamas on couldn't have been very comfortable. There are rips all over them. You're lucky you didn't hurt yourself worse, you know. You would be better off with your hands in the garden today instead of going to that school. But since you insist on it, you're excused from your chores so you can stay clean. You will, however, wipe up the mess you made downstairs before you go."

"I will, Tutu, every bit of it. I'm sorry. Thank you. I love you."

Tutu got up, shaking her head. "And I love you too, but this is getting a little out of hand."

When she was gone, Mahina fell back onto her bed, exhausted. Maybe it *would* have been a good idea to take the day off. But she really wanted to tell Koa what happened, and she certainly couldn't do that on the phone in the kitchen.

By the time she ate breakfast and scrubbed all the dirt and blood out of the floors and rugs, she was almost too tired to put on her backpack and walk the length of the driveway to catch the bus. Her sore feet ached with every step, and even unlatching and swinging open the gate took a herculean effort. When she finally climbed onto the bus, she collapsed into the first seat available and realized that closing her eyes was more important to her at that moment than doing her neglected homework. She put her backpack against the window as a pillow and promptly fell asleep despite the bumpy road and the exhaust fumes that always seemed to swirl inside every school bus she had ever ridden.

Normally, she could get last-minute assignments done on the bus despite the discomforts, but not this time. Today, she would just have to face the consequences in class and not make excuses. What was she going to say, anyway? *Sorry, I didn't do your assignment last night because I was too busy flying around like a bat and going for a barefoot hike in a lava tube without a flashlight?* That excuse was as bad as *The dog ate my homework*, which she also could never use after Tutu stopped keeping pit bulls because they had the bad habit of falling into the cave holes and killing themselves.

She herself felt like dying when the bus stopped at school and she had to get off. The jostled sleep had done nothing to help her wake up, but she dragged herself down the steps of the bus and across the lawn to the big tent for the morning assembly. There, miracle of miracles, was Koa sitting in the back row waiting for her with a black coffee from Moonbucks.

"Are you kidding me? How did you know?" she said, plopping down next to him.

"Oh, this isn't for you," said Koa, frowning. "Ms. Reynolds asked me to get it for her."

"Oh," said Mahina, disappointed.

"Just kidding!" said Koa. "Of *course* it's for you! I'm not her servant!" He handed the grande cup to her and picked up his own from under his chair. "What? Did you really think Ms. Reynolds would ask me to support a mega-giant, small-town-business-slaying corporation like Moonbucks?

"No! And *I* don't like the idea, either. But wow, this tastes amazing, you don't know ..."

"Yeah, my dad got a gift card yesterday from a client, so we walked over there this morning before school. But you only get the coffee, because we ate all the scones."

"That's all right. Thanks. I really needed this." She felt like she might cry.

"Hey, you look a little ragged. Did you stay up all night doing homework? You weren't online, and I thought about calling you, but ..."

"Yeah, I know, no cell phone, and the kitchen phone is ..."

"Not private, I know. That's why I didn't call. Was something going on?"

She glanced around at the crowded assembly that was about to start and gave him a significant look. "Yes, something. Something important. I'll tell you at the tree. Thanks again for the go juice."

It wasn't her usual style, but she discovered that if she sat silently and just nodded in history and English class, she could hide her lack of preparation and pretty much figure out what she had missed homework-wise. Only Ms. Reynolds gave her a look when she wasn't her usual talkative self, but Koa covered her by being engaged enough for both of them. Math class would be a different story, of course, but that didn't happen until after lunch.

The hardest part about listening extra carefully in class, though, besides her sore body and caffeine-fueled jitteriness, was not going over and over in her mind what had happened to her last night.

Had she actually flown? Or was the flying part just a dream, and she had somehow sleepwalked through the lava tube into the cavern? If so, why were her feet not already cut up when she woke up there in her pajamas?

In real life, Tutu couldn't send Olina flying off to drag her into a lava tube, so that obviously was a dream. Tutu feared the caves. Maybe her dream somehow took Tutu's fears and made them true. After all, Tutu had told her she might end up naked and lost in there. Maybe Mahina's Moemoea mind picked up on that as a suggestion. How did *that* work? She wondered if bad things happened in the cavern only around members of her family who were afraid. Or was everyone vulnerable to fear? Maybe that's why Tutu thought the dreaming and the caves were evil—because there was so much more fear around these days. The earth has fear because of all the horrible changes that are happening, and the people have fear about the consequences of what they have done to the earth.

She needed Koa to help her figure things out. He was the only one who had gone to the cave with her and knew what she was going through with the dreaming, except Tutu, who refused to discuss it and would certainly get upset if Mahina told her what she and Olina had done to her in her dream.

"You still look ragged," Koa said, sitting down with her next to the tree when lunch rolled around. "Maybe we should sign out and split for another coffee before we talk?"

"That's a tempting idea, but I don't think I can walk that far." She slipped off her sandal and showed him her bandaged toe. "Let's just sit here and eat first. I need fuel."

"Whoa, gruesome! Fine by me, but I'm dying of curiosity. Eating, yes! I'll race ya!" He tore open his lunch bag, unwrapped a sandwich, and took three fast bites in a row and then a bite of an apple, his lips smiling while he did so.

"Stop it! You're going to choke," she said, laughing. Sometimes he could be such a goofball.

"I'm just trying to get to the part where you tell me one of the pigs on your ranch bit off your toe while you were dancing naked in the moonlight."

"You're not too far off, buster, but just give me a minute to eat. This isn't going to be easy."

"Not easy, huh? What? You're breaking up with me because you actually *like* getting bit by a pig? Wait, you fell in love with one?! No! It's an abusive relationship! Don't drop me for that swine! He'll never stop with just your toes!"

"Will you shut up? How can I eat when you're making me laugh?!"

"Okay, I'll shut up. Enjoy your *ham* sandwich."

"It's peanut butter, you idiot."

They ate quietly until every scrap of her sandwich was gone. She felt better afterward, but how to begin telling him about what happened last night was escaping her. She decided once again to just dive in and trust that Koa wouldn't conclude she was a hopeless nutcase.

"I flew again in my dream last night."

"Oh, yeah? Tell me more." Koa popped a last mini-carrot into his mouth and set his lunch sack aside.

"It was the best yet. I did the concentration thing, and I floated my way through the cave until I found the cavern, and then I zoomed out the hole into the night air."

"Yes! That's so cool. I bet it felt better even than surfing?"

"Well, it ended weirdly, but I have to say, it *did*. Better, even, than *anything*. It was like, I don't know, all the pleasures of life at once. It had all the *doing*, the movement that the most enjoyable parts of life require, and all the *freedom*. But not the freedom of escaping from something; it was more like the freedom of finally *belonging*. I don't know, it's hard to describe."

"Belonging ...to what?"

"To everything, to the world, to the universe, I guess ..." She looked at him searchingly and realized that up until this moment, the problems at the end of the dream had made her forget just how great the flying had been at the beginning. Remembering the comfort of the cavern, the sound of her mother's voice, then leaving to go outside, the wind in her face, the absolute beauty of it all. The sense of belonging and freedom. Tears formed in her eyes.

Koa studied her carefully. "Sounds pretty great. I'm jealous. I mean, I feel connected that way when I'm playing in the waves sometimes, but I can't imagine *flying*."

Mahina smiled. "Why am I hearing that song in my head from Peter Pan? "I can fly, I can fly, I can fly!"

"I don't know, was Peter Pan up there flying with you?" Koa smiled back at her. As if on cue, the wind started blowing hard enough to make the pine needles swish above their heads. He looked up and laughed.

"No," she went on, "but here's the thing. You're going to think I'm crazy. It was really great for a long while, but then I realized I was *getting used to it*, like it was normal. I was looking for other people to share it, like doing it itself was not enough. It was still totally fun, of course, but eventually not that much different than the fun of surfing, or riding a horse, or even just walking around."

"That's amazing! Like you were a bird doing your everyday thing, no big deal?"

"Yes, and it was still very enjoyable, but I wanted to share it. But when I flew by the house and saw my tutu sitting up in her bed, she got insanely mad at me. After that, the dream became a nightmare, like I was required to pay a price somehow for all the special, everyday fun I was having. Right after Tutu yelled at me, Olina dive-bombed onto my legs and dragged me out of the air with her claws."

"What, did you forget to feed her last night?" He paused, but she didn't laugh. "Wow, that *was* a nightmare," he said, immediately changing his tone. "Like being caught in a wave and running into the seawall."

"Worse, because, well—you're not going to believe this. I woke up in the cavern."

She watched Koa take this in and realize she was serious. He stared at her and frowned in concentration. "The actual cavern? The one in your dreams?"

"Yes, with the hole in the ceiling, exactly as it was in my dreams, and it was *huge*."

"You *woke up* there?"

"Yes. Barefoot and in my pajamas. It was cold and wet there, worse than where we were in the lava tube."

"Wait a minute, are you telling me ...?"

"Yes, I was stuck."

"But you're here now, so you figured out a way to get out, obviously. Through the hole?"

"No, it was too high up to climb to."

"Tutu rescued you?"

"Nope. She was the one who sent me there, I think. Or at least, her dream self did. I walked out with my pajamas wrapped around my feet."

"Give me a break, for real? How?"

"I remembered how I got there in my dream and felt my way back using the map in my brain. Except, my body glowed when I was floating in the dream, and it wasn't glowing last night, so I had to walk out in pitch blackness to find the entrance."

"Show me your feet again."

She kicked off her sandals and rolled up her jeans. The cat scratches on her calves were red and inflamed.

"You got the scratches from the grass walking back to the house?"

"No, from Olina flying into me and dragging me through the air. I don't remember anything after she attacked me. It was like being slammed by a truck, but we must have gone down the ceiling hole. All I remember is surrendering to the power of her claws sinking into me and then waking up in the cavern."

"This is freaking me out. But why didn't you just fly out of there?"

She stopped for a moment to consider that. It was a good question. Why didn't she?

"Wow, Koa, I didn't think of it. I was awake. I only fly in my dreams. It never occurred to me to try it while awake. Huh. On the way out, I even got mad at my mom for not letting me float back to the entrance, and *still* I didn't think of it. I always believed that flying was up to the dream gods, or my mom. I never thought that it could be up to *me*, but I should have at least tried! Or maybe I didn't think of it because Tutu and Olina were the ones who sent me there, and Tutu doesn't want me to dream and fly."

"Wait, your *mom* was there? Oh, right, I remember—the guiding voice. Hmm, so what did you tell your tutu when you got back to the house?"

"I wasn't going to tell her anything, but she found the blood from my feet on the floors in the morning, so the cat was out of the bag, so to speak."

"So she knows now. About everything? Did she remember you seeing her in bed?"

"No, I don't think so. She didn't say anything about that. Probably she would feel bad about it if she did, but I don't know. It might have been a dream for her too, one she may or may not consciously remember. Since she always goes nuts when I talk to her about flying, I let her think I had a sleepwalking session that took me outside, and she let it go at that. I don't think she guessed I was in the cave. Knowing that would have freaked her out even more than she already was, and she already thinks the dreaming thing is totally evil."

"Maybe that's what you think now too? I mean, obviously, it's dangerous. Look at you! What if you had a dream and woke up in the volcano?"

"I'd be toast!"

"Yes, literally." Koa laughed.

"I don't know, Koa. We can laugh, but I don't know what to think. I *do* think it's dangerous. There's so much I don't know about this! It's complicated, like trying to predict the weather."

"Well, you know what *I* think? Your dream came true. I don't mean it was a dream come true that you were stuck in a cave, but you know, you dreamed something, and then it became reality. You dreamed you were in the cave, and then you were."

"Okay, and ...?"

"Well, what if dreaming about flying is the same thing? You dreamed it, and ... What if you *should* have tried to fly in the cave? What if you really could have?"

Her mouth dropped open and she jumped up, forgetting that she hadn't put her sandals back on yet. She yelped in pain and sat right back down, rubbing her toe.

"Koa," she said, "I think you might be right! One of the things my mom's voice was telling me in the dream last night is that the Moemoea duty to the people and the earth is for each generation to help the next one to be even more powerful. Mom wants to nurture me to fly, to birth my power, but Tutu doesn't. But what if something is forcing Tutu to do her duty? What if part of her dreaming mind sent me back to the cavern because it *had* to? Tutu said she was afraid to nurture the power in Mom and me, but maybe the dreaming part of her knows she should help the dreams grow. Obviously, what sent my body to the cavern was a power, either hers, Mom's, or mine. Or maybe it was all of ours. But it doesn't matter whose specifically. The fact that it happened means that the power *has to be real*!"

Koa handed Mahina her sandals. "You know what I think? As soon as your wounds are healed, I think we better buy some headlamps and try to find the way to that cavern!"

Chapter Nineteen

For the rest of the week, Mahina soaked her feet in the bathtub, caught up with her homework, avoided the subject of the "sleep-walking" incident with Tutu, and somehow managed to sleep through the nights without dreaming. Did her mind give her a break because she was afraid of waking up somewhere again in her pajamas? Maybe, she thought. She also noticed that Olina had shifted to sleeping with Tutu, but who knew if that meant anything because she liked to rotate between them sometimes. Cats were as mysterious to figure out as dreams!

In any case, for whatever reason, she was glad her life returned enough to normal that she began to feel her old energetic self again. Did she feel better because she wasn't dreaming? If so, then Tutu might be right that dreams were unhealthy for her. They'd certainly put her in a tough predicament recently. But even if she was feeling better, the attraction of the cavern tugged at her like an obsession.

In English, because of the hurricane, Ms. Reynolds assigned a research project to find and discuss poetry written about storms and other recent climate disasters.

"It may not be the most pleasant subject in the world," she said, "but poets have always been the first to tell the truth about things, even when the rest of the world wasn't ready to listen."

Each student was given a class period to present the poems they chose and lead a discussion about the changes in the world the poems highlighted. An automatic A would be given to anyone who wrote an original Shakespearean sonnet thematically related to the poems they found.

On Friday, Mahina got permission from Tutu to go over to Koa's house after school to work on the assignment. They settled in his room, and a simple Google search for *poems about climate change and global warming* yielded a ton of results.

Poetry about plastics in the ocean and how they were poisoning the fish and making them sterile intrigued Koa. Mahina couldn't make a choice. Air pollution, droughts, forever chemicals, depletion of usable soil for growing crops, coastal flooding, sea level rise, melting ice caps, and species extinction all made tears come to her eyes as she read the pain in the poets' lines and the longing they felt to return to a healthy planet.

"Who *are* these people doing this to the environment?" she asked Koa. Mr. Kahale had ordered them pizza, and they decided to eat it upstairs while his mom, dad, and younger sister watched *Moana* downstairs for the third Friday night in a row.

"People with power," answered Koa. "Greedy people with power, I should say. Not everybody with power is corrupt."

"But a lot are," said Mahina. "Oil company executives, for instance. For decades, they pushed petroleum as the only source of energy while knowing exactly what burning them would do to the environment. They should pay to take the carbon back out of the air."

"Yeah, but they won't. They'll defend their choices to the end."

"But why? They're clearly at fault, just like the cigarette companies are at fault for all the lung cancer they caused."

"I know that, and you know that, but the executives running those companies only care about their power and money. It's the way of the world, the way it is."

She finished a slice of pineapple pizza and tapped on her laptop for a while. "What do you think of this for a sonnet?" she said and read out loud:

Because we need to get from here to there

We burn the plants that once had turned to coal
And now we live when no one seems to care
That life today is falling in a hole
You can't escape the feedback loop today
The winds of change are ripping out the trees
The animals are dying in dismay
We're making drones instead of saving bees
The life of earth is in the melting ice
A river of despair will cause our flood
Who has the right to throw this fateful dice?
And spill what's left of Paradise's blood?
The world explodes because of all their lying
And no one now can live the joy of flying

"I think it's worth an A!" said Koa, and hugged her. "But it's sad, of course."

"Yes, it sucks what's happening to the world. We're going to see some horrible things in our lifetime. And our children, I can't even imagine ..."

Suddenly, there was no more questioning in her gut. She could feel the heat again. While it was good to read her poem in English class at school on Monday, her gut was telling her it was more important to get back to the cave.

"You know, Koa, we need to do something about this, not just study it in school."

"Do you want to go on strike like Rita Thinberg?"

"No, that was her thing. I want to do something more than that. The world is dying. No one is going to be able to surf anymore."

"Well, actually, with all the storms, the surfing will probably rip!"

She slapped him on the arm. "You know what I mean."

"Yeah, I know. We have to do *something*. We all do. But what?"

"That, I don't know yet." She sighed. "For now, let's think about how we're going to get back into the cave this weekend."

"I found some headlamps in a box in the garage. Dad bought them a long time ago to take a group of friends night hiking to the Kilauea lava flow. I put new batteries in them, and they work fine. Here's what I think we can do ..."

THE NEXT DAY, SHE TOOK off on her bike after chores. She told Tutu that she was going to the farmer's market that was held every Saturday at an old stable on the big ranch property nearby. "Alone?" she asked.

"No, Koa's going to meet me there, and we're going to pedal out on the old road toward Waipio afterward. Koa's trying to get in shape, and Mr. Kahale is too busy these days to take him surfing."

"We could be too busy out here on the ranch, too, you know," said Tutu.

"I know, Tutu, but I also need some things in town."

"What things? We got everything we need here."

She thought fast. "*Personal* things, you know."

"Oh. You can't get that stuff at the farmer's market, girl!"

"I know that. I'm just going to go to the pharmacy first and then bike with him. I packed a lunch, and I have a lot of water."

"Well, okay, I guess. You be careful. Is your toe okay for that much exercise?

"All healed now, Tutu. Thanks. See you after lunch!"

She grabbed her backpack and walked her bike to the end of the driveway and through the gate. The wind was mild, and the sun was bright. If it was going to rain today, it wouldn't happen until the afternoon, so there should be plenty of time for their plan.

She mounted the bike with her backpack on her back. The peak of Mauna Kea was glowing brightly in the distance. As she always did, she marveled at how beautiful the ʻāina was where she lived. How anyone could only look at the earth as a resource to exploit just to make money was beyond her. *Maybe the rest of the world isn't as beautiful as it is here,* she thought. But no, she'd seen the pictures on the web. The world was gorgeous pretty much everywhere.

Pedaling her bike in jeans and hiking boots did bother her still-healing wounds, but not too badly. Mostly, the scabs just itched now. Twenty minutes later, she was at the farmer's market, which was mobbed by tourists as usual. For a while, Tutu used to drive early here to get sourdough bread from the local bakery until she figured out how to make it herself. Hers wasn't as good as the bakery's, but they couldn't really afford the bakery's prices. "A special treat every once in a while," Tutu said when she quit going.

She thought about buying Tutu a loaf today to surprise her, but she only had enough cash for the feminine product she didn't really need but had to come home with because of her lie. Again, she felt the pang of regret and loneliness that came from being deceitful toward Tutu. The feeling went away, though, when she spotted Koa, also dressed in jeans and hiking boots, at the grilled cheese sandwich cart. He had on a baseball cap and looked rugged, ready, and gorgeous as usual.

"You want to split this with me? I got here early for this," he said, showing her a golden, grilled monstrosity oozing with flowing white cheddar. He handed her half when she got off her bike.

"Thanks! You ready for this adventure?" She took a bite and sighed. "Wow, that's *ono*!"

"Right? I get one whenever I come out here. And yeah, I'm ready."

"Look, I know we need all the time we can get today to be safe, but I've got to stop at the shopping center for a minute first."

"No problem. We can polish these off on the way. Let's go!"

He stayed with the bikes while she went inside the grocery store and bought the smallest and cheapest box of generic pads she could find. She hid them in her backpack as soon as she got outside. It's not that she was embarrassed about buying that kind of stuff in front of Koa. She just didn't want to relive feeling bad about lying to Tutu that morning.

When she rejoined him again by the bikes, she was relieved when he just said, "Got what you needed? Okay, we're out of here!"

They mounted their bikes and headed back toward her ranch.

Tutu always did what little shopping was required during the week when the grocery stores were less crowded, but there was no predicting when she might decide to go to the feed store or the hardware store. If she saw them on the road, the plan was to tell her that they changed their mind and were biking past the ranch out the road to Mauna Kea instead of to Waipio. But they never saw her rusty pickup. No one she recognized had passed them on the road by the time they reached the start of the Moemoea fence line.

When they could hear that no cars were coming from either direction, they pulled over onto the grassy shoulder, and Mahina carefully crawled under the bottom strand of barbed wire into the corner of their pasture. Koa followed, quickly lifting the bikes over the fence to her. In a flash, they walked their bikes behind a small hill with several eucalyptus trees at its base. They hid them safely between two large boulders where they wouldn't be seen or rubbed against by the cattle.

"Perfect," Mahina said. "This way."

Beyond the hill, she found the cow path she was looking for that led them out of sight along the road until it cut into the heart of the property. Several dozen black steers mingling with cows were munching on the grass and ignoring them.

"Those guys are huge!" said Koa.

"Not as huge as the bulls we keep in the back pasture," she said. Just then, a pheasant exploded from under a bush next to their feet and flew off across the pasture, flapping furiously.

"Yo, that woke me up!" shouted Koa, laughing.

"No kidding! But let's try to be quiet now. We're getting close. The barn and everything is over there about a mile. It's a long way, but sound carries around here. Tutu's probably out in the garden. If we cut this way, we'll run into the new streambed that flows down from near the entrance. It will keep us hidden until we get to the concrete blocks."

Koa gave her a thumbs up. Then he whispered, "Maybe we should put the headlamps on now, so we don't have to do it in the open by the entrance?"

"Good idea," she said. It was warm out. Biking and walking in jeans, long sleeves, and hiking boots had made her sweat. She was looking forward to the coolness of the cave despite having almost shivered to death in there. Koa adjusted a headlamp and handed it to her and then adjusted his own. He showed her how to focus the beam and turn it on and off by twisting the end of the lamp, and then he put his baseball cap into the backpack and gave her a gentlemanly bow, gesturing dramatically for her to lead onward.

Entering the cave quickly so they wouldn't be seen was a good thing, and not just because of the welcome cool air. It gave them no time to change their minds. They both squeezed quickly through the busted-out opening hidden behind the grass and moved as far as they could into the tunnel, using the available light before turning on their headlamps.

"Okay, cool. We did it," said Koa.

"We're in. So far, so good," she said, breathing hard. Unlike the last time they were here together, she felt a warm electric current flowing across her skin. Was it chicken skin from the cold humidity, or something else? She wasn't scared, exactly, but her body's senses were definitely on high alert. The air felt energizing and refreshing this time, except for the musty cave smell that reminded her of being lost.

"So, we go the way we went before, right?" asked Koa.

"Yes, the same left turns. But let me lead because the turn we missed, the one I took on my own when I came back through, was lower and kind of hidden behind a boulder. I only found it because I was touching everything on the walls with my hands. It's up ahead, but not for a while. Come on."

They moved slowly and carefully along the lava tube, their headlamps cutting through the darkness like lightsabers. The floor of the tube was mostly easy to walk over, but in some places, piles of sharp rocks had collapsed from the ceiling. She couldn't believe she had walked over them in just her bare feet wrapped in pajamas. That was crazy. It was definitely easier to do it in hiking boots.

She also felt better having Koa along. It kept her from worrying too much about Tutu's warnings and the fact that she was again going back to the very place where her parents lost their lives. Would it matter to Tutu if she knew she heard her mother talking to her in here? She doubted it. Probably Tutu would just say that it was the evil dreams messing with her head or that she had violated a sacred space without permission or awareness of the dangers.

It was also good having Koa along because she could tell him what she was feeling, and he wouldn't laugh at her. The electric current on her skin was increasing the farther they walked into the tunnel. It felt like the same feeling she had when she was glowing in her dreams, but it sure was a different experience being in here awake with Koa. Awake, she felt she had to analyze the heat that was happening inside her. When she was here in her dreams, she seemed to know what she was feeling without having to think too much about it.

After a while, she said, "That big boulder up there might be the one."

"Yeah, I think the first big split we came to is just beyond it," said Koa behind her. "There's a passageway?"

"Yep, here it is!" she said, peering between the boulder and the side of the lava tube. Koa caught up to her to look at it and pulled his smartphone out of his pocket.

"This boulder must have cracked off from the ceiling when the lava cooled and almost blocked it," he said. "No wonder we didn't see it before. Do you want to go in now, or should we go on a little bit first?"

"You mean go on just to be sure that where we went the first time is on the other side of the boulder?"

"Right. And, you know, we should probably make a map. We better take some pictures of each turn." He snapped a few shots that flashed like lightning bolts with his phone, and then they maneuvered their way around the boulder. The split they took before was just a dozen yards beyond. They were on track. Koa took a few more photos, and then they turned around and went back.

"You know what's crazy?" she said. "We took two left turns when we were in here last time together because they seemed to head upward, but in my dream, I took two right turns, one here, and one just before a narrow passageway that almost drowned me. Then, when I was awake in my pajamas, I found my way back by taking two left turns."

"And?" asked Koa.

"Nothing. I'm just trying to keep it straight in my head, that's all. You know, what is dream reality and what is real reality."

"I get it, but you don't need to worry. I'm taking pictures, we have reliable headlamps, and I'm very good at remembering the reality of where I've been. Shall we?" Again, he bowed dramatically and gestured for her to enter the tunnel.

Chapter Twenty

Once Mahina and Koa squeezed past a few boulders that had fallen just inside the entrance, presumably along with the big one that had almost blocked it, the lava tube opened up to be just as large as the first one. At places along the way, a school bus could have fit inside it easily, and at other places, Mahina could touch the ceiling if she jumped.

They moved ahead slowly with their light beams slicing the ground in front of them. She looked carefully for the next turn she took in her dream. After a few minutes, there it was on the right, a large opening that quickly narrowed when they entered it. The tube snaked forward, leading to who knew where. Probably a whole labyrinth of lava tubes was ahead. Her body zinged at the thought of exploring them.

"We're getting close," she said. "Whoa, I can feel it in my bones. This is the last right. See how it gets narrow deep inside there?"

"Mahina, your voice is getting kind of dreamy. Stay with me here, okay?" Koa put his hand on her shoulder.

"I'm okay," she said. "I'm glad you're here. I see water on the walls up ahead, so let's go." Koa nodded his headlamp and took some more pictures. She nodded back and entered the narrow tunnel.

Just like in her dream, this part of the tunnel went on for a while, but finally, there were ten yards or so of narrowness where they had to go single file. There was water seeping down the walls and disappearing through the floor. Not very much, but enough so that everything was dripping and smelled even more like a wet dog than the rest of the cave. With a few more splashing steps, the tunnel opened up into the cavern. They were through!

"Oh my goodness, it's so big!" said Koa, shining his headlight about. She could see it really was. If a school bus could have fit in parts of the lava tube behind them, a whole fleet of them stacked on top of each other could fit in here. "Are we inside a hollowed-out hill somewhere?"

"Must be," she replied, staring at the bright hole in the ceiling far above her. "We haven't angled downward at all, and look how tall it is!" Her voice echoed off the craggy walls.

She tried to think which hill in her pasture was big enough to hide a space this large. There were six or seven possibilities. Maybe once they made their map, they could figure out where this particular one was. Or maybe not. There were dozens of hills with open holes on the property. She memorized its shape so she could look for it from the outside.

Mahina moved her gaze from the ceiling to the floor trying to find the spot where she had woken up. "Turn off your headlamp for a minute," she said. "There's enough light. I want to see if it looks the same." She turned hers off.

When his went out, there were beams of daylight, not moonlight, cutting through the darkness from the opening, but right away she knew. She was standing right on it. For a blindingly scary moment, she felt like she was alone again in her pajamas. She glanced at Koa and reached down to touch her blue jeans. She shuddered at the feeling of Olina scratching on her calves, and how cold she had been waking up here.

"Right here," she said, straightening up. "I woke up right here."

"Wow," said Koa, his deeper voice echoing stronger in the cavern than her own. "Do you want the light back on again?"

"Not yet," she said. The burning urgency in her body was intensifying as she remembered everything about the dream that deposited her here: the thrill of flying, the progression into accepting the thrill as normal, seeing Tutu, getting attacked by Olina.

Was this all inside her, these amazing feelings? Or were they coming from this cavern? Was it her mom making her appreciate her dreams and the gift she has of being alive? She started to cry. Oh, if her mom were truly still alive!

"I do appreciate it, Mom! I do!" she said out loud.

"Mahina, what's happening?"

"It's okay, Koa. I'm making my own map. A map of my feelings. I think *feelings* are the key to the dreams, to my parents' deaths, to why my body needs to be here."

"Okay. Can I do anything for you?"

"You're here. It's enough. Like my dad was here for my mom."

"Hey, does this mean we're going steady now?"

"You make me laugh, Koa. My dreams helped me choose you. We're connected now, forever, whether we're going steady or not. Come closer to me. There's something I want to try. Hold my hand, please?"

When she felt his cool firm palm in hers, she whispered, "I'm going to try to go into my dreaming state again to see if, well, if I can do it, like we talked about. It may not work. You're here, and it's different than being asleep, but ..."

"I was in your dream before, right? So, I can be here. Go for it!"

She smiled at him, feeling his support. She felt her mind slip back into the sacredness of this temple of dreaming, the concentration, the lifting, the flying.

She whispered, "I have to accept—accept that I'm not normal, accept that there is magic in the world, in here, in this cavern, on this ranch, connected to me, connected to my mother, connected to Tutu, connected to her mother and her *tutu,* our big, powerful "Moemoea family. Oh, Mom, help me to see back through all of us to be the strongest in the line! Help me to help you! Help me to take care of the world, as you tried to take care of it. I love you, Mom. Help me to understand life the way it really is, in all its glory, in all its love. Guide me, Mom. Please guide me!"

The light from the ceiling brightened and descended, and along with it a beautiful wave of molten ecstasy shook her body from the top of her head downward through her arms and torso to her waist and legs.

When the tingling fire reached her toes, she focused all the electric currents, the belonging she was feeling, into pure concentration. She was still awake, and she loved the reality of Koa's hand she was holding as she loved herself, but that didn't alter the strength of her dreaming focus.

She felt the womb of the cavern envelop her, connect with her, as if she were the cavern and the cavern was her, and warm light glowing from her skin illuminated everything. "I can fly now," she said out loud. "Don't let go of my hand, Koa."

"Mahina, um ..."

She just smiled, and in her heart the voice spoke. "*Sharing is your power*," her mom whispered inside her and from the glowing cavern walls. "*You were born to give. Your gift will change everything. Rise, Mahina, rise!*"

Awake, but still wonderfully in a dream, she felt her heels lift from the ground and bend toward the back of her knees. She settled onto the steamy air below her and willed herself up, pulling Koa's hand until she was like a hot air balloon tethered only by the strength of his grip.

"Join me, Koa. You're part of the reason I can do this. Mom says. Bend your knees. *Believe*. We are in the cavern of life, where everything is possible and having nothing is more than enough."

And then he was next to her, his knees bent, floating there, his mouth open in astonishment. "I mean," he stuttered, "I guess I sort of thought *you* might be able to do this, with your dreaming and all, but I never thought *I* would be able to fly!"

"Oh, yes, you can. *We* can, I should say." Sure of her power, she willed herself and Koa farther up into the shimmering air of the cavern. She remembered all the lessons from her flying dreams and said, "Your mind is your steering wheel. Your feet are the accelerator. The higher you lift them, the faster you fly. Bend the left knee when you will yourself to go left, and the right knee to help you go right. Will yourself to be perfectly still in the air, and you can straighten your legs to rest them. That's how it works. It's easier than surfing, Koa. Try it!"

"Mahina, am I dreaming? Is this for *real? You're glowing so much! I can feel your heat!*" Koa's breath was coming in and out fast as he turned with her left and right.

"We're awake, Koa. You know we are. Yet we're also in my dream. *Our* dream now. *Your* dream later, maybe, after we finish. That's the way it works, I think. *Right, Mom?* Come on!" She let go of Koa's hand.

"No! Don't let go of me! I'll fall!" Koa screamed, but he stayed floating right next to her.

"See? You won't fall, your vibrations will harmonize with mine as long as we stay close enough to hear each other's voices. Even if we drift too far apart, or if your doubts get too strong, I'm sure all we have to do is start over at the entrance to the cave."

That was the lesson of all the nightmare failures, right, Mom?

"Hey, try following me!" she said.

She willed herself to fly the length of the long cavern, but something in her gut warned her not to touch the walls.

"Whoa! I'm doing it!" she heard Koa say behind her. "This is so cool!"

Yeah, it is, she thought, but you'll get used to it. *Thanks, Mom. I get it now what you need from me, to use my goddess power to make the extraordinary ordinary, so that the ordinary has a chance to become extraordinary once again.*

They flew upward together and followed the curve of the ceiling past the hole and a long way into the depths of the cavern until it curved down and ended at the continuation of a narrow lava tube. "Don't land or touch the walls until I tell you to," she said loudly. "Let's go back and do that again!"

"Oh, I could do this all day!" said Koa, not breathing quite as hard now. He followed her back to where they entered the cavern, dipping and zooming back and forth.

"You lead this time," Mahina said. "Use your mind to stay afloat."

"Okay. This is unreal! It's like flying in a video game when you forget you're holding a joystick, only it's *real*!"

"It's *real-ly* unreal!" Mahina laughed. "Now you know how I feel every morning when I wake up from my dreams!"

She followed him, mimicking his dips and turns like they were on a wave in the ocean. Their whoops and laughter echoed loudly off the moist walls. When they got to the far end again, she looked back at the distant dot of bright light calling to her from the ceiling. Was Olina out there? Did Mahina dare go through and breathe the air of the world outside?

Yes, you can do it, she heard in her heart. *And you must.*

"Are you ready to see if we can do this outside?" she said to Koa, who was carefully doing a forward flip with his backpack falling up onto his head. She reached out and kept the pack from floating away as he completed the maneuver.

"Thanks," he said. "I forgot I had this thing on!"

"Yes, they kind of lose their weight, don't they? Along with everything else, like problems, frustrations, and the feeling you don't have enough or are missing out. Come on, let's see what we can do in the fresh air! Stay close behind me but don't touch the walls or the grass in the hole. I think it's big enough if we go through one at a time."

Back they flew, and up, until they were hovering right below the jagged-edged hole. The light was bright, not direct sunlight, but close enough that Mahina had to wait a few moments until her eyes adjusted.

"Will yourself straight up and keep your hands to your side," she instructed. "Think of the ground as capable of stopping the electricity that flows between us. I don't know if it works that way, but that's the message I'm getting."

"Wherever you're getting your messages from, I'm glad you are listening to them!" said Koa, below her.

"Remember, you have a backpack on, so keep the walls closer to the front of you to make room for it." She willed herself upward, and like red lava powerfully emerging from a volcano, she rose through the walls of rocks and into the sunshine of the day.

"Ah, so this is where we are," she said to herself, looking back at the line of hills between her and where she knew the ranch house was hidden. She shifted her gaze from there to the backside of the hill where the entrance was. The feeling was like seeing the layout of the ranch from the roof of the barn, only better and from a different angle. Koa emerged from below her and floated up next to her.

"Oh man, I got chicken skin!" he said.

She pointed south. "That's where the ranch is, below those hills over there, and that's where we went in, below that hill where all the cows are. No one can see us up here, except the birds."

"Or somebody driving by?"

"I don't think so. The road winds its way between the hills. As long as we don't fly too high, no one will notice us."

"Oh, man, I want to fly around the mountain! Look at it!"

Indeed, Mauna Kea was beautiful, with traces of snow shining in its high valleys and just a smattering of clouds around the peak to give it dimension. Did the power of her family's ranch come from the lava tubes and their connection to the earth, or from the volcano and its connection to the sky? Probably both, she thought. The universe is massive and all-powerful. She turned to look at Koa.

"We'll skip the mountain for now. Someone would probably see us."

"Smile!" he said and snapped a photo of her with his cell phone.

"Hey, I don't think that's a good idea. Erase that, will you?"

"Uh, okay, why?" said Koa. He swiped on the screen and zipped the phone back into his pocket.

"We can't tell anybody about this. This place would get mobbed, and Tutu would disown me."

"You're right. Sorry. I didn't think about that. Wow, Mahina! We're flying!"

"I know! Note where we are, and let's not fly any higher than just above these hills. There's nobody to the northeast of us. We should be able to stay hidden if we're careful."

"How fast do you think we can go?"

"This is my first time, too, partner. Let's be careful and stick together. Maybe we can see."

She turned to the northeast and willed herself across the pasture between the hill they emerged from and the next big one a few hundred yards away. The wind blew through her hair, just like in her dreams. Could she follow it over Kohala Mountain and down to the surfing area? She felt she probably could, but her gut was telling her not to venture too far from the ranch, and maybe not just because of the risk of being seen. Gone were the days when she doubted herself when her body sent her warm messages like this. No, today they would stick as close to the ranch as possible. There might be time later for longer flights.

Flying was like riding a rollercoaster as they popped up over the gentle hills and dipped into the small valleys between them. The only dangers, easily avoided, came from errant branches of eucalyptus trees and the occasional ohia tree. The power and phone lines mostly ran along the road, so they weren't a problem either. They frightened a few cattle egrets from the backs of steers, but the big white birds never got in their way.

"It's too hard on the eyes to go very fast," said Koa, after they paused above a hidden valley to catch their breath and rest their ankles and calves.

"Yeah, I know what you mean. But do you care?"

"Nope," said Koa. "It's as much fun hovering or moving just a little bit as it is to get someplace in a hurry."

Maybe that's one of the lessons of all this, Mahina thought. "Hey, we should test the feeling I have about not touching the ground and see if it makes any difference."

"Here?" asked Koa, looking down on a few black steers below.

"No, let's fly back to the bikes. But when we get near the entrance, we need to be as quiet as possible and keep our eyes open. Tutu likes to ride sometimes on Saturdays.

"Okay, but we'll do this again soon, right?"

"I sure hope so! You're getting used to it, huh?" She smiled.

They had flown farther than they thought, but just like on a hike, the way back seemed shorter than the way out. Fifteen minutes later, they were hovering ten feet above the ground over the bikes.

"It's a little more challenging to fly so close to the ground," observed Koa.

"Yeah. But just like anything, you get better at it as you go along. Okay, stay right next to me as we land, and be ready for anything."

"You're making me nervous."

"Don't worry. We haven't seen Olina flying at us with her claws out, have we? I think we'll be okay."

Mahina descended to a flat area next to the bikes. Koa descended next to her but was a few feet higher than she was when her hiking boots touched the grass. Gravity pulled him down like a hay bale tossed from the back of a pickup truck. He rolled immediately to lessen the impact.

"Ouch!" he said.

"Are you okay?" The ground was solid against her feet just like it normally was, and she felt a chill run through her body. "I guess that answers that! Boy, these packs are heavy again!"

"Yeah, I'm okay. It just surprised me, that's all," said Koa, shaking himself off. "Man, we did it! That was *so* cool!"

"Let me try to fly again. Take my hand," she said. The skin of his hand was cold from the wind, as if he had been riding a bike barehanded on a freezing day. She closed her eyes and concentrated, trying to feel the power, the connection with him and her mother that she'd been feeling all day. Think up, believe, she told herself, but she realized it was no good. Not only could she not fly again, but she didn't get any of the bodily feelings that led up to it.

"Nothing, huh?" said Koa when she opened her eyes.

She shook her head.

"Interesting," said Koa, looking longingly at the sky behind them.

"There's a lot about this I don't understand. I mean, I knew this would happen, that if we touched the ground, the flying would stop. But I don't get *why* I knew that. You know what I mean?"

"Of course. I totally understand. Your feelings. Your dreams. They're complicated. I mean, this is all a huge, beautiful mystery, isn't it? Maybe we can find someone who can help us explain it. A psychic, or something."

"No!" she snapped, her knees buckling. Koa rushed to catch her and keep her from falling over.

"Are you okay, Mahina?"

"Dizzy," she said. "I'm really tired for some reason all of a sudden and a little cold."

"Come over here, sit down on this log." He helped her take off her headlamp.

He supported her shoulders until they could both sit on a fallen eucalyptus limb. The minty smell of the leaves entered her nostrils like Vicks VapoRub, reviving her a bit. Or maybe it was just the warmth of Koa's arms around her that made her feel immediately better.

She was grateful to him for coming along with her into the tunnel, but the image of Tutu sitting up in bed and scolding her harshly flashed into her mind. She had to make absolutely sure he wouldn't let it slip to a psychic or someone else what they had done.

"You cannot even *hint* to anyone what happened to us today, Koa. You have to promise me that."

"Of course. I promise. But, hey, when can we do it again?"

"Soon, but look, I'm serious about this. Tell *anyone*, and that's the end. If you do, I'll have to deny everything to protect Tutu and the ranch, and we're through."

"Do you mean with flying, or with going steady together?"

Was he serious or joking? "Don't make me think so hard right now, Koa. You get what I'm saying. You've been wonderful, but I need to go home now, maybe have some hot tea and cuddle with my cat. Obviously, there's a next move. There's got to be. But I don't know what that move is except to keep this a secret. Today was important, and it happened to us for a reason. What that reason is, though, I don't exactly know. Right now, honestly, I can barely move I'm so tired."

"Like after a big day of surfing, yeah, I get it. Give me your backpack, and I'll walk with you to the fence. I'll carry everything for us in two trips. If you get lightheaded, just tell me. We'll sit down again."

"Thanks, Koa," she said.

As she stood and leaned into him, her energy was a little better. Her body felt beaten up, but she also felt relieved. At least she had someone she could count on who took her seriously and understood what was going on with her.

They had *flown*—like in her dreams, but awake! She did understand Koa's impulse to ask somebody for help with this. She wanted to do that too. But as comforting as that might feel, she knew she shouldn't because no one in their right mind, even a psychic, would believe them without proof.

It was true that she couldn't have done what she did today without him. But as she ducked under the barbed wire that Koa held up nicely for her with a concerned look on his face, she wondered who she really was to have this power, and toward what adventure her life would take her next.

Chapter Twenty-One

Mahina was on her bike, and the distance from the beginning of their fence line to her driveway was only a little over a mile, but it felt like running a marathon. Koa, meanwhile, was full of energy, laughing and trying to cheer her up by popping wheelies on his mountain bike.

At the gate, he leaned his wheels against the fence and opened the gate for her, while she rested her head on her handlebars and tried to catch her breath.

"Do you want me to go in with you?" he said, coming close to her and putting his arm around her shoulder like he did before.

"No, I'm okay," she replied, again getting a small boost of energy from his touch. She straightened up from the handlebars and wobbled off her bike. He stayed close, steadying her. She turned to him when she regained her balance. "Thanks again, Koa."

"Mahina, thank *you.* This was so incredible today. I'll never forget it. I feel *changed*, you know? Like there was my life before, and now there's my life ahead, and it's going to be so much better!"

He hugged her. It felt really comforting, and had she not been so tired, she might have even kissed him. Instead, she peeled away reluctantly and walked her bike through the gate.

"I'm going to feel better after I rest," she said, feeling like she was apologizing to him. "I'll call you tomorrow if I can, or I'll see you Monday at school, okay?"

Koa swung the gate shut behind her and watched her move slowly down the driveway. She turned and waved to him at the end, and he smiled and saluted her back.

She put her backpack down and opened the barn door to hang her bike back on its hook in the storeroom, or maybe just leave it on the floor and hang it up tomorrow when she had more strength.

"Did you have a nice ride?" said Tutu's voice, startling her. She was in the nearest stall, brushing down Ikaika.

"Oh, hi, Tutu. Yes, thanks. It was great, but I'm worn out."

"There's a beef stew on the stove if you're hungry, and I made biscuits."

"Thanks, Tutu. That sounds great. Did you go for a ride?" *Did you see us flying through the air?*

"I wanted to ride the fenceline like you and your cowboy did to check things out for myself."

"So, were we right? Was everything okay?"

"I don't know, I decided not to go. Something told me not to, so I changed my mind and just stuck around here. I let Ikaika graze around the perimeter of the garden while I pulled a bunch of weeds. I don't know, maybe I'm getting scared of riding alone in my old age."

"You're not old, Tutu. Something told you, huh?" *Was it you, Mom? Thanks.*

"Yeah, in my gut. You know how I am sometimes about that. Intuition. I wouldn't have stepped in a hole, but who knows?" Tutu laughed. "Anyway, I had a wonderful and safe day planting tomatoes and taro, even though I missed you. I'll be in when I finish up a few things here. You go ahead and eat without me. You look hungry."

"Yeah, I'm pretty tired. Thanks, Tutu." Mahina managed to lift her bike onto its hook only because Tutu was watching her. She didn't want her to think she couldn't. Then she left the barn.

She picked up her backpack and trudged into the kitchen. Olina greeted her by walking between her legs and then prancing into the pantry for her supper. "I'm glad Tutu didn't send you out flying today, you little rascal," she mumbled and followed her dutifully to put a scoop of kibble in her bowl.

The stew was delicious. She ate a big bowl with two biscuits and butter and some homemade fig jam that she had made with Tutu last summer. By the time Tutu came in from the barn, the moon was shining, and she was passed out on the couch with Olina. Tutu shook her awake, and she woke up disoriented and scared. Then with relief she realized where she was and gratefully trudged upstairs with Olina to go to bed. She fell asleep thinking about her mother and dreamed ...

Chapter Twenty-Two

I am there again, the entrance, only this time there is no concrete wall. Koa is with me, only he's not Koa. He's much older. He looks like me, and I love him *so much*, but I love what I have to do with my power even more. He understands that and forgives me. He hugs me and looks up at the sky with a worried expression.

"If we're going to do this, there's not a lot of time," he says, turning on his flashlight.

We walk into the lava tube. With my power, I smooth the way ahead of us, making the path easy, but I leave the big boulder where it is. I am afraid of it for some reason. It is powerful, and it hides the way so cleverly. As we walk, I let the path behind us return to how it was, rocks jostling into each other as they snap back to their proper places again.

"Hana, you're sure?" he asks when we reach the cavern. No light is streaming from the sacred opening above, only dark clouds and the swirling of wind. The first arm of the storm has arrived.

"This place is the honored source of our family's power. It called us to this island to tend to its mana because we are strong. Here resides the guiding spirit of the earth, and we are its servants. But we are failing. Mother neglects our destiny to build on our powers to fight the changes and dangers, not hide from them and weaken our powers out of selfishness and fear. I have just given birth. What kind of messed up world will my daughter have to live in? This growing chaos is not okay. We can't sit back and accept it. This island is our *home*. We've been over this so many times. You know I need to try, Kiawe. We can stop this storm"

"I know you can, but the risks! Won't it eventually happen again—and everywhere, not just here?"

"Then we will stop it everywhere, until we can change and get back to living in harmony with the earth." Tutu and Great-Tutu would agree. "If not me, who? If not this cavern, what? If not now, when? We have a new child who will need the earth to remain its nurturing self, a child who will one day care for it, and for the people—because she must, as we must, as every person in the Moemoea family must."

"I love you."

"And I love you, Kiawe, my man of this world, the chosen one of my dreams. It is time. Hold me."

I sit and root my crossed legs into the floor of the cavern. I concentrate on the sacred goddess power burning within me and stare upward at the storm. Lightning flashes in the hole. I feel my strong, faithful man sitting behind me, his arms wrapped across my chest giving me his warm mana. I rock back and forth with him. We are one.

When I am ready, I birth my will upward into the storm clouds. Lightning flashes into my mind. *No, that's not okay,* I answer the storm, returning lightning bolt for bolt until I have its attention.

Yes, I understand why you are angry, but you don't have to do this. You are afraid and confused, but this will not help. Turn back! Give your rain to the ocean instead. You must stop this madness because it is wrong! This is our home and you love us! It is not the way you should act, and you know *it!*

More lightning, wind, and blasts of thunder. My head is splitting, but I try again.

What good does it do to be angry? You are resilient and strong beyond all measure. Absorb the carbon and adjust as you once absorbed the fumes from the birth of these sacred caves. We are your children. Trust us! Obey me! Yield to my power! Give us time. I'm begging you, no, as your child, I am commanding *you to stop this temper tantrum and spare our home!*

More lightning. I fight it burst for burst and turn the furious wind gusts back onto themselves, but the storm will not be denied. It does not turn away.

Yet, I stall it, a temporary standoff. I am its child. I strain against it, feeling its love, but then it pushes even harder against me, draining my mana, dropping its tears in drowning sheets. The storm weeps in pity for my foolishness. I am human and the servant of the caverns, and the world loves me, but too many of my kind have not loved the world back.

The storm invades the sacred portal above. I have lost the battle. I cannot stop it. Failure flows through my veins sputtering my fire. I stand up. "Wake up, Kiawe! We have to get out of here!" But he is unresponsive, crumpled on the cavern floor, worn out from giving me all his mana.

I shield my head from the deluge and weep. "Oh, Mother, I love you. Why didn't you help me? I needed your mana, too! Your powerful wisdom! What have I done? You knew I would fail, didn't you? You could have helped me find a better way! Oh, Mahina, my baby, I am sorry. What was I thinking?!"

Now a torrent gushes toward us from across the cavern. I turn my will to stop it, but the best I can do is divert the flood around us. It rushes by, inches from our bodies and roars into the lava tube.

Higher and higher, the tears of the earth's storm rise. The angry sadness of everything flows over us now. I can't hold it back. It is too powerful, too heavy. I slip. The tears rush in mingling with my own.

Oh, Kiawe, I am sorry! Oh, earth, I am sorry! Forgive me for what I've done to you, what the people have done to you! Take me, if you must! I give myself to you! You are the cavern, the understanding, the love!

The swirling water douses the remaining fire of my will. Kiawe's body is torn from my feet and disappears down the tunnel. I reach for him, and I lose my anchor. I too am swept away. My head bangs on many rocks until the boulder snags my body. I am not allowed to leave. My spirit is stuck here forever, but not until it guides sweet Kiawe to the glittering mindfulness and acceptance of everything that is the ocean.

Chapter Twenty-Three

Mahina awoke with a start, her pillow soaked with sweat. Her throat was swollen, and tears were flowing from her eyes.

"Oh, Mom," she whispered. "I'm so sorry." She reached out next to her, searching for Olina, then sat up and saw her silhouetted in the light of dawn on the windowsill.

"Come here, Olina," she said in a halting voice, but Olina just ignored her and turned around to bite an itchy spot on her back. Mahina felt alone and exhausted. She collapsed again onto her pillow.

As usual, the dream settled into her waking mind with a feeling of reality that seemed more real than waking up. Never had she felt so close to her mother, or learned so much about her, but could she trust what was revealed? Had her dreaming mind only imagined how her mom had died? Or had she truly just relived her mother's death from inside her mind and body?

No matter which, the awful emotions were the same. What a horrifying way to pass on to the next world! Never had she missed her mother more, or her father. She wished she could have dreamed *his* emotions from inside of him too like she just did with her mother, but maybe that wasn't how the power worked. He must have loved her mother very much. He gave her everything, including his life. As she always did every morning no matter how the dreams left her feeling, she stared at her parents' picture on the wall taken when they were young and in love. Oh, how she wished that they were still alive!

She thought of Koa and how he had blended with Kiawe in her dream. She needed to talk to him and find out what he was feeling this morning. But then she remembered it was Sunday, and she had already been gone from the ranch the whole day yesterday. There was a five-gallon bucket of potato eyes in the barn waiting to be planted for the next crop. Tutu would keep her busy all day for sure. Plus, there was homework to catch up on.

Mahina sighed. Did Koa have a nightmare last night too? She doubted it. He seemed more energized after their flight than exhausted. Knowing him, he probably went home and dreamed of flying around Mauna Kea. Why had she felt so groggy? Was he sapping her energy somehow? No. He *gave* her energy, just like her father did to her mom. Besides, she had always been a little tired after flying, even when it was in a dream and she had been sleeping. It didn't matter before. The dreams were great, the reality of them, the flying, everything. But lately she wished the dreams weren't so draining and scary, with the flooding, the harsh words from Tutu, Olina attacking her, and the feeling of being confused and lost most of the time. She'd gotten what she asked for—more adventure in her life, and some answers about her dreaming and her mother. What she hadn't bargained for was all this mysterious danger. But nature was mysterious, powerful, and changing, and so, she supposed, was she.

She rolled out of bed and wiped her face on a tissue, then blew her nose. That cleared her head a bit, but her brain was still out of it. "Come here, you cute cat! I need to pet you."

Amazingly, Olina left her perch immediately and trotted over to rub herself on Mahina's legs. "Have you been a good kitty? What were you doing all last night? Prowling like a vicious and merciless hunter in nature? Are you ready for your breakfast? Do you want your breakfast time?"

Olina looked up at her and dropped her jaw to answer in a sweet *meow*. Mahina laughed and shuffled to the bathroom with Olina at her heels impatiently trying to redirect her downstairs to the pantry.

As usual, even on a Sunday, Tutu was already outside when she descended to the kitchen. Mahina scooped the kibble, made herself some coffee and eggs, chowed them down on a bed of toast, and stepped outside in her work boots to a gorgeously sunny day.

Tutu waved good morning from the garden as Mahina walked into the barn to feed the chickens and the pigs. Mahina looked at her bike hanging in the storage room and remembered how she could barely hoist it onto its hook yesterday. She didn't feel a whole lot more energetic today, although the coffee was slowly kicking in.

Stepping out of the barn into the sunshine again reminded her of the beauty of emerging from the cavern hole at the start of her outside flight with Koa.

"I'm a person who can fly," she whispered out loud to herself. Would she ever get used to that fact?

How could she? It was so cool. But really, she realized, walking into the garden where so many wonderful things grew was almost the same sensation. It all depended on how you thought about life, she decided. Whether you were paying attention. Hadn't flying even gotten a bit routine after a while? Weren't all things like that? Did the fact that she got used to experiencing the beauty of the ranch and the garden make them any less beautiful? No, she didn't think so. But she sure could use someone to help her think these things through.

She looked at Tutu, who was standing over a long row of bare earth that she had already turned over. Oh, how Mahina longed to tell her what was going on, what her dream said about her mom and how she died, that she could fly, that she knew about the sacred cavern.

Tutu smiled at her as she approached, and she realized she loved Tutu like a mom. Moms weren't supposed to be your friends, she'd heard. But why not? She'd feel so much closer to her as a mom if only Tutu weren't so fearful and quick-tempered.

"Good morning, sleepyhead. Feel better after your thirteen hours?"

"Hey, Tutu. Yeah, I guess. The chores are done."

"Thank you, and I suppose you want to bike off and do something again with your cowboy friend today?"

"No, Tutu. I want to help you in the garden. You asked me, right?"

"Good! There's so much to do, and it will be good for you. Feel that beautiful sun! And almost no wind. Planting. Nothing restores mana better than digging in the ground and planting something. The earth gives everything to the plants and to us. Grab yourself one of those paring knives and a handful of seed potatoes from the bucket. We'll work together going down these two rows I've prepared."

Despite the predictable mini-lecture, Mahina did already feel more energetic just being in the garden. As she followed Tutu's actions, carefully cutting off sprouted chunks of potato with her knife and burying them a few inches deep and a few inches apart in the long trench, the work cleared her mind and calmed her worries. It is always this way, working in Tutu's garden. What seems like a chore at first turns out to be pretty great.

Mahina watched Tutu work beside her and wondered if she felt the same way. Yes, she had the nervous habit of always wanting to move on to the next thing that had to be done as if there was never enough time, but once Tutu was actually doing something, she worked as if she had all the time in the world to do it right.

"We're going to have a lot of potatoes," Mahina said, reaching into the bucket.

"Potatoes are amazing. They don't take much, and they give and give," said Tutu, smiling. "I've been putting the straw and manure from the horse stalls on this section of the garden for the past six months. I wouldn't be surprised if we get a thousand potatoes."

"Yeah, you told me about that, and I can see the results. Building the soil. The cycle between animal waste and growing plants."

"Animals eat the plants, and plants eat the poop and pee, and eventually the animals' bodies too, if we let them. It's the way of the world. But it's not the whole story, Mahina. Bacteria are involved and all kinds of other living things in the soil. They are the mana movers, living full lives just like we do, only on a microscopic scale. A trillion stories unfold every day in the lives of trillions of beings in this soil." She held up a handful of the rich dark earth and smiled at it with reverence.

Mahina looked at her own hands covered by the dirt as she poked another sprouted potato eye into the ground. Could she feel the mana Tutu was feeling? She thought if she concentrated, maybe she could.

About halfway down the row, Tutu spoke again. "You know, child, it's more than what we were just talking about."

"What do you mean, Tutu?"

"This garden. It's more than just a good garden."

"Yes, it's amazing how well everything grows here."

"Bigger and tastier than anybody else's I've ever seen on the island, and you know, our soil isn't even as good as on the other farms. It's nowhere near as deep or rich, because the lava flows are newer here."

"New, like several centuries old."

"Right, but it takes a long time to build good soil on lava rock, and our ranch is still working on it. The cattle and horses help, but no, what makes this garden so good is the Moemoea ranch mana. It's the same life force that makes our cattle bigger and stronger than anyone else's. It's nowhere else on this island. Well, the mana is everywhere on this island, I should say, but it's strongest right here. You can feel it, you know. At least *you* should be able to. You, me, your mom, my mama, her mama, from the beginning, we all knew how to feel it. Just close your eyes and bury your hands like this in the soil."

Tutu had given Mahina this lecture many times before, but Mahina didn't mind. Tutu was never more open and gentle than when she closed her eyes and wiggled her hands deep into the soil. Mahina did the same, grateful that Tutu had mentioned her mom again. Maybe they could talk about her again. She hoped so.

At first, the soil just felt moist and a little cool. It smelled like everything smelled on the ranch—pungent and rich with complexity. *Life is like that,* she thought. *Never just one smell, one emotion, one possibility. Always choices and forces pulling everything this way and that. Nothing is simple, even though we dearly want it to be. We so want to feel like we understand it all and are in control.*

Mahina felt a warm tingle at the tips of her fingers. It spread into the palms of her hands and up her arms into her shoulders. When it reached her head, it lapped at her consciousness like a sun-baked wave on the beach until her whole body was humming with the heat of it.

She swayed and almost fell over. This was the same feeling she had before her body glowed in the cavern, the same exact sensation as when she bent her knees and soared through the cavern. For a moment, she was afraid she would float right up out of the garden and reveal her secret to Tutu, so she snapped out of it and yanked her hands out of the ground. Immediately, she was back in control of herself again. The tingling all over her body faded but didn't disappear.

She turned, astonished, toward Tutu, who was nodding and smiling knowingly at her. "See what I mean?"

"Tutu, it's like ..."

Tutu frowned. "Don't say it! Don't say it's like your dreams! It's *not* like your dreams, Mahina. Not at all! It's *real.* It's the ranch. It's the *spirit* of this place, the mana that emanates from the earth here.

Dreams do not nurture us like the land nurtures us, like nature, like this soil. We are earth's children, *not* the children of dreams."

"So when you're out here every day ...?"

"I'm communing, Mahina. Building my strength. Living in the mana, worshiping it, humbling myself to it, grateful for all of its gifts. That's what life is all about, Mahina. Or it should be, anyway."

Mahina thought about how great the tingling feeling still felt in her body, and said, "Life on this ranch, you mean."

"We're lucky enough to live away from all the pollution, but no, I mean everywhere. Anyone can feel it anywhere if they just slow down, nurture the soil, live simply, not show off, help the neighbors, treat animals with respect, love the miracle ..."

She wondered what Koa, Ms. Reynolds, and the other members of her English class might say to this argument. Could they truly understand it without experiencing the feeling of their hands in this soil themselves? Maybe it was wisdom only people in her family could understand.

But she was convinced that Tutu was right. Whether she was flying, glowing with insight, or just performing this simple act of connecting with the earth, the feeling was the same—intense, beautiful, life-fulfilling even, like loving her mother. Not for the first time did she understand and respect Tutu's life choices. If she had to argue for Tutu in class, she would say that if everyone had the same outlook on life as Tutu had, there wouldn't be a climate crisis.

How many other people in her life were like Tutu? None, she thought. Maybe Tutu was afraid of the cavern, like Mom said in the dream, but she wasn't afraid of the cavern-like feeling of the garden. Maybe that was good enough. Maybe she was right that the caverns were dangerous, and her mom's fear of the hurricane and of the earth getting destroyed was what led to her death. If she had followed Tutu's advice and not thought about her dreams so much, she herself might not have ended up naked and stranded underground. She felt very lucky.

"I love you, Tutu," Mahina said, smiling at her. "Thanks for showing me all this. Let's plant the rest of these potatoes—I want to get my hands back into the soil!"

She would remember the loving look Tutu gave her for the rest of her life.

Chapter Twenty-Four

The good feelings in Mahina's body stuck with her all day through supper and homework. She woke up on Monday morning not only not having had any dreams, but feeling refreshed and full of energy again. Maybe Tutu was right about planting potatoes, she mused, holding onto Olina, who chose to be with her last night. Or was it planting the onions, taro, carrots, green peppers, and tomatoes? It had been a productive day, but the conversation never got around to her mother.

Koa was waiting for her when she stepped off the bus. "Hey, partner," he said, glowing. "I guess you couldn't call yesterday?"

She shrugged, and he just laughed and said, "Hey, it's a compressed schedule today, did you get the message? The lower school needs an audience for a play they're doing!" He was dancing around like this was the most exciting news in the world. She felt good today, but apparently not as good as him.

"Oh, so that means English is in the third period and math is right before lunch," she said.

"Right, and no study period, but eat with me?"

"Sure thing. See you at the tree."

Why teachers always had to dump tons of new stuff and homework onto their laps on Mondays, she didn't know. Did they have nothing else to do on weekends but make devious plans to keep their students overly busy? By the time English rolled around, every last tingle from the weekend had disappeared from her fingertips. She forced herself to remember that she liked school and its many challenges.

When she saw Koa again in Ms. Reynold's section of the temporary classroom building, his energy hadn't diminished a bit. He was alive and enthusiastic about the climate change poetry presentations starting today.

After a while, though, even Koa lost his good mood when presentation after presentation delivered desperate and horrible news about what was happening to the environment. As she heard about cancer-causing pollution in the water and air, the scourge of plastics in the ocean, the disappearance of the rainforest in Brazil, and the destruction of the reefs in the oceans, Mahina remembered her hands in the soil of their garden back home. How could people ever let this happen to the earth? What was the matter with them?

Ms. Reynolds, annoyed that her class had been cut short by ten minutes, still managed to leave some time for discussion at the end. Mahina raised her hand and asked, "What is the *matter* with them?"

"Who, Mahina?" Ms. Reynolds replied.

"The people who let this happen. Are they stupid?"

"Any ideas, class?" asked Ms. Reynolds.

"It's money and greed," said the girl in the back who gave the presentation about plastics.

"Elaborate on that," encouraged Ms. Reynolds.

"Well, the plastic people, like the cigarette people, just wanted to make a lot of money selling their products. If they knew how bad plastic was for health and the environment, they didn't care. It wasn't their problem, or that's how they thought about it, anyway."

"I see," said Ms. Reynolds. "Some people say it's the structure of big corporations that's to blame. The job of the people in charge is to make money for the people who own the stocks of the company. They don't care about anything else, and the stock owners don't care about the specifics of running the company, so ultimately no one is responsible."

"But is that true?" challenged Koa. Ms. Reynolds nodded for him to go on. "Every company has a leader, a CEO, or a president. That person has to worry about bad publicity. Hurting the environment is bad publicity, so isn't he or she at least partially motivated not to let their company rape the environment?"

"Maybe," said Ms. Reynolds, "if the consequences are obvious enough and directly linked to the actions of the company. But take plastics, for instance. They're used in practically everything. Are all companies who use plastics to blame for fish in the oceans losing their fertility?"

"Some companies are switching to biodegradable alternatives to plastics," Mahina piped in, "and it's helping their sales. The Korean restaurant in town here uses only biodegradable packaging for its takeouts now."

"Yes," said Ms. Reynolds, "I noticed that."

"Whoever runs that restaurant decided to do something that wouldn't hurt the environment," continued Koa. "That made a difference."

"My mom runs a company," said a usually quiet Asian boy named Jacob, "and she says it's the tall, white men with cell phones who are to blame." Ms. Reynolds just looked at him like she couldn't believe what he had just said. "Yeah," he went on. "She says tall, white men in suits with cell phones are the most dangerous animals on the planet."

"Well, Jacob, perhaps we can express that differently. While it's true many leaders of the world's largest and most polluting companies are men, and the majority of those men are statistically taller than average, it doesn't mean they are, as a group, necessarily the most dangerous people on the planet. Maybe we can say leaders of companies who are out of touch with the needs and wants of the average multicultural families in our world are the ones who need to change."

"If they change, though, and lose their jobs, there are always more of them willing to replace them," pointed out Koa.

"Not if they do it right," Ms. Reynolds said. "The economics of healing the planet can be profitable for companies. It just takes creativity."

"And the will to do it," Mahina said.

"Exactly, and the will to do it. That's why these presentations you are doing are so important. People with power need to know what is happening to the planet, and they need to know that people care about that, if they're going to summon the will to make the necessary changes. Okay, class, nice job today! We'll have the rest of the presentations tomorrow. Remember, the play starts at one o'clock in the theater."

Mahina packed her backpack and maneuvered her way through the exiting students to walk next to Koa.

"One more to go," she said.

"Math!" he said, pumping his fist.

She looked at him. He wasn't being sarcastic. "You're a weirdo, you know that?"

He just laughed and linked arms with her as he danced out the door.

"You're too much," she said. "I'll see you at lunch."

She sat as far away from him as she could in math, but he kept making her laugh by sneaking glances at her and fluttering his eyebrows. He was always serious in English, but he could do math perfectly in his sleep, so she had to forgive him. Still, she knew because of his distracting antics, she would need to go over the problems again at home to understand them. Also what was distracting her was wanting to snarf down her peanut butter sandwich at the tree with him and talk about the weekend.

At lunch, their friends had caught on that when she sat at the tree with Koa, they didn't want to be disturbed, so she was less worried this time about checking around every ten seconds for eavesdroppers, even though today was probably the most top-secret tree discussion yet.

Surprisingly, Koa sat down with her and was immediately serious. Was it because of his smarts that he could turn his moods off and on like that? Who knew, but she appreciated his businesslike attitude because they didn't have a lot of time before the assembly show, when they would have to clap and laugh at the antics of the little kids to make them feel good about being on stage.

"I've got to tell you that what I was saying at your gate Saturday is absolutely true. I'm a happier person right now," he said.

"I can tell," she said.

"What about you?"

"I was just tired. I'm better today. I had a good day outside in the garden yesterday."

"Yeah, that's the thing. I didn't do anything yesterday either, but whatever I did, even brushing my teeth, I *really* enjoyed it." He looked at her very seriously to make sure she knew this wasn't a joke.

"You enjoyed brushing your teeth?"

"Yes, *ecstasy*. And don't get me started on making my bed, or taking the dog for a walk, or doing my homework, even. It felt the same as flying."

"It can't be the same as flying, those things. Really? Zooming around the hills with the wind in your hair?"

"I know it doesn't make any sense. Maybe if I'd been flying alone, I would view doing that as way better than doing those things, but I don't know. I'm, like, on some kind of high that doesn't go away, and I think it's connected with you."

"Huh, really?" she said. She hadn't felt connected to anything after the flight until she got her hands in the dirt. Maybe she had been too worried about everything. She needed to learn to take things easier, like Koa.

"Yes, with you, or the experience in the cavern, or something. And yes, it could be flying. I do want to do it again, but you know, I don't *need* to do it again. It's not really like a drug. It's more like ... a revelation."

"I wasn't trying to convert you to anything, Koa. I'm still trying to figure this out myself, remember?"

"I know. That's not what I meant. Maybe I meant 'education,' not 'revelation.' Yes, I feel more *educated* somehow, more connected. Like a mystery has been solved in my brain."

She looked at him pulling on his curly locks and looking pensive. "I had a nightmare Saturday night," she said.

"You were in the cave?"

"No, not me. I was my mom in the cave, with my dad. I died trying to use my power to stop the hurricane."

"Hurricane. The one that ..."

"Yes, the one that drowned her and my dad, who was kind of you in the dream, by the way, even though he looked like me. Not to worry, you weren't really him."

"I'm not worried. I like being in your dreams. Your mom, huh? That must have been really hard for you." She could see a tear of compassion form in his eye.

"It was, but I learned a lot about her and our family. She could have given a hell of a good presentation today in English class, I tell you!"

"I bet. Sounds like she cared a lot about saving the environment."

"That's the main point about what I learned. Helping the world stay steady has been the family thing. She gave everything for it."

Koa wiped his eye with the back of his hand and took a breath. He looked her in the eye again, and the tingling sensation returned to her hands. He whispered, "And if she had been in English class today, do you know what she would have said?"

Do I? she wondered.

You do. You are finding your path, came the voice from Mahina's heart. The tingling sensation increased. Her heart warmed and her hands began to glow. She looked around and quickly hid them under her shirt.

Koa seemed not to notice. He said, "I'm pretty sure that if I were the head of a huge chemical company right now, and I felt the way I do after flying with you, I would do everything I could to stop my company from polluting ever again."

A vision flashed in front of her mind of tall, white men with cell phones digging up the lawns of their corporate headquarters and planting potatoes, not caring that they were getting their fingernails dirty and their fancy suits ruined. She brought her pulsating hands to her face and laughed until tears streamed down her face. She turned to Koa, smiling.

"Looks like you're the one in a good mood now!" he said, reaching out to touch her.

She squeezed his hand then wiped her face with a napkin. "Let's finish our lunch and see if Ms. Reynolds can talk after the assembly. I think I know what I want to do next, but it's time for some help from an adult we can trust. Someone who has *connections*."

Chapter Twenty-Five

Mahina had just enough time to eat and to lay out her thoughts to Koa, then they had to hurry to the theater. Although the little kids were very charming in their pirate outfits, she had a lot of things on her mind, particularly how to get Ms. Reynolds to believe in what was going on with her without thinking she was crazy. Having Koa there for the conversation would help, although there was a danger Ms. Reynolds would think it was a prank, given his reputation for being a comedian.

Maybe talking to her was a bad idea, and they should try to contact people on their own. But who did Mahina know who ran big polluting corporations? No one, and she doubted Koa did, either. Their parents? Well, Tutu was out obviously, but Mr. Kahale? Maybe, but he would probably freak out too if they told him, then he would surely say it was too dangerous. She laughed out loud imagining him making them wear parachutes and football pads to be safe enough in the air. Koa looked at her strangely. Apparently it wasn't the right time in the play for laughter. She smiled at him and shrugged.

They could try going to Mr. Kinkle, Head of School, but she highly doubted he would take the chance to help them, even though it was her fundraising project that had saved the school.

No, Ms. Reynolds was their best hope. A lot of teachers talked about wanting the world to change, but Ms. Reynolds had been an actual environmental radical in her youth, and, unlike Tutu, she didn't cut you off as if you were a child when you brought up hard topics. But how to bring the subject up with her? The assembly ended before she could come up with a plan, but she stood up and clapped and cheered along with everyone else. One thing she loved about this school was that the students all supported each other no matter what. Aloha spirit, the best thing about Hawaii.

"Are you still up for this?" whispered Koa in her ear as they left the theater.

"Yes," she whispered back. "But I don't have a plan. Swear her to secrecy first, I guess. After that, I don't know."

"Well, don't worry. I think it's going to work out great! Just get into your zone and go with your gut. What's the worst that can happen?"

Mahina didn't answer, but she could imagine a lot of bad things. They emerged from the theater, and she checked the clock outside the administration building. They had a half hour before she needed to be on the bus.

They walked across the lawn past the construction workers hammering on the new classroom building toward the temporary trailers and found Ms. Reynolds with her head resting on her desk with her earphones on. Mahina recognized the tune buzzing from them: "Sugar Magnolia" by the Grateful Dead.

Ms. Reynolds sat up when she saw them and removed her earphones with a sheepish look on her face. "I love show tunes, but they get stuck in my head. I have to listen to something else right afterward, or I'm toast." She laughed, then hit the pause button on her phone and put it away in her woven Peruvian purse. "What can I do for you guys? Is it about the class? I know this stuff can be hard to take ..."

"No, no," she said. "Class was great. Actually, we wanted to follow up on it. But is there someplace we can go that's more private than this trailer?"

"Uh, sure. Let me think. Privacy can be pretty hard to come by around here. Oh, I've got an idea, the skateboard park across the street! I'm an adult, so guaranteed no one will come within twenty feet of me if I'm around there. Even though, just between you and me, when I was at Berkeley, I could thrash with the best of them!" She smiled.

Koa laughed long and hard at this. "That, I'd love to see!" he said.

The three of them crossed the street into the park and to a cypress tree next to the skateboard park. Ms. Reynolds was right. It was like she had a force field around her, although Mahina thought it was her teacher vibe more than her adult vibe that kept the skaters far away from them. They were alone, and the wind rustled the leaves above them. No one would hear their conversation.

"Okay, what's up with my two favorite students?" asked Ms. Reynolds, her flowing skirt gathered over her knees as she sat cross-legged against the tree.

"Oh, we know you, Ms. Reynolds. You don't play favorites!" said Koa, smiling.

"But we did make a pretty good team for the concert," Mahina said.

"Unforgettable," agreed Ms. Reynolds.

"Okay," Mahina said, "you know how we talked in class about the tall, white men problem?"

"Oh, wait. Don't we ...?" said Koa, putting his forefinger to his lip.

"Oh, right. Secrecy. We need you to promise that you will keep this a secret. It's important."

"I assumed that's the case, and it shouldn't be a problem unless either of you are in danger or being abused somehow. Then I would have to ..."

"No, it's nothing like that, Ms. Reynolds," Mahina said. "We're fine. It's just that this can't get out, *ever*."

"Okay, you have my word. So, you were talking about the corporate leaders, many of whom happen to be tall, white, and male? Let's not be prejudiced, now."

"Yes," Mahina went on. "We're all aware that there are lots of tall, white males in suits with cell phones who aren't eco-rapers, but you know what I mean. The challenge is to do something about the attitudes of people in charge no matter what they look like, right?"

"Uh huh. As we discussed, the will of CEOs of companies to change policies that pollute *can* make a difference," said Ms. Reynolds. "It's not easy to do that, though."

"Yes, the love of money and the structure of corporations stand in the way. We get that, but what if we told you we might have a way to help despite all those problems?"

"Oh, you do? Interesting. I take it you mean more than just sending out copies of your presentations, something I'm planning on doing, by the way." She smiled again.

"Yeah, something more than that," she said, swallowing and glancing at Koa. She took a big breath and pushed on. "What if we told you we could give those leaders an experience so cool and amazing that it would change them once and for all into people who would *want* to stop climate change?"

"I'd say, wow! What is it?"

"Well," Mahina said, then she hesitated.

Koa jumped in. "Just for the sake of argument, let's just say we did have something very unusual and special for them to experience, something uniquely mind-blowing that makes them see the error of their ways, and I mean *really* see it, and we could prove to you that it works. Could you help us bring these leaders to the island?"

"Secretly," added Mahina. "It would have to be a secret."

"I don't know. I mean, I suppose I could *try*. We do have a pretty extensive list of celebrities and wealthy donors collected from the concert. But why do you need me? You have the same list, don't you?"

"We could come up with it," said Mahina, "but this is different from kids saying come to a concert to help build a school building, Ms. Reynolds."

"Yes, this is pretty far-out stuff and way bigger," Koa went on. "So much bigger and far-out that no one would take us seriously, even though it is real and could change the world and stop climate change. We need an adult to convince them that it's worth their time."

"And to do it discreetly."

"You keep saying that. What, is it a drug trip or something? What are we talking about here?"

She and Koa both shook their heads. "Not a drug trip," Koa said. "Way better. Life-changing, in fact, as we said."

"So?" asked Koa.

Ms. Reynolds straightened her back and gave them both a long look. "I don't know," she said. "You want me to get on the phone and convince celebrities I sort of know, some through the donation list and some, I guess, through connections I have from Berkeley and NYU, to quietly fly out here to do something with two high school freshmen that will change their lives forever?"

"Right. To stop the climate crisis," said Koa. "Celebrities came for the concert when we didn't think any of them would come. They'll come for this, too." Mahina nodded.

"I don't see how I could answer that question without knowing what it is you would do to, or with, these people. You swore me to secrecy, so maybe now's the time to tell me? I mean, sure, if this experience is safe and is as transformative as you say it is, then how could I *not* help you? I'm as anxious as any other thinking person to save humanity and the environment. I don't understand why you have to keep it a secret, though, unless it is ..."

She looked at Koa and didn't say anything.

"Unless it is what?" asked Koa.

"Well, I know how connected Mahina is with her dreams, and I can see how much you two support each other in class, even though you aren't afraid to challenge each other too. So I just wonder whether your reluctance to say what this idea is might be because it's kind of a dream. It's not unusual for smart people your age to dream of a better world, to dream that they can make the world better, and to feel frustrated that things aren't as good as they should be. Maybe this thing that you want to do with celebrities and world leaders seems like a solution to you, but could it be that you just *want* things to be better so badly that ..."

"We're not *delusional*, Ms. Reynolds!" Mahina said with some heat. "You must know that about us by now. "The idea for the fundraiser came from my dreams. Was that delusional? I don't think so!"

Ms. Reynolds put her hands up. "No, I understand that. It wasn't. It was nothing but great. I apologize—and nice use of that vocab word, delusional, by the way. But can you please just tell me what you're talking about so we can get out of the hypotheticals?"

Mahina nodded at Koa, and he said, "There is a cave on Mahina's property, a lava tube several thousand years old. It's connected to the earth. Well, obviously it's connected to the earth, but I mean connected to the *spirit* of the earth. It's sacred and magical, that's the only way to describe it."

"It's where my mom and dad died. Mom speaks to me when I'm there, and sometimes when I'm not. She was a goddess fighter for the earth way back when Earth Day was just beginning."

Ms. Reynolds nodded. A skateboarder crashed in the far corner of the park and cursed loudly. Mahina glanced briefly at him and went on.

"You see, Ms. Reynolds, I have these dreams about flying. They always start in the lava tube. They're not always good dreams, but the flying part is amazing. There's a cavern in there with a hole at the top of it. It's kind of like a womb, but the details don't matter right now ..." She looked up at the leaves of the tree in frustration. *This is where I blow it with my favorite teacher,* she thought. *She's never going to believe me.*

"The lava tube is real," said Koa. "We've been inside of it."

"It's just like in my dreams, Ms. Reynolds. I relived my mother's drowning death in there. My skin glows with light in there. I fly in there—well, mostly in the cavern. In the lava tube itself, I pretty much just float. It's a Moemoea family thing, this power I have. I concentrate and raise my feet behind me and fly in there, and also out the hole, and all around the ranch."

Ms. Reynolds looked at her with a concerned expression on her face.

"She's not lying, Ms. Reynolds. Honestly, she's not. I thought she was at first too, but then I went with her. We *flew* together, Ms. Reynolds, awake and in the daytime, and it changed me even more than surfing has. After flying with Mahina, I cared more for the earth and its magic than I ever did before. The earth is so much more than what we give it credit for. It's amazing, and we've got to keep it from turning to hell!" Koa had a far-away look in his eyes but then turned them to look at Mahina with purpose and love.

"It's the truth, Ms. Reynolds. I really can do all these things, *have* to do them, in fact. It's the reason my mother gave birth to me. Trying to take care of people and the earth, it's our family's purpose in life, and now it's more important and dangerous than ever before. Koa and I are begging you to come with us into the cave so you can see for yourself." She swallowed and forced herself to look her favorite teacher in the eye.

"Well, that's quite a tale. If true, it's beyond anything any human has ever done before. Dreaming about flying is common, but actually *doing* it—without wings and motors, I assume—yes, that *would be* transformational."

"So you'll go into the cave with us, or at least with Mahina?" said Koa, excited.

Ms. Reynolds took a deep breath. "No, I'm afraid not. I'm not much of an outdoor adventurer, and your grandmother has made it abundantly clear that I'm not welcome on your property. I have to respect that."

"But she would never know," said Koa. "It's a mile away. You can get to the cave without going anywhere *near* Mahina's house."

"Doesn't matter. It would be trespassing not only on her property but on her wishes as well. But that doesn't mean I'm not taking you seriously. The idea that leaders in this country need to learn that the present beauty and magic of the earth is enough is a good one. All their changing it and polluting it because of striving for more money and power than they need is unnecessary. Yes, you are totally right about that."

"So you won't help her fulfill her dream?" said Koa, his buoyant mood crushed.

"I *will* help her, but maybe not exactly in the way she wants." She turned and took her hands in hers. "Your dreams obviously give you great ideas, Mahina. They're not only helping you to process the tragic loss of your mother, but shaping your priorities for the future. I have no doubt you will help the world, both of you. Maybe these recent dreams you guys are processing together are the seeds of a work of art? A novel, or maybe a play, or a series of short stories? At the very least poems!" Ms. Reynolds let go of her hands and clapped them together.

Mahina just stared at her. Koa's mouth was hanging open.

"Oh," he said. "I get it. An idea for some writing. That's great. Spoken like a true English teacher." He gestured with his head to

Mahina. "Um, looks like we've got to go, Ms. Reynolds. Your bus, Mahina?"

"Yes. Well, thanks anyway, Ms. Reynolds. Looks like I've got to fly," she said ironically.

"Oh, I get it! Good one!" said Ms. Reynolds. Mahina choked up and shot her a dark look from her watering eyes.

"Wait!" Ms. Reynolds said, stopping them. "Look, I was wrong to trivialize this. I'm sorry. It's just hard to wrap my brain around something so surprising and strange, that's all. Mysterious things do happen, I know. I appreciate you trusting me with this, and I promise I'll think more about what you asked. You really are my best students, and I wish there was a way I could help you with this."

The best Mahina could do was give her a nod. She was too upset. She should have known. She *did* know. *What a fool I've been,* she thought. She took Koa's arm and let him walk her to the bus.

Chapter Twenty-Six

That night, Mahina dreamed ...

SOMETHING IS STRUGGLING in my backpack, but the opening into the cave is clear. I walk forward, sure of my way, unsure of what I carry. Olina trots next to me, meowing like she's hungry.

"I can feed you when we get there," I say to her, but I don't know how I'll do that. So many things I don't know, and yet I walk on.

Then it's time. I concentrate and raise my feet. My boots graze the bottom of my backpack, startling the thing inside and making it thump against my back, like a child throwing a temper tantrum.

Olina and I float past the boulder and are pulled toward the narrow place. Olina is sucked through ahead of me like a spider in a vacuum cleaner hose, but my backpack grows bigger and catches on a rock. I am stuck there, squeezed by the walls, my hair pulled forward and whipping against my eyes.

The suction is merciless. Saliva blows out of my mouth. My ears roar. The backpack rips apart behind me, releasing me, and I fly forward into the cavern, empty fabric flapping on my back.

Bright in the beam of the day's sun, I float just below the opening. Olina, no longer hungry, basks next to me and fills the cavern with purring. Then I turn to see what I left behind. Staggering out of the narrow place is a woman with wounds on her neck and arms. Instead of red blood, many colors ooze from her skin and form pleasing designs on her billowing clothing. She pulls a ham and cheese sandwich on white bread out of a plush, woven handbag. Olina meows and flies to land next to her. The woman gives her a bite of her sandwich.

"Thank you for believing in us," I say.

Chapter Twenty-Seven

The next day at school, Mahina decided it was best to forget about it all and just have a regular day. She could do that. What was the use of all the suffering, and who did she think she was, anyway? Madame Pele? Someone who could *save* the world? *Give me a break.* She would have to just put up with her dreams, or do what Tutu wanted her to do and ignore them.

Koa was his usual bouncy self between classes. He didn't suggest a tree discussion at lunch, and she didn't either. Maybe he sensed her need to get back to normalcy after their disappointing discussion with Ms. Reynolds.

The school day went on as it usually did. English was a little tense with Ms. Reynolds occasionally looking at them with a worried expression, but all they had to do was listen to the rest of the climate presentations. Not that the presentations weren't interesting and horribly depressing. They were.

The climate crisis was a bummer, but Mahina supposed it was something they would just have to live with. Apparently, there was nothing she could personally do to fix it, even if she did have the power to change people, or at least Koa, in profound ways.

On the way to the picnic table for lunch with their usual group of friends, Koa piped up and announced a game he wanted to play. "I don't like what my mom packed me for lunch. It's good and everything, but I've had it too many times. How about today is Guess What Someone Is Having For Lunch Day? Guess someone's lunch, and they have to share it with you!" Mahina rolled her eyes at him and snorted. If she had changed Koa somehow, it wasn't in this. He knew how to make people have fun.

There were some smiling groans, but everyone sat down and waited cheerfully for the specifics. Then Ms. Reynolds sauntered up and squeezed her way in next to Koa like nothing had changed. Maybe she was trying to have a regular day today, too.

"No, Ms. Reynolds, you can't open your lunch here," said Koa authoritatively. Ms. Reynolds' face dropped. "At least not yet. We're guessing each other's lunches, and if you're right, you get half the lunch. It's a way of diversifying our caloric input."

"No, it's a way for Koa to get an upgrade from the cat food his mother packed for him today," said Jacob.

"Wrong guess, Jacob. Cat food? My mom is a gourmet lunch packer. You don't get my lunch! Anyone want to go next?"

"Hey, that's not fair! That wasn't my guess," said Jacob, pretending to be angry.

"Okay, we'll let you have a freebie. Consider it a demonstration of how *not* to play this game!" Everyone laughed, but Mahina didn't feel like joining in for some reason. Normally she liked lunchtime banter. It was great to be outside in the fresh air and sunshine. But today, she felt a familiar tiredness gripping her from the dream last night. Maybe she should see a doctor and get some sleeping pills? Do they make any that get rid of dreams?

She glanced at Ms. Reynolds across from her, eyeing her lunch bag. Koa called on someone else, who made a wrong guess at what he had in his lunch box, but Mahina suddenly could hardly follow what was going on. She felt faint and hot. Time slowed down, and there were tingles in her gut again. Her hands were brightening. As quickly as she could, she put them on her lap under the table, but they seemed to descend through the air in slow motion. Had she hidden them in time? Would her face start glowing too right there in front of her friends? She concentrated hard on not allowing it to do that.

"Your turn, Mahina," she heard Koa say, as if from far away. "Whose lunch do you want to guess?" Part of her mind understood this, but the dreamy part of her mind heard, *And whose hunch do you want to test?* She raised her head slowly and stared at Ms. Reynolds.

"I know who I want to test," she mumbled. She saw Koa and her friends look at her strangely. She felt her mind detach from her body and hover above the table. Instead of Ms. Reynolds, she was looking down at the woman from last night's dream who had shared her food with Olina. "I mean," she said quickly, "I want to guess yours, Ms. Reynolds. It's a ham and cheese sandwich on white bread."

Ms. Reynold's jaw dropped. She laughed and said, "You're right, Mahina! How did you know?" She unwrapped it to show the table.

"Wow, great guess!" said Jacob. "Wait, do you have that sandwich every day, Ms. Reynolds?"

"No, first time in ages."

"Well, Mahina, you win! And you scored half a sandwich," said Koa. "Hey, that actually looks delicious. Did I tell you that a portion goes to the referee as a game fee?"

"That's okay, you can have my half," Mahina said. "But I want at least a bite of it to take home to my kitty. It'll be a *dream* come true for her." She gave Ms. Reynolds a piercing look.

"How'd you guess that, Mahina?" someone asked.

"I'll bet it was a gag! You guys set us up, didn't you? Good one!" said Jacob, starting in on his own lunch.

The rest of the table followed his lead, laughing and shaking their heads. She peeked at her hands in her lap. Not glowing. She opened her lunch bag and started munching along with everyone else. Slowly she came back to reality, but the fatigue lingered. She let Koa's entertaining banter wash over her and the table like an energizing shower, but she couldn't avoid the eyes of Ms. Reynolds questioning her the rest of the lunch period.

Chapter Twenty-Eight

That afternoon, the school secretary discreetly entered Mahina's last-period math class and slipped a folded yellow note onto her desk.

Please meet me at the skateboard park after school today.

– Ms. R.

Mahina refolded the note and stuck it in her backpack. Was there a chance Ms. Reynolds had changed her mind? She debated telling Koa about it but decided this one should be between her and Ms. Reynolds because only Ms. Reynolds had been in her dream.

At the park, the same teenage skateboarder who crashed so spectacularly last time was there again, trying to defy gravity. *I could give him a lesson or two,* Mahina thought. She found Ms. Reynolds on the far side of the tree, well hidden from the gossiping eyes of students and parents jockeying their cars into the pickup line.

Ms. Reynolds stood up from the tree.

"We can sit," Mahina said. "I have a half hour again. My bus is always the last one in line."

"Thanks for not ignoring my note," said Ms. Reynolds tentatively.

"You're my teacher," she said, shrugging. They sat with their backs to the tree trunk and watched the skateboarder crash and curse again for a moment. The crash wasn't as bad as the one yesterday. He was getting better.

"I'm more than your teacher. We did the fundraiser together. I'm your friend. You want to tell me how you knew what sandwich I packed today?"

"Would you believe me if I told you the truth? You probably think I peeked during English, or Koa did and told me."

"My lunch bag was in the teacher's lounge all morning. I doubt either one of you would be that daring. So ...?"

Mahina took a deep breath. Was this worth one more try? She could just say it was a lucky guess. She looked up at the sky and thought about the storms coming in the world's future. She put her hand on her belly and felt the stirrings of the spirit of a daughter she would most likely give birth to one day, as every woman in her family had before her. What future would her daughter face in this already damaged world? Trying to ignore it didn't feel right. Didn't Mahina have a responsibility to help her in any way she could? Didn't she have a responsibility to help the *world*? She decided she did. And Ms. Reynolds had been the most open and thoughtful adult she'd ever met. She took a deep breath.

"I didn't fly last night, Ms. Reynolds, but I did dream. I had a dream about *you*."

Ms. Reynolds didn't say anything for a long time.

"It had a sandwich in it. Yes, the ham and cheese sandwich—white cheese, by the way, just like the one you ate today at lunch. So it was a guess, but a pretty easy one given the way my dreams go and what my gut tells me about them. My family's been pretty good at that—*knowing things*. At least, my great-*tutu* was, and her mother before her."

"Oh," said Ms. Reynolds.

"You want me to tell you what else I learned about you in the dream? We were in the cave, by the way, all the way into the sacred cavern."

"I don't know ..." said Ms. Reynolds, but Mahina could sense in her fingertips that Ms. Reynolds did want to know. The tingling moved up her arm and then down into her belly, and she slipped again into a dream state. She lowered her voice to barely above a whisper.

"You say you don't know because I am a student, and deep in your heart you are sick of being carried around by your students, your life controlled by them. For too many years, students have carried you on their backs, like a book or another temporary piece of their education in a backpack. They use you. While they like you, and you like them, they don't necessarily know you for who you truly are."

Ms. Reynolds stared at her and swallowed. Mahina's hands warmed, and she hid them under her shirt again.

"You feel the squeeze, the walls literally closing in on you. But the more they squeeze, the more you grow. You grow to the point where you desperately need to break free. Cuts and bruises won't matter because it's time to move forward. You know you will bleed, but the blood you shed will make new patterns for your life, better roles to play, patterns you have dreamed about forever."

In a trance, Mahina's vision was back in the cavern again, looking down at Ms. Reynolds feeding Olina. Her body swayed as if hovering in the air.

Tears trickled down Ms. Reynold's cheeks as she stared at her.

"You *care*, Ms. Reynolds, but not just about the students around whom you must always be so cautious. You care about animals, especially ones that fly, but also cats. You shared food with one in the cavern. You don't want beautiful, flying souls to die, and so many of them are dying now. All the presentations in your class were about terrible losses in our beautiful world, but dying animals struck you deepest in your heart."

"Yes," whispered Ms. Reynolds. "So sad, so very sad. The birds! So many gone! I never said anything. How do you know these things? No one can be so insightful! I'm ..." Ms. Reynolds held her face in her hands and sobbed.

Mahina channeled love and compassion and sent them to her teacher. She slid one glowing hand discreetly across the grass between them and into Ms. Reynold's hands. Ms. Reynolds stopped crying and stared in amazement at the soft human skin illuminating her own.

"I believe you now, Mahina," she whispered. "I don't know how you and your family know these things, but I guess no one knows how someone like Shakespeare could have known so much either, yet magically he did. Something similar is moving inside you, I think, something creative—no, *more* than creative: godlike. Forgive me, please, for yesterday."

Ms. Reynolds pressed Mahina's hot, glowing hand then let her take it back to hide it from the skateboarders. She wiped her eyes, looked directly at Mahina, and said, "I don't know what it is, this energy of yours, but it feels good. It feels right, and it feels *important.* I want to learn more. Thank you for not giving up on me. I'm sorry. I want to help. If you're still willing, please take me to see this cave."

Chapter Twenty-Nine

The scheme for sneaking Ms. Reynolds onto the ranch wasn't the greatest, but it would have to do, Mahina thought, sitting low in the grass next to her hidden bicycle by the road at the corner of their fence line.

This morning she could see in Tutu's eyes that she didn't buy Mahina's story about wanting to go to the farmers market again to listen to a slack key guitarist who had performed at the benefit concert, but Tutu let her go anyway.

The plan was for Koa to use the same excuse with his parents, then bike out and meet Ms. Reynolds coming in her Prius. Dressed in running shoes, they would blend in with the handful of joggers and bikers that always parked in a pull-off just a few hundred feet from the fence line.

She kept her eyes on the section of the road visible between the tufts of grass. As usual, it was mostly pickup trucks and four-wheel drive vehicles going by. She recognized the Kealoha's red pickup with surfboards in the back headed west into town, but most were locals heading east, presumably to conquer the all-day scenic drive around the mountain.

As long as Tutu's pickup didn't cruise by while Koa and Ms. Reynolds were walking from the car, they should be okay. Tutu hadn't mentioned going to town this morning, but she never shared her daily plans unless she needed help with something. Mahina hoped she wouldn't drive to the farmers market to check up on her.

She heard Koa's voice saying, "Here's the hill with the trees."

Mahina met them at the fence. "Hi, Ms. Reynolds," she said, and Koa lifted his bike over to her. She laid it down on the ground and raised the bottom strand of barbed wire so they could climb under.

"Just like old times, eh, Mahina?" Koa laughed. "This is getting routine. What a beautiful day to be outside!" He was dressed in long sleeves and hiking boots again, and Mahina was glad to see Ms. Reynolds dressed similarly. She hoped he remembered to bring the headlamps.

As they walked his bike to hide it with hers, Koa said, "I brought three headlamps ready to go, and the map I finished sketching out for us. And my cell phone, although with the map, I doubt we'll need any pictures to figure out where we're going. Weather looks good, too."

"Don't worry, Ms. Reynolds," she said reassuringly. "I know this cave pretty well. We're just being extra careful. We won't get lost."

"I appreciate that, Mahina. I trust you." Ms. Reynolds opened her arms to the hills in front of them. "What a beautiful ranch you've got here. I can understand why your grandmother wants to keep it a secret."

"Well, not exactly a secret. She just doesn't want to see it get wrecked. There's a lot of meaning in it for her, and for me too, I guess."

"You don't have to say, 'I guess.' I get it. I feel attached to it too, and this is only the second time I've been here! I want you to know I get that this is a sacred place, and it's not just because of your parents. It's everything, and I respect that, especially how it's shaped you, *and* what you told me yesterday."

Mahina always felt bad about sneaking around Tutu, but her heart warmed once again toward her teacher, and she was glad things worked out and she was sharing this special place with her.

"Thanks, Ms. Reynolds. Come on, it's this way, about a half mile. We need to keep our voices low. Sound travels far on this ranch, and the house is just beyond those two far hills."

As they wound their way through the cow trails to the entrance, she kept glancing back at Koa, who was smiling contentedly and walking with calmness and confident energy. He was always a happy person before, but it was true that now, *everything* seemed to make him happy.

They paused behind the last hill before the entrance to put on their headlamps, and then quickly crossed the clearing and slipped through the hidden opening in the concrete blocks.

"Feels like I'm in a Murakami novel," said Ms. Reynolds, with a bit of awe in her voice. She shined her light around the walls of the lava tube and glanced back at the daylight streaming in from the entrance. "At least this is not a deep well with no way out..."

"If all goes as planned, we'll leave a different way," Mahina said.

The damp cold of the lava tube felt comforting to her today in a strange way. Could something that once made you shiver to your bones still feel like home? She saw Koa pull the map from his backpack.

"We're here," he said to Ms. Reynolds, showing her. "Up ahead we'll go right, see? It's a little tricky to see the turn, but we've got it down thanks to Mahina feeling her way out of here in the dark one time. Then we go here, through here, and into here."

"You had to feel your way out of here in the dark, Mahina?!" Ms. Reynolds asked, horrified.

"That was a while ago. Long story with a happy ending. Just be happy you don't have dreams like mine to contend with in your life."

"Huh, I guess, except I'm here right now with you, aren't I? I'm not much of a cave person. Give me a rocking chair and a book on a nice sunny porch. That's more my style." Her voice sounded a little shaky.

"Lanai. We say lanai here. Feel whatever you feel, Ms. Reynolds. That's part of it. I've been scared here plenty of times in my dreams. The fear sucks, but I come back because it's worth it. But if it gets too much for you, we can always turn around. Just let me know."

"Thanks, Mahina. I'm okay, I think. Let's keep going."

"That's the attitude!" said Koa. "On to the cavern!"

As they made their way through the lava tube to the hidden passageway and then to the narrow tunnel before the cavern, Mahina kept thinking about the dream with Ms. Reynolds in her backpack, struggling to escape. She hadn't known what the dream meant when she was having it, or even when she woke up. Only when she was remembering it and interpreting it for Ms. Reynolds at the skateboard park tree did the significance of it become clear to her. It reminded her of discussing books in Ms. Reynolds' English class. Sometimes you have no idea what a scene in a book has to teach you until you talk to others about it. So it's worth paying attention to everything that happens in your life because you never know what might be importantly meaningful later on.

When the narrow passageway opened up into the cavern, Ms. Reynolds was standing in the light from the ceiling, just like she had been in Mahina's dream, except this time dressed in blue jeans and a long-sleeved shirt rather than in a blood-stained skirt and blouse. Mahina felt the rightness in the blending of dream and reality.

Her body began to tingle as she thought about this. Ms. Reynolds was in the cavern now, but she was also in the cavern before now because of her dream, and Ms. Reynolds would likely be there in the future too, in reality, or in further dreams by both of them, or even Koa. From the viewpoint of this ancient cavern, perhaps these appearances were all one event. Maybe all of them were there, and all of them were elsewhere, everywhere, at once in reality and in their minds. She could feel this thought resonate in her bones, and her hands immediately glowed.

The heat inside her began as she smiled at Ms. Reynolds and Koa, who were both looking upward at the daylight knifing through the opening and softly illuminating the silver, black, and brown walls of the cavern. She focused on their faces as she concentrated with all her might and gently willed her heels to rise.

"Hold my hands," she whispered to them. "In here, with me, you shall fly."

Their hands felt cool in hers. She floated slightly above them and gently lifted their arms upward.

"Up, up, up," she said. "Concentrate on floating up. *Believe*!" She felt her knees resting on the cool damp air, and she willed Koa's knees to do the same, then Ms. Reynolds'.

"Whoopee!" said Koa. "Just as I remembered it!"

Ms. Reynolds gasped. "I can't believe this is happening to me!"

"It's happening, Ms. Reynolds," Mahina said. "This is not a dream. Or maybe flying is life, and the reality outside is the dream—I haven't quite figured that out yet. But, whichever, it's okay to say whatever you want and to let go of hands. You're okay.

"Think where you want to go, and you'll go there. Will yourself to stop, and you'll stop. You can rest and hover with your feet down. When you touch the rocks or anything connected to the ground, the flying will end, so stay carefully in the air until it's over."

"You got this, Ms. Reynolds!" said Koa. "Watch my knees. See, I bend my right one and it helps me to go right. Now I'll go left. See my left knee, and what it's doing? My mind keeps me from hitting anything. Now you try!"

Ms. Reynolds followed Koa upward and managed to fly in a circle with him around the shaft of light. "It's like getting a ski lesson!" she laughed. "Wow, I can really fly! The birds, they must feel like this! Oh, the birds!"

Mahina smiled and led them up and down the cavern a few times. Then, when she was sure Ms. Reynolds was in control of herself and Koa was calm enough to stay focused, she led them carefully up and out of the hole and into the beautiful sunshine that made the rolling hills of her ranch glow verdantly beneath them.

"You've got to stay low over the hills for this part," warned Koa, "but not too low. Don't touch the grass!"

"Yes," Mahina said, scanning the hills and valleys for trespassers who might see them, or worse, Tutu on one of the horses.

The coast seemed clear, so as she and Koa had done before, she led them northeast toward the most remote part of the ranch, where they zoomed through the valleys and between the eucalyptus trees.

"It feels so right!" said Ms. Reynolds after a while. "Like I *belong* here, in the air."

"You *do* belong here, Ms. Reynolds," replied Koa. "The earth loves you, like a mother does. Like she loves all living things!"

"Like she loves the birds! Oh, I'm a bird! I'm free!" exclaimed Ms. Reynolds.

Congratulations, Daughter. You have found the path, and you will return again. Now go. Immediately! You must go back. Now*!*

Mahina felt her heart leap into her throat when she heard her mom's warning. She waved her hands frantically and called out to Koa and Ms. Reynolds. "We need to go back! To the bikes. Now! Follow me and stay low. If we see people, we'll just land and pretend we're on a hike. Come on!"

She flew low, southwest between the hills, and followed a cow path back toward the road. At the entrance to the cave, they turned up the cow path to the hill where the bikes were hidden. She hovered over the bikes next to the tree and lowered her legs. "Touch down when I touch down. That way, you won't land too hard."

"Yeah, I learned that lesson the hard way last time!" said Koa. "Here, hold my hand, Ms. Reynolds!"

She waited until she knew they were both watching her and slowly willed herself to the ground. No one even stumbled. It was like they were stepping off the back of a pickup truck.

"Oh, my goodness! That was so great!" said Koa, a little too loudly.

"Shhh!" Mahina said. Ms. Reynolds looked a little unsteady on her feet, but she too had a big grin on her face.

Then Mahina saw Ms. Reynolds gasp as if she had seen a ghost.

Mahina heard the hoofbeats just as she turned to look where Ms. Reynolds was staring. Like a nightmare, trotting toward them on the path from the road was Tutu riding Ikaika.

Ikaika spotted them and lurched sideways, and Tutu pulled the reins hard to stop her and to keep from falling off. Ikaika calmed down when she recognized Mahina and stood breathing hard.

"What are you doing here, Mahina?" said Tutu.

All Mahina could hope for was that maybe Tutu hadn't seen them in the air. Mahina's mouth was open, but she didn't know what to say.

"Hi, Mrs. Moemoea!" piped up Koa with a big smile on his face. "Beautiful ranch you've got here!"

"Hello, Koa. Didn't expect you out here today. Thought you two were listening to music in town? And what are *you* doing here?" said Tutu to Ms. Reynolds, who just stared back at her with a frightened look on her face. "I thought I told you to stay away from here!"

"I invited her, Tutu," Mahina said, barely getting her voice back.

"Yeah, we were waiting for the music, and we decided it was too nice a day to waste with a bunch of tourists, so we came out here for a hike," continued Koa with a grin. "Nice day for a ride, too, and you're smart to ride Ikaika. That Costco is a handful!"

Ikaika started to get antsy again, so Tutu swung her leg over the saddle and stepped down, holding the reins. "And you couldn't come in the front gate to let me know you were back, Mahina? You had to wait until I came riding along and happened to hear you laughing up here? What's the matter with you? And you, Ms. Teacher Lady. No one teach you any manners? Where'd you park, anyway?"

"We were looking for birds, Mrs. Moemoea," said Koa.

"Ms. Reynolds really loves birds, Tutu. We saw her at the farmer's market and started talking about the pheasants that live out here. She didn't believe that we had them on this island, so we wanted to show her some. They like this part of the ranch the best, you know, so we just came here. Sorry."

"Yeah, and I almost didn't come because I have to get back by noon to help my dad today," continued Koa. "But I'm excited because we saw *three* of them, so see, we were right, Ms. Reynolds, weren't we?"

She knew Koa was trying his best, but she could see Tutu wasn't buying it. She felt sick to her stomach.

"I'm sorry, Ma'am," said Ms. Reynolds, nodding at Koa. "You're right. I should have driven in the gate. It was rude of me not to. I get excited sometimes, and I don't think. I didn't mean to be disrespectful. I'm embarrassed, and I'll leave your property right now. Mahina, thank you for inviting me and showing me around. I'm sorry I put you in this position. I should have known better. The pheasants were beautiful, dear, and I learned a lot today, but I shouldn't have thought it was okay just to go under the wire with you. I agree with Koa, Ma'am. You have a special place here, extremely beautiful. Koa, do you need my help with your bike and Mahina's?"

Tutu took this in and, frowning, got back on the horse. She looked at Mahina pointedly and gestured for her to get on home, then turned Ikaika around and rode away.

As soon as she was out of sight, a wave of dizziness overtook Mahina. Koa and Ms. Reynolds fetched the bikes and headed for the fence but dropped them when Mahina staggered and dropped to her knees. Dimly, Mahina saw them running toward her.

"Are you okay?" said Ms. Reynolds.

Was she? She felt so tired again. Always after these flights, such overwhelming fatigue, and this time with guilt and sadness piled on top of it.

"I'm ..." she said, then swayed.

"Just sit there for a minute," said Koa.

"I don't think she saw us," Mahina managed to say.

"No, I agree," said Ms. Reynolds. "What would she have done if she had?"

She felt both of them holding her. "I really don't know, but I better get home right away. I feel exhausted." She struggled back to her feet. "Help me with my bike, will you? And remember, you guys, *secret*, this is a secret. It's got to be, otherwise ..." She shook her head.

"We understand," said Koa. "We're in enough trouble as it is without blabbing our mouths about what we were actually doing here. But really, thanks, Mahina. Go home and rest. We'll figure this out later. You've made flying feel so cool and normal for me!"

"Yes, thank you," said Ms. Reynolds. "I'll never be the same! I hope you'll be okay?"

Mahina was not okay. She felt a cold darkness pushing in on her eyes, draining her almost completely. She wanted to feel energized because the flight was so successful, but she could hardly move. Seeing Tutu reminded her of being lost in the cave and how horrible it was, but it wasn't just being caught that made her feel drained. This was something more. She couldn't help wondering if maybe this good thing that was happening wasn't so good after all. She loved these people and what they were doing for her and the world, but right now all she wanted was her bed and her warm cat.

"Yes, I think so. I'll be okay," she managed to reply, "but I'm afraid I need your help to get me to the gate."

Chapter Thirty

After she mumbled goodbye to Koa and Ms. Reynolds at the top of her driveway, Mahina walked her bike slowly down to the house.

What was she going to say to Tutu? Stick with the lie? Tell her the truth? Her brain was too foggy to make any decisions, even though she knew she had to say *something*.

She leaned her bike against the side of the house and staggered up the stairs to the door. She hardly had the strength to turn the knob, and when she finally got it open, she zig-zagged to the nearest chair to rest. She sat awkwardly, and her head flopped forward on the kitchen table.

"Chasing pheasants wear you out?" Tutu said, appearing in the doorway from the living room.

She lifted her head and mumbled, "Oh, Tutu, I'm so sick!"

Then everything went dark, and she slipped off the chair onto the linoleum floor.

When she woke up in her bed, it was light out. She vaguely remembered Tutu shaking her awake on the living room couch and helping her walk up the stairs to bed. She had a splitting headache, she had to pee, and her mouth was completely dry. Where was Olina? She got up and walked to the bathroom, rubbing her eyes. When she returned, she saw a glass of water by the side of her bed. Was that there all night? She drank it gratefully and climbed back into bed.

Deeply asleep, she vaguely heard her door open and close several times. Must be Tutu coming to check on her. Waking a little more, Mahina was grateful she wasn't having another dream. Remembering

Tutu discovering them was enough of a nightmare. Was that yesterday? It must have been. She could see sunshine on the leaves of the trees outside, so it must be Sunday afternoon.

She heard her door open again slowly and saw Tutu peeking in, holding a mug. "You're awake, finally," she said. Olina scampered in behind her and jumped on the bed.

"Yes, finally."

"How are you feeling?"

She ran her hand down Olina's soft back, and answered, "I'm better. Still tired. My head hurts."

"I've got some fresh chicken broth for you." Tutu brought the mug to her bedside table and picked up the empty water glass. She then put her hand on her forehead. "You don't seem to have a fever."

"That's good," Mahina said, sitting up to take a sip from the mug.

"Your mother used to get these spells too. I'm worried about you. Sneaking around with Koa and now with your teacher. Do I have to ground you so I can keep an eye on you?"

"I'm sorry, Tutu. It won't happen again, I promise."

"I know it won't because that's the end of your relationship with Ms. Reynolds."

"What do you mean, Tutu?"

"I mean that's the end. You'll need to get out of her class or do whatever you have to do because I forbid you to speak with her again."

"Tutu! I can't do that. I can't just switch to another class."

"Well, you'll just have to figure it out or drop out. That woman is coming between me and what I know is best for my grandchild. Look at you! So sick you can't even do your chores!"

"Tutu, I'm sorry about the chores. I'll do them now." She got out of bed.

"Don't bother. I covered your chores for you this morning. Use this time to figure out if you want to stay in that school or not. If you do, no Ms. Reynolds."

"I'm staying in the school, but I don't see how I can do it and not be in Ms. Reynolds' class. She's the only English teacher."

"Hmph," said Tutu. "Well, then you have a problem, don't you? Now get dressed. You need some time in the garden. Mama always said, 'If you're feeling sick and there's no fever, get out into the sunshine and fresh air.'"

"I don't want to."

"Yes, you want to, and you'll do it as soon as you have something in your stomach."

"Okay, but I'm going to school on Monday, and I'm not cutting Ms. Reynolds out of my life. You can't make me do that. It's not fair."

"Oh, yes, I can. You can cry about it planting onions today. Finish that broth and the chicken sandwich I made you downstairs, and I'll see you in the garden."

It was all garden business with Tutu the rest of the day, with Tutu giving orders and Mahina following them reluctantly. Tutu was angry with her, and the way Tutu showed it was by working three times as hard as Mahina. That wasn't hard, considering that Mahina was still exhausted from the flight and sick with worry. Whenever she tried to talk with Tutu, in the garden and later during their late supper of garlicky chicken soup and cooked carrots, all she got was silence and angry stares.

Monday morning, she felt strong enough to go to school, and when Tutu let her board the bus, she hoped that Tutu had changed her mind about Ms. Reynolds.

But on her way to afternoon math class, she was startled to see Tutu walk purposefully into the old cabin that served as the office of the Head of School. Tutu *never* came to school. This wasn't good.

A half-hour later, the school secretary slipped another yellow note into Mahina's hand. *You're needed in the Head's office immediately.* Koa got one, too, and shot her a worried look.

"What's up, do you think?" said Koa once they left the trailer.

"I don't know, but I saw Tutu on campus. She wants me never to see Ms. Reynolds ever again."

"What? Look, don't worry. I don't think that's going to happen. I think it'll be okay," said Koa.

"How do you know? When Tutu gets something in her mind, no one can stop her," Mahina said, opening the door to the administration cabin.

"I don't know, I just have a feeling. Things have a way of working out if your heart is in the right place." Koa gave her an encouraging smile and followed her inside.

In the foyer, she could see Tutu through the glass, sitting in the Head's office and gesticulating wildly. Her voice was loud but muffled. Sitting near her was Ms. Reynolds, looking serious and a little bedraggled. Mr. Kinkle was listening calmly in another chair instead of behind his desk. He looked up, saw them, and opened the door. "Hello, Mahina, Koa. Please come in and join us," he said, shaking their hands. Behind him, Tutu fell silent.

"Hello, Mrs. Moemoea. Hello, Ms. Reynolds," said Koa.

"Tutu, what are you doing here?" Mahina said.

"Have a seat, please, you two," said Mr. Kinkle. "Your grandmother tells me you had a little adventure on her property yesterday without permission."

"Yes, they did!" said Tutu. "After I specifically requested this teacher to never set foot on our ranch again. I want her *fired* for cavorting with minors outside of school!"

"Tutu!" Mahina cried. She looked from her to Ms. Reynolds, who shook her head worriedly and looked downward.

"Now, Mrs. Moemoea, I told you, we want to get the facts first before we jump to conclusions and call for someone to lose their job. This is a small school that prides itself on relationships with students that go beyond the classroom. Ms. Reynolds has been nothing but professional since she's been here, and you yourself said they were out looking for birds. So let's get the story straight first. Mahina, let's start with you because, obviously, it was probably you and Koa's idea to bring Ms. Reynolds onto your ranch?"

"It was my idea, yes," Mahina said.

"To look for pheasants?" asked Mr. Kinkle.

"We saw pheasants, yes," she replied, "and Koa and I both know Ms. Reynolds loves birds. I wanted to show her the birds, but ..."

"Go on," said Mr. Kinkle. She felt Tutu's eyes boring into her. Ms. Reynolds was looking earnestly at her, too, and Koa was calm and smiling gently.

The bird lie wasn't going to cut it. Not only did it feel wrong in her gut, but Tutu was going to have to know the truth at some point, whether she wanted to hear it or not. Mahina had a life to live that was her own, and the ranch was as much her home as it was Tutu's. She looked at Tutu's angry face and how different it was when they had their hands working in the garden together. Now, Tutu was in Ms. Reynold's garden. Maybe Tutu needed to realize that Mahina got as much energy from this school as she got from home.

"That's not really the reason we were there, Mr. Kinkle," said Mahina. "We were there because of my mom." Tutu's eyes flared, and Ms. Reynolds frowned questioningly, but she pushed on. "Mr. Kinkle, you might not know this, but my mom and my dad died on the ranch a few days after I was born."

"Yes, I'm aware. You mentioned it in your application essay, and it's in your file, of course." Mr. Kinkle's eyes were compassionate.

"Well, ever since they died, I've been trying to find out more about them, who they were, why they were in the lava tube during the hurricane, and, well, Tutu, you don't ever want to talk about them with me, especially not about my mother. I understand why, and I don't blame you, but *I have to*. I'm connected to you, Tutu, really strongly. You mean more to me than anyone alive. But I'm also connected to my mother, and Koa is the one I recently opened my heart to about this. And now Ms. Reynolds because of the literature and the climate crisis we've been studying in class."

"And because you worked closely with Ms. Reynolds on the concert and our fundraiser," said Mr. Kinkle, nodding.

"Exactly," Mahina said.

"But why the trespassing on your own land?" he went on. "Ms. Reynolds, can you explain yourself?"

"I've apologized to Mrs. Moemoea. I shouldn't have been on the ranch without her permission, but Mahina asked me to. She's been very thoughtful lately about her mother and father, and a little sad. She needed to explore her feelings and begged me to help her with that. She knows her mother loved the land, and Mahina wants to connect to the ranch like her mother used to, not just how you do, Mrs. Moemoea, although she likes that too. I know kids need adult guidance when it comes to personal loss. I sure did, when my mother passed away. Anyway, Mahina wanted to show me where they died and have me there to help her process her feelings. I knew that you would say no to that, but Mahina said she could never talk to you about her mother and begged for my help. Aside from upsetting you, it was actually a healing experience for her, I think, and one she is still working hard on."

"You think it's your business to talk about my daughter and to try to heal my granddaughter?" said Tutu, a tear forming in her eye.

"I think it's the business of every adult, especially teachers, to help as many people heal as we can. We all have pain, Mrs. Moemoea, but not all of us have people who care enough to help us get rid of it. I assure you, I am on your side when it comes to your granddaughter.

She's an amazing person, and I love her for who she is, and I know she cares about you and the ranch more than life."

Silence fell in the room. Tutu looked from Ms. Reynolds to Mahina and finally to Koa, whose eyes had nothing but love in them for everyone in the room.

Tutu blinked away tears and spoke directly to Mr. Kinkle. "This is embarrassing. I've never been much for school, Mr. Kinkle. The Moemoea Family is a very strong and proud family on this island. The people of this town always used to travel to our ranch for wisdom and guidance. Not so much from me or my daughter, but from my tutu and her mother, oh yes. *Not* to schools. But I see now that I have not been that same source of wisdom for my own granddaughter, at least not about the loss of Hana, my daughter, her mother. Maybe school has filled in a little bit for what I can't provide for her. I'm not happy about that, but I know that our family is no longer as complete as it used to be, and I supposed I should be grateful for the help.

"This is not easy for me to say, Ms. Reynolds, but when I first heard about you and the rumors of your antics in Berkeley and New York, it reminded me of Hana. How foolishly stubborn and confrontational she was, especially just before she died. But I know that's not fair to you, and I will try to see beyond my issues with your generation. Mahina has grown by knowing you, and what you did together for the fundraiser was remarkable. It's clear to me from this conversation that you love my granddaughter and have her best interests in mind. And you, Koa, I can see that my granddaughter loves you, and I have no reason to feel that she shouldn't. You both shouldn't have done what you did, but I see why now, and I forgive you. You are always welcome, Koa, at our ranch." Tutu paused, then went on. "And you, Ms. Reynolds, have my permission to come to the ranch anytime as well, but I hope you'll remember to let me know when you do."

"Thank you for that," said Mr. Kinkle.

"Yes, thank you," whispered Ms. Reynolds, her face streaked with tears.

"I love this school!" said Koa.

"Mahina," said Mr. Kinkle, "today's issue seems to be settled, but I have one more thing to say. It's a gentle suggestion, actually, something for you and your grandmother to think about." He paused to look at both of them thoughtfully before going on. "I hope that both of you will find a way to talk more about your heritage, your family, and especially your mother and father, Mahina. If there is one thing I know about families, it's that old wounds heal best when exposed to fresh air."

Mahina nodded.

"What you're asking for is complicated, Mr. Kinkle," said Tutu, "but I understand what you're saying." She stood up, and Mahina was grateful to see her shake Ms. Reynold's hand. Mr. Kinkle opened the office doors and walked them onto the front lawn of the school.

"See that new classroom building going up right there?" said Mr. Kinkle. "There's a proposal coming before the board to name it after your family because of what Mahina has done for the school."

"Oh, we don't want that," said Tutu, but then she hesitated and added, "but I suppose it's best to leave that decision up to Mahina and Ms. Reynolds."

Chapter Thirty-One

On the ride home from school, Mahina was both worried by how exhausted she felt and relieved that Tutu had calmed down about Ms. Reynolds. Despite how well it went in Mr. Kinkle's office, she was still worried about so many things. What good would it do to take people flying if it ruined her health? She stared out the window of Tutu's truck and let her mind mull things over.

She had managed to get Ms. Reynolds into the air, but she hadn't yet had a chance to find out how she felt about it afterward. What if Koa was the only one transformed by the experience? What if Ms. Reynolds didn't feel the same enlightened things Koa did? What if she didn't agree with them that celebrities could convince corporate executives to come to the cavern and stop climate change? And what about the problem of Tutu not wanting people to mob the ranch? How was *that* supposed to mesh with their plan? Sneak them in a better way, somehow? Obviously, the best way would be to convince Tutu to help them, but Mahina was convinced that if they tried, she would cement up the entrance again.

There was so much to think about. It was overwhelming, trying to save a planet! Plus, she had the usual boatload of Monday night homework to do when she got home. She yawned and looked over at Tutu behind the steering wheel and wished she hadn't caught them on Saturday. There would have been a lot less fuss if Tutu just hadn't come snooping around. Now Tutu knew not only that Mahina wasn't ignoring her dreams, but also that she was physically exploring the ranch to learn more about her mother.

As if Tutu had read her mind, she looked over from the driver's seat and said, "I've told you this before, Mahina, but you remind me more and more of Hana every day. It doesn't surprise me, what you were doing with your teacher and Koa. Hana was obsessed with the ranch and used to explore it all the time, even when I forbade her to."

"Why did you forbid her to? You showed me how to put my hands in the garden to feel the mana of our land. You must have shown Mom that too?"

"Oh, I did. She used to roll around in the garden all the time. There was no keeping that child's clothes clean! Not that I ever wanted them to be. But there's a difference between getting dirty in the safety of the garden, on the surface where we belong, and putting yourself in danger going where she insisted on going."

"The caves, you mean."

"Yes, the caves," replied Tutu. "Get the gate, please, would you?"

Mahina was almost too tired to move, but she got out as she was told. She swung the gate closed behind the truck and climbed back in.

Tutu didn't say anything more. She drove down the driveway and parked the truck by the house. Inside, Tutu heated some frozen homemade beef stew, and Mahina went into the living room to study, but concentration became impossible when the growing aroma from the kitchen made her stomach growl. She gave up and went to sit in the kitchen. Tutu set two steaming bowls on the table and sat down wearily with her.

"Tutu, I know it's hard for you to talk about Mom, but I have a confession to make."

"I figured you might," said Tutu, blowing on a spoonful of stew.

"There's more to what happened on Saturday than we talked about in Mr. Kinkle's office."

"I know that, dear."

"Did you see us ...?"

"I wasn't following you around, no. I had a nightmare about the fence line. It was catching people and ... But you don't need to know the details. I don't dream very much. As you know, I ignore them, but lately, my nightmares have started up again. Bad ones. I haven't had those since Hana was alive."

"Because of me."

"Yes. Probably because you told me you were dreaming and liked it. Hana told me the same thing before she ... Anyway, I felt I needed to ride the perimeter and check the fence right away, so I did. Then when I saw the grass pressed down under the barbed wire as if someone had crawled under it, I followed the path and found you."

She breathed a sigh of relief and then felt guilty about it. She wanted to tell Tutu about the cave, the flying, and her and Koa's plans to save the earth, but in her gut, she knew she couldn't. Not yet. Maybe not ever. She would block the cave again for sure if she knew. Tutu knowing she was venturing into the very same lava tube that killed Hana? It would put her over the edge.

It's okay to tell her about me, though.

Mahina looked hopefully at Tutu to see if she had heard Hana's beautiful voice, too. It didn't seem like it, and that made her sad.

"Tutu," Mahina said softly, "we went out there because I've been hearing Mom speak to me in my head."

Tutu put her spoon down and looked at her intently. "Oh," she said.

"Yeah, but only when she wants to. In my head and in my heart. I can't start a conversation with her whenever I want to or anything, but when I hear her, um, my hands sometimes get warm and glow."

"I see," said Tutu, glancing down.

"I figured if I got closer to where she died, I could speak to her better, or at least she might speak to me more, about more things, like her life, and why she died, but I didn't want to be out there alone, and I didn't want to ask you."

"Do Koa and your teacher know what's happening to you? The voices, the heat in your hands?"

"They might have noticed my hands, but we've never talked about it. It doesn't happen often, and I didn't tell them about Mom talking to me. But listen, Tutu, these are my *friends*. I trust them. They would never gossip or do anything to hurt me, or you, or this ranch."

Tutu looked steadily at her for a long moment, then picked up her spoon and started eating again. Mahina did the same.

After a few bites, Tutu put her spoon down again and said, "I had a nightmare a few nights ago. I dreamed I was serving drinks to people on an airplane, which is weird because I haven't been in an airplane since I had to go to Oahu to get my gallbladder taken out two decades ago. You were in the dream. You and Olina were in the cockpit, flying the jet, and Olina went wild and did something to the controls. The drinks spilled out of my hand as the plane tilted downward and started to fall. I tried to reach you, but you were too far below me, all alone in the cockpit with your cat going crazy, steering the plane toward the ocean."

"That's horrible, Tutu."

"Yes. I'm trying to forget about it. In this family, paying attention to dreams is dangerous. But I'm worried about you."

"I'm not going to die, Tutu."

"And yet you spent the weekend in bed after your little adventure, didn't you?"

She thought about that. Tutu was correct that dreaming about flying, and then actually going into the cavern and flying, were the two most exhausting things she had ever done in her life.

"I was very tired afterward, you're right," she admitted.

"Mahina, a while ago you made a promise that you were going to ignore your dreams, and now all this other stuff is happening. I know it's your Mom and all that, but you need to try harder to keep your word. This is not child's play you have gotten yourself into. I don't know what your capabilities might be, but our family power increases with each generation, and with more power always comes more risk and more danger.

"I know you aren't a kid anymore, and you've done some incredible things, but you know what I'm saying. This is *serious.* There are powerful volcanic forces at play on this ranch, and not all of them are safe to mess around with, especially the ones in the caves. Even the garden can be dangerous if you don't have the right mindset, the mindset that I know works, the one that I have been teaching you."

"I will try to be better, Tutu."

"You need to do more than try, Granddaughter. You need to be strong, like me. We already lost your mother and father to this. It would have been much better to have Hana around for real than just you hearing her voice every once in a while. I love you. Be careful with your power and who you trust to know about it. It's sacred."

"It helps to talk with you about it."

Tutu sighed. "Maybe, but there's been a lot more words spoken today than I'm used to. You're not the only one getting worn out by this, you know. Come on, finish up and wash your dish. Have you fed Olina? I think it's time for both of us to go upstairs and call this day done."

Chapter Thirty-Two

The next morning at school, Koa wasn't waiting for her as usual when the buses arrived, so she went to look for him around the classroom trailers. She found him with his dad outside Ms. Reynolds' classroom, unloading scrap lumber from the back of Mr. Kahale's truck.

"Hey there, Mahina!" said Mr. Kahale. Koa smiled at her from behind an armload of plywood.

"The plywood can go in that corner," said Ms. Reynolds, pointing. "Oh, good morning, Mahina! Look at all the great wood Mr. Kahale is donating to our project!"

Project? Had Mahina forgotten about an assignment?

"Um, good morning, Ms. Reynolds, Mr. Kahale! What project?" she asked, taking in everyone's big smiles.

"You'll find out in class," said Ms. Reynolds. "I had a dream last night that all the birds on the island were losing their homes. Then I got online and found out it was true! There's been so much human development that the birds don't have enough safe places away from rats and cats to raise their young. So I decided we're going to build birdhouses! But then I looked at lumber prices online and, whew, they are out of this world! Who, I asked myself, might have some scrap lumber hanging around they could donate? Mr. Kahale! I called him up first thing this morning, and look at all this great wood! The birds are going to tweet about this, I tell you!"

"We're going to build birdhouses in English class?" she asked. Koa smiled at her and gave her a thumbs up.

"Poetry houses, I'm calling them," continued Ms. Reynolds. "Everyone makes a cool bird house and then writes a 'save the birds' poem on it with permanent markers before we install them around the school! Isn't that cool? We can help the birds!"

Mahina smiled at her teacher, who seemed to have swallowed the same happy potion that flowed through Koa's veins. "That's a great idea, Ms. Reynolds. I have a design in mind already. Is it okay if you and I hang one off the campus property? I know a great tree near the *skateboard park* that definitely needs one." She winked.

"Well, I suppose, but we better go check it out first," said Ms. Reynolds, catching the hint. "Why don't we go over there at lunch today and see? Want to join us, Koa?"

"You bet!" said Koa.

English class was fun. They worked on birdhouse designs and started composing poems for them. Mahina's went like this:

Every bird who flies deserves a rest
Here lies one who's safe inside her nest
It's not as easy to soar as it might seem
Yet life above the clouds can be a dream.

At lunchtime, she and Koa checked out at the office and headed for the skateboard park. "I'm glad you're feeling better," said Koa as they crossed the school crosswalk together. "Your tutu seemed okay yesterday when we left Mr. Kinkle's office?"

"She was okay, not great," Mahina said. "We reached a kind of understanding. She's still worried that I'm going down the same path that led my mother and father to their deaths, especially because I've been so tired, but I can't figure out if she's worried about me or about her not wanting people to know about the magic of our ranch. Both, I think."

"That's going to make it hard for you to get the movers and shakers to the cavern, isn't it?"

"I know. It's a problem, and I wonder if it will even work if I do get celebrities to fly with me. Could they really convince oil company executives and other people with power to come to the cavern? And would it have the same effect with them as it did with you and Ms. Reynolds?" She spotted Ms. Reynolds waiting for them under the tree.

"I don't know, but look at Ms. Reynolds. I don't think it's an accident that she's all obsessed now with helping the birds."

"Hi, guys!" said Ms. Reynolds when they approached. "We've got to talk fast. I need to get back for a Zoom meeting that just came up."

"Okay," Mahina said. "I'll start. So, Koa, you said that when you flew with me in the cavern, it radically deepened your love for the world and made you even more committed than you were before to stopping climate change. Was it the same for you Ms. Reynolds?"

Ms. Reynolds held her hands open by her sides and said, "Without a doubt. It was so amazing, even with the scare at the end. The feeling of flying, which is the best feeling there is, as you know, is still with me no matter what I'm doing. Just standing here talking to you, I have the same feelings running up and down my spine as I did flying with you over the ranch."

"That's right," said Koa excitedly. "It transfers to everything. It's like a weird combination of the greatest pleasure ever and never really having to worry about it again because it's always with you."

"Even when things don't go the way you want them to," added Ms. Reynolds. "Like when I smashed my thumb today because I'm a klutz with a hammer. It hurt like crazy, but I just accepted it and laughed. It was a cool experience, just like any time you're alive is a cool experience. Before Saturday, if I smashed myself like that, I would have gotten down on myself and maybe given up."

"So, if we can manage to find powerful people," Mahina said, her hope growing, "and if we can manage to sneak them into the cavern with me for a 'session,' do you think it might motivate them to do more good in the world instead of causing pollution?"

"Definitely!" said Ms. Reynolds. "I am fully committed to what you want to do. You're truly a gift from the heavens, and I think your vision can make a difference in this world! Look at me. I'm a nobody, but after what you did for me, I'm at least teaching people to put up birdhouses." She pointed at a large branch above them and smiled. "And this, by the way, *is* a great place for one. I've always liked birds, but now I'm *nuts* about saving them. What do you think I would do if I had real power to change things? I'll tell you what I would do for this world that gives me so much pleasure just for being alive in it—*everything I possibly could*!"

"Well, that answers that!" Mahina laughed. She felt a warm glow in her chest, like lava ready to erupt and spread love over the entire world. "So this might just work! Now the problem is how to get the most influential people in the world to come here and fly with me, and how to do that without Tutu finding out."

"Leave the first part to me," chimed Ms. Reynolds. "I'm already on it. That's what my Zoom meeting is all about. I'm working my way down our celebrity list and looking at who they probably know. We'll see, but people will usually do whatever their favorite musician asks them to do, and I made friends with a lot of them at the fundraiser!"

"And leave the second part to me," said Koa, smiling as usual. "I think I know the perfect way to keep your tutu occupied while you do your thing."

Mahina looked at him with surprise. She'd expected Tutu would be her problem to deal with.

"Hey, I've got to fly," Ms. Reynolds said suddenly. "I have a Zoom date with a country rock star!" She took off jogging back toward the school, her dress flowing behind her in the wind.

"Wow, this is really happening!" Mahina said. She wondered if her chest was glowing under her shirt. She looked at her hands. They were normal. "So, what's your idea for Tutu, Koa?"

"A garden club, at your ranch, sponsored by the school somehow. Kids come out to help your tutu at the same time as you take fancy executive dudes into the cavern for a spin over the hills."

"Hmm," Mahina said, "but Tutu doesn't want a lot of people on the ranch, Koa."

"These wouldn't be just people. They'd be children. And they'd come only on Wednesday afternoons and Saturday mornings. I'd get the children to ask her for permission. I don't know a Hawaiian auntie on this island who wouldn't do anything for keiki who sincerely wanted to learn something. I'd set it up as some kind of outreach project for the school, or maybe as an independent study for me in how to help kids learn to garden. That way, I can be there and make sure your tutu stays in her garden and is looking downward at the kids and the plants."

"I'm not sure you can get her to agree to this," Mahina said.

"As I said, leave it up to me. I've got it cogitating up here," he said pointing to his head.

She laughed. "Okay, Einstein. Somehow I believe that right now, you could pull off *anything* you put your mind to!"

"You got that right! Where there's a will, there's a way. Just like cleaning up the environment, right? We can do this, Mahina! Just give me a day or two to think it through with Ms. Reynolds."

"I will, my friend," she said and gave him a quick but very sincere hug. "Want to eat here or at the table?"

"At school with all our friends!" He laughed and sprinted back toward the picnic table. She ran after him laughing, too, with her feet on the ground, and her heart in the air full of hope. Could life be any more beautiful?

Chapter Thirty-Three

Even with her hope, Mahina sincerely doubted whether Koa could convince Tutu to teach gardening, but she had to admit afterward that Koa played her perfectly.

First of all, he and Ms. Reynolds convinced Mr. Kinkle to let him do an independent study project about sustainability on Hawaii Island and the best ways to motivate kids and their parents to grow food.

Then, through his dad and through contacts with the Po'okela Academy Lower School, he rounded up a pack of third- and fourth-graders whose parents were willing to let them come to the ranch on weekends and select school-day afternoons to work in the garden and learn gardening tips from the "famous Auntie Moemoea."

Then, when Mahina was at school, Koa got his dad and Mr. Kinkle to bus some of the kids out to the ranch to knock on their door. Koa said that at first, Tutu said no but then relented when the kids begged her to "help them grow carrots and stuff."

When she talked to Tutu about it, Mahina admitted to Tutu that she knew ahead of time about Koa's independent study idea and was surprised that Tutu had said yes.

"Me, too," said Tutu, "but I decided other kids deserve to feel the good mana of the garden's soil." She shrugged her shoulders. "Besides that, Koa is a charmer and a good spirit. Reminds me of my husband when he was his age. I can understand why you like him so much."

The plan for the first Saturday was set. Ms. Reynolds would convince Slide Pickens to come back to the island in his private jet with an invited oil company executive. Ms. Reynolds would drive the bus from school with Koa and the gardening students. Mahina would free herself using the excuse that Koa didn't want her in the garden distracting him from observing the students. Everyone was excited.

The big day arrived. Mahina said goodbye to Tutu after chores and rode her bike into town to the tree by the skateboard park. She locked it there under the new birdhouse to wait for Slide Pickens.

It was overcast and windy, but not rainy. For a moment, she was afraid he would pull up in a limousine, but Ms. Reynolds had done her job. It was a red jeep, so commonly rented by tourists that she almost missed him waving at her from the passenger seat in his signature cowboy hat and sunglasses.

She hopped in the back. A tall, white man was driving. She smiled and said, "Hello, Mr. Pickens. Very nice to see you again! I'm Mahina, in case you forgot."

"How could I forget, Mahina? Especially after all the things your agent told me about you! This is, um, well, we'll just call him Mr. Smith. He's flying a little under the radar, so to speak." Slide laughed.

"Good to meet you, Mahina." Mr. Smith's voice was deep and gravelly. Was he a smoker? She didn't smell any smoke on his clothes. Maybe he used to be, she thought.

"Likewise. Thanks for coming. You guys are kind of the first, but hey, Ms. Reynolds is my teacher, not my agent. I'm not talented enough to have an agent. Not like you, Mr. Pickens!"

"Call me Slide. So, where do we go for this, ahem, special place we've got to see?"

Mahina pointed. "Pull out here and go left at the intersection. There will be a stoplight soon after that, where we'll turn left. Then we drive for a while toward the mountain." Mr. Smith did as she directed.

After a few turns, they were on the road to the ranch. Mahina told them that the road also went on beyond their property to encircle Mauna Kea, which meant “white mountain” because it so often had snow covering the peaks and valleys at the top.

“Snow in Hawaii,” said Slide. “Blew me away when I first saw it.”

“Yep, pretty amazing,” Mahina agreed. “Sometimes people even ski up there, but there’s no chairlift or anything.”

“Skiing. Maybe when I was younger,” said Slide. “It’s hard now for me to even walk a couple of blocks these days without getting tired.”

She wondered how well he’d do in the lava tube. She’d just have to keep her fingers crossed. Mr. Smith looked like he was in decent enough shape despite the gravelly voice.

When they approached the beginning of their property fence, she directed Mr. Smith to park with the joggers. They were out in full force today, which for this area meant six or eight vehicles. She asked Slide to leave his cowboy hat in the Jeep, and he reluctantly complied. They got out and walked slowly along the road until they got to the fence line and the hill with the eucalyptus trees. Slide was stiff and limping at first, but then seemed to warm up. Neither of the men particularly liked crawling under the fence, though. There was a lot of groaning, and even a “Are you kidding me?” mumbled under Mr. Smith’s breath.

She handed them the headlamps and silently asked her mother to help her. No answer, but strong warmth in Mahina’s heart signaled her presence.

“We’re going into an old lava tube. It’s a place of ancient and great power. It’s going to be dark and moist, and the footing is uneven. We’ll go slow. I’ve been in this cave many times, so don’t worry, we won’t get lost. If all goes well, we’ll come back a different way, an easier way. As I hope Ms. Reynolds told you, you need to please keep an open mind and trust me. Okay, ready? Follow me.”

"I don't usually trust kids in high school, even if they are polite," said Slide playfully, "especially ones who take me on ruggedly impossible hikes."

"I wouldn't make you and your friend do this if I didn't think it was *very* worth your time, but remember, you're on your honor not to reveal to the public what happens here today. Not yet, anyway."

"Yes," said Slide, "that was what made this so interesting, right, Mr. Smith? We're the first!"

Mr. Smith just grunted skeptically.

"You can, of course, recommend others to come. We *want* you to. That's part of the deal. You like it, you put others in touch with Ms. Reynolds. You'll see. It's just not possible to describe it convincingly in words. People would laugh at you."

"Hmm," said Mr. Smith, even less convinced.

That's all right, she thought. I would think this was a scam too. The only reason he's here is because of Slide.

Except for Slide having to suck in his stomach a little bit to squeeze through the cement blocks, they made it to the boulder in front of the hidden passageway without anyone stumbling or falling.

"I need a rest," said Slide. "My foot is a little sore."

"Sorry, the rocks can be a little hard to walk on," she said. She waited while Slide leaned on the boulder and caught his breath. After a moment he pushed himself back upright, and they entered the next leg.

Just before the narrow part, Slide sat down again with a big grunt. "I don't mean to be childish, but are we there yet?"

She aimed her head beam at him. He looked red in the face and very worn out. What to do? She couldn't have him pass out in here! If he did, and he sure looked like he might, she'd have to go back and call an ambulance, and that would bring all kinds of people to the ranch and ruin everything!

"Slide, listen. I can see that you're very tired. We're almost there, but I think I'm going to try something right now that I don't usually do until we get to the special cavern."

Please, Mom, if ever I needed your help, it is now. Help me with these men.

"Mr. Smith, stand back a bit, please, behind Slide. That's it. Thank you. Mr. Pickens, take my hand, okay? And just relax and feel the mana, the energy, of this cave. It is sacred to my family and to this island. The spirit of my mother dwells here, and I am the newest and most powerful daughter of the family of Moemoea."

She closed her eyes and concentrated hard, focusing her will and her love as she had done so many times in her dreams and in reality, inviting both states of mind to blend together.

She breathed deeply and let the air in her lungs escape slowly through her mouth, inviting the mana of the cavern to reach her through the passageway.

Up, up, up, she thought.

Believe, said her mother's voice.

Mahina's hands grew warm and glowed. Her heart pulsed with love.

And there was Olina, claws out floating next to her, ghost-like.

"Olina, wait, no!" she said out loud. "No need to be afraid. I love you, too. Come here, my sweet kitty. Let me hug you." Olina retracted her claws and floated closer. Mahina hugged her soft body. Olina licked her face with a tongue that was no longer rough then wafted her way alone back through the lava tube toward the entrance.

"Up, up, up," she said again.

And up she floated, pulling Slide's hand and arm with her.

"What is going on?!" shouted Mr. Smith, his voice hurting her ears in the confined space.

"Shhh," said Slide. "Let the young woman do her thing!"

She willed Slide to slowly release from the ground and float upward toward her.

"Wow," Slide said. "This ain't no stage trick!"

"Relax and float with me. We'll do more once we reach the larger cavern. I'll pull you along, Slide. Just try not to touch the walls or the boulders on the path. Mr. Smith, follow us on foot. I'll get you up in a little bit, too, don't worry."

Her mind guided them down the lava tube and through the narrow tunnel.

They emerged into the cavern, with Mr. Smith stumbling and gawking close behind them. As usual, the daylight streaming in from the hole in the ceiling made the space feel like an ancient and powerful cathedral.

"That sure beats walking!" said Slide. "Wow, look at this place! It's like John Lennon's first solo album. You know, the one in the forest with him looking up into the sunshine? Beautiful!"

"Slide, just let your feet relax. I'm going to let go of your hand, and that's okay. As long as you can see me or are near me, you're fine." She let go of his hand.

"Momma!" exclaimed Slide. His grin was enormous.

She willed herself down next to Mr. Smith. "Are you ready for the ride of your life, Mr. Smith? Take my hand, please. Relax. Let the power of this cavern, this Moemoea world, infuse your body and mind."

Her hand was glowing brightly now, warm and powerful. He took her hand and they rose slowly, as Slide had.

"Oh, no. Oh, no!" he said, panicked, looking down at his feet.

"No need for fear, Mr. Smith. There is strength in fear, but fear is weak compared to the strength of flying. You'll see. I've got you. It's okay. Everything is okay."

Slowly, Mr. Smith's breathing returned almost to normal. "I'm floating! I'm flying! I'm really flying!" he said.

She willed herself and Mr. Smith into a circle with Slide.

"Look at my feet," she said. "Your mind is the accelerator, but your mind also contains your body, so where you place your legs matters. Bend your right knee to go right, like this, and your left knee to go left like this. You can rest your legs completely when you hover. Follow me now for your first flight. Will yourself to stay in the air without touching the walls or anything connected to the ground. You are flyers now, creatures of light and air."

Watching the men carefully, she turned and led them upward a bit and then down the cavern, turning at the end, resting, and then flying back with them to where they started.

"I feel so powerful!" said Slide. "Like I can do *anything*!"

"And you can, Slide, just by sitting still and letting earth's mana and love flow through you. This feeling that you have now, this amazing feeling of flying, that's the very feeling of life itself, the wonderful gift of the earth. Come, let's enjoy it now in the fresh air! Mr. Smith, you're doing great!"

"I can't believe this is happening to me!" Mr. Smith said.

"It's happening to you because you're alive, Mr. Smith. You just might not have fully realized that miracle before."

She led them to the opening. "Remember, will yourself to be in the air only, not landing on any trees or boulders, and think up, up, out of the earth! When you emerge, stay close to me and don't make too much noise. We will only fly where there are no people, but sound travels far in these hills, and we're not doing this to show off. Not everyone is ready to understand what we're doing yet. Beautiful things get ruined if they become popular before they're fully understood and appreciated."

Up Mahina flew into the sunshine. Quickly, she scanned the hills and valleys. No one was near. She hovered over the opening and waved for the men to come up. Slide rose first, his face radiant, then Mr. Smith, also smiling.

Taking them on the rollercoaster ride of zipping above and around the rolling green hills was thrilling, like teaching surfing except through the air without anything holding you up but your mind. She was free, unfettered, giving, and full of power.

And yet it was *connection* that created the power, she thought, not independent freedom. It was connection with everything, with the world, with these students who happened to be adults, like when her hands tapped into the miraculous mana in Tutu's garden, only the garden she was flying through now was much larger. This garden was *everything* around her and inside her that she could see, hear, smell, and feel, and even other things in the world too, like the guiding spirit of her deceased mother, and the spirits of all the people, plants, and animals that vibrated across the planet no matter what the state of their bodies. She was of the world and creating it at the same time. She was in the now, and in all time.

She led them over the ranch to the far northeast corner and back again toward the road where they began. Behind her, her fledglings found their wings. Gamboling, she thought, a new word she learned recently in English, along with delusional. They're gamboling in the pungent high-country air, drinking in the feelings, transforming their hearts and minds, *maturing*.

It felt so good to her, so right what she was doing, creating flyers. And how could it *not* help the earth? These men would be forever changed for the better, she was sure.

This time, the fatigue set in earlier, while she was still instructing them how to descend safely to the grassy ground. But because she was expecting it, she accepted its gut punch and pushed through.

They landed, and Slide said, "I sing a lot about flying, but nothing compares to the real thing. That was *surreal*!"

"I never knew I could feel this way," said Mr. Smith. "*Thank you*, young lady!" She thought the look of awe on his face made him look ten years younger.

On the way back to the car, Mr. Smith was practically skipping, and as soon as he saw the fence, he immediately went ahead to hold up the barbed wire for her and Slide with a smile on his face. Slide himself was also moving without his previous limp.

There was no Tutu on horseback this time, and the ride back to town was all about Slide and Mr. Smith joyfully bantering and rehashing the experience.

"I feel so good in my body right now," said Mr. Smith. "I'm driving this clunky gas-wasting vehicle, and yet I'm still in the air flying."

"I know!" agreed Slide, with his hat on again. "Just sitting here right now watching these simple country hills go by is like the best feeling ever!"

Even though she was ready to pass out from fatigue in the back seat, Mahina smiled. *I'm creating a tribe of Koas,* she thought, laughing to herself, and closed her eyes to let their excited voices wash over her until they reached the skateboard park.

"I hope you'll take us out again, Mahina," said Slide, parking by her bike.

"Yes!" said Mr. Smith, "please!"

"I will," she said, opening the door to step out. "But first, I need your help to discreetly bring others here who have the power to change the world for the better—that is. if you think it's a good idea?"

"Young lady," said Mr. Smith. "This was no gimmick. You have helped me see things in a whole new way. The beauty of this island, this world! My gosh, I never noticed it before!"

"You can be *sure* we'll help you," said Slide. "I know a lot of people who could really use this experience, people I have argued with for years to stop destroying nature just for money. You've got my word, Miss Mahina, that I'll be contacting your agent, Ms. Reynolds, with them in tow. You'll see me again soon. Count on it."

"Thank you," she said. It was amazing. This was working!

"No, thank *you*!" said Mr. Smith. "You are the wisest and most inspirational person I have ever known."

She finished getting out of the car, but her legs buckled under her suddenly, and she crashed into the open door. Slide leaped out and helped her up.

"Are you okay, Mahina?" he said.

She straightened up and set her shoulders back. "I'm fine," she said. "I just stumbled on that rock."

"Are you sure? You look a little pale."

"No, I'm fine. No broken bones or anything. I need to get on my bike now. Remember, what happened today is a secret."

"You have our word, Mahina," said Slide, "and our lifelong respect for you and your family. Aloha, as they say here. It means 'love,' right? We aloha you! Until next time!"

"*Aloha, a hui hou,*" she said and turned to unlock her bike. The men honked and waved as they pulled out. There was satisfying warmth still in her heart, but her body was cold and tired, and the ride home was going to be a slog.

Chapter Thirty-Four

By the time Mahina wearily walked her bike down the driveway, Koa and the lower school gardeners were already gone, and Tutu was no longer in the garden. Must be inside getting lunch, she thought.

Not wanting Tutu to see her barely able to move, she left her bike at the top of the garden and lay down between the rows of tomatoes in the warm sun. It looked like the young gardeners had been busy pruning and tying up the long branches of the tomato plants. There wasn't a weed to be seen anywhere, either. She felt happy for Tutu.

She lay back and looked through the young tomato leaves at the northern sky where she had recently been flying with her first "clients." But it wasn't a moment later before her eyes closed, and she started to drift off. She let her hands dig into the freshly turned soil. *I'm like a computer plugging myself into a charger,* she thought. She felt instantly better, almost as good as cuddling in her bed with Olina.

The sun had moved a bit in the sky and wasn't quite as warm anymore when footsteps awoke her. "Well, Mahina, I see you've discovered my favorite place to nap!" said Tutu.

"Oh, hi, Tutu," Mahina said, sitting up slowly and brushing the dirt from her arms. "I conked out. How were the kids and the gardening lesson?"

"You better be careful. Your cowboy has a whole new slew of admirers, that charmer!"

"I don't want to hear about it," Mahina said with a joking eye roll. "Looks like you got a lot done. The garden looks great."

"Yes," said Tutu, "they were actually pretty good workers after they got all their questions answered, and oh, did they have questions! I had to lie down here myself for a while to recover after they left. I'm not used to talking so much!"

"Yep, teaching can be tiring. Sounds like fun, Tutu."

"It was, in a way, and in another way, not. I realized it is important to pass on the knowledge that we Moemoeas have, but it also reminds me of how little of that I have really done in my life." Tutu sighed. "Have you had lunch yet?"

"No, not yet, but I'm starving."

Tutu nodded and turned to walk back to the house. Mahina put her bike back in the storage room and followed her inside. She felt a little better, but she could still easily sleep the rest of the day.

In the kitchen, Tutu had a kettle of tomato soup bubbling on the stovetop. "I showed the kids how to boil down tomatoes today after we picked the last of them from the old plants," said Tutu. "The youngsters got a nice taste of down-home freshness. Koa and his dad brought some sea salt from the rocks at Puakō. It gave this soup a nice flavor, along with the basil from the garden, of course."

"Thanks, Tutu, for doing this. It smells wonderful. It means a lot to the kids, and to Koa too."

"You could be there, too," said Tutu, hinting.

"I know," she said, "but I like my garden time with you alone, if you know what I mean."

"Hmm," said Tutu, ladling a bowl of soup for her. "And by yourself, I see. Well, I can't argue with that. I feel the same way about the garden most of the time—like it's special for me only. The whole ranch feels that way to me."

"But it's good of you to share, and to pass on your gardening wisdom, right? Thanks," she said as Tutu gave her the bowl.

"Yes, I know, but it's not easy. It's about all I can handle, you know, of the family tradition," said Tutu sitting down with her. "Your great-grandmother, my mama, when I refused to go into the caves to learn to read people's fortunes as she did or do whatever the caves had in mind for me, she said I was missing out on learning how I was even more powerful than she was. But I didn't want to be more powerful than her, or Tutu, or anyone. I was scared. So I never found out.

"Anyway, when I put my foot down and wouldn't go anywhere near the lava tubes, Mama said that she still had to pass on something to me because I was her daughter. It was required. I never asked her who required it or why. It just was. It was Hana who told me much later on that she felt the requirement was from the spirit of the earth, to protect the earth and the cycles of the people and animals on it, and I think she might be right. So hard to do with all the pollution going on, though."

"So your mom taught you how to garden, right?" Mahina took a spoonful of her soup. It was delicious.

"Yes, it was a compromise for her, but she taught me to *feel* the garden with my hands, just like I showed you. Even though I never did what she really wanted me to, that's how I came to believe I was helping the world as I should, by preserving the ranch, growing food, and knowing in my fingers the creative power of the soil to sustain us."

"And now you can teach others that. That's good enough, right?"

"But as I said to you in the garden just now, I still don't *want* to share it, even though I should. I want the garden to myself. Because I'm afraid." Tutu lowered her eyes in shame.

"What are you afraid of, Tutu?"

"I'm afraid people will ruin my connection to it, ruin it like they ruin everything in the world, by not respecting it."

"Did you think Koa and the kids disrespected the garden, Tutu?"

"No, honey, I don't. That's what I'm trying to tell you. I'm *grateful* they came. They were wonderful, so alive and interesting. They were lovely, like the plants themselves. My connection with the garden is growing, I think, because of them."

"I'm so happy, Tutu."

Tutu got a faraway look in her eye. "You know, people used to line up at the gate to come to see Mama and Tutu. I used to not like them coming around, but Mama and Tutu always greeted them with a smile and many words of wisdom. Maybe today I got a little taste of what they used to feel."

Mahina had the thought that maybe she had been too hard on herself about upsetting Tutu's life by doing what she had to do with her mother. Being forced to learn new things about yourself is a good thing even for someone as old as Tutu. Maybe none of us ever really escape school in this life even if we try to hide ourselves away for a whole lifetime. "I love you, Tutu."

"And I love you, too, Mahina."

Tutu stared at her quietly for a few moments, then said, "It's not enough, though, these kids and Koa in the garden. They make me feel ashamed. It's too little too late, I'm afraid. I didn't do what I was supposed to do."

"I don't understand."

"I had my chance, and I didn't do it." Tears were trickling from Tutu's eyes. "I can't explain it to you. There are things I refused to learn, from those who loved me, and from the earth. Things I have been avoiding for far too long. Now I am old, and I know I will never rest easy unless I dare face what I was too afraid to face before." She looked at her pleadingly. "But I can't do that alone. I need your help. I need you to show me the place."

"What place?" she said, suddenly afraid.

"Where *she* talks to you. Where you went with Koa and your teacher. We can take the horses after lunch."

"Why, Tutu?"

"Because it's time for me to apologize to her."

They put on their boots and walked to the barn. Any fatigue Mahina was still feeling after the day's flying session disappeared with the nervous adrenaline that was flowing through her body as they saddled up Ikaika and Costco in the barn. This was her chance to tell Tutu about everything, but she wasn't sure she wanted her to know that she's been going into the cave. She needed to figure out how to handle this.

By the time they mounted the horses in the yard, she decided there was no way she would take Tutu into the cavern. To do so would be to risk Tutu blocking the entrance again, or worse, disturbing her mother's spirit. She was afraid that Tutu's inner strength and fear of the caves would destroy the magic in the cavern that allowed Mahina to teach people how to fly.

Funny, she thought, I'm more worried about not being able to teach others to fly than not being able to fly myself. She knew what she was doing was important and excited that her plan was working. She must make sure it didn't get ruined!

As they passed through the gate to the vast back pastures of their ranch, she decided the best idea was to keep an open mind and just see. She knew Tutu loved her, and that the death of her daughter was devastating. Could Mahina have lived her life perfectly if the same thing had happened to her? She doubted it. Tutu had backed off of the idea of forbidding her to go to school, and she even just admitted that she had done some things wrong. Tutu was changing. She would let whatever was going to happen this afternoon happen, even if it disrupted her plans.

She looked ahead at the hills and wondered if her mom could feel that they were coming. *Guide me*, Mahina whispered to her.

"Where we went is this way, Tutu," she said, taking a path that leads to the east side of the hill away from the entrance to her mom's cavern. She steered Costco toward where she figured the lava tube snaked its way underneath the hill to the big cavern under the far hillside. That's close enough to not be lying about where we went, she thought, but her nerves were getting jangled. The afternoon winds began blowing the grass and the branches of the eucalyptus trees as they rode.

"This is the area, Tutu," she said. "All around here."

"Yes, we're near where she and Kiawe perished. I can feel that," said Tutu. "I usually never come to this part of the ranch."

Mahina's hands were suddenly very warm holding the reins. "We can go back," she said.

"No. We should tie the horses up, over there under those trees."

They used the halter ropes they brought to secure the horses, and Mahina followed Tutu toward the big hill. She felt her mind slipping into the state right before she concentrated and lifted her ankles. Only, this time, Tutu's mana was blending with her mother's. Mahina felt like she could fly, but she certainly didn't want to try.

"If you hear your mother's voice, I want to know," said Tutu. She paused to place her hands on the ground then continued, "The vibrations, they're so powerful here. She's near. I can feel her! We need to go this way." They headed up the gradual rise to the edge of the hill. Their lungs began to work harder.

It amazed Mahina that Tutu was in as good a shape as she was, or maybe adrenaline was taking over for her too right now. There was a powerful mix of hot mana entering Mahina's chest that she had never felt before even inside the cavern.

The wind began to blow harder. Mahina's mind was fizzing with power, half in the outside world and half in her dream world as they approached the top. She held her hands up to her face. They were glowing stronger than they ever had before, even in the bright sun.

Just before the summit, Tutu collapsed to her knees. Mahina rushed forward to make sure she was all right.

Tutu wailed, "Oh, my dearest Hana, my beautiful daughter, I hear you crying!" Mahina knelt next to her in the wind.

Tutu lifted her head from the ground and raised her red eyes to the sky. "Take me closer to you. I need you in my heart again—the way you are, not the way I wanted you to be!"

Tutu paused, listening, then crawled forward across the deep grass until she reached the opening.

"Tutu, don't fall in!" Mahina said, her vision blurred by the waves of vibrations washing through her mind.

"No more fear, Mahina. Not from you. Not from me. And never from my daughter, my brave, brave Hana!"

Tutu wedged her hip against an upturned hunk of lava at the opening and leaned over the damp air rising from below. She reached her hands over the opening.

Tutu let loose a long cry of utmost despair. "I'm sorry, Hana. Your strength of purpose made me afraid. I didn't try hard enough to understand you. I was wrong. I wasn't enough. I have failed you. I have failed our family!"

"Tutu! Be careful!"

She grabbed Tutu's leg, but Tutu kicked her hand away. Far below, she could see Tutu's shadow wavering on the cavern floor and heard little rocks pelting the ground below.

Tutu cried again, "I could have helped you, Hana, and I didn't. My life was a lie! The garden wasn't enough. You needed my strength, my knowledge, and my support *here*, where everyone went but me. Moemoeas do special things in the world, great things, as we were charged to do. It is our destiny because we are chosen. We are goddesses of the earth. But I failed. I was too afraid to be special and became a nobody instead.

"I'm sorry, my magnificent daughter. I let you down. I let my family down. I let the earth down, even though I love her with all my heart. I did not seize my chance, my time to help you, my time to seize my destiny, to make a difference, to become who I was supposed to become!

"I did not see that you *had to be different*, that you had a right to be mad at me. I did not realize we *all* were different. It was right that we were different, each in our own way. I see that now. Your daughter has taught me that. I wanted you to be like me because I needed to feel good about myself, even though I knew I didn't deserve to. Strength without courage, without love and acceptance, is not strength at all. It is a wasted gift. And now my time has passed, and yours was robbed from you because of me. Oh, *because of me*!" She teetered forward, weeping uncontrollably.

Help her, Daughter. It's not her time!

Mahina lunged and grabbed Tutu's leg and dragged her back from the edge, setting loose a small avalanche of rocks into the cavern. Tutu collapsed at her feet gasping and thrashing in grief. Mahina knelt and held Tutu with her glowing hands, loving her, and letting the boiling tears from her own eyes fall on Tutu's heaving back like rain.

Slowly, as the sun dipped below the foothills of Mauna Kea, their sobs finally abated. Tutu rolled over and squeezed Mahina's hands gently, reverently. Then she stood up, sadly wiped her face with her sleeve, and walked down the hill toward the horses.

Before following her, Mahina turned to look back at the opening to the cavern and heard her mother weeping softly deep inside. *I love you, Mom. Thank you.*

Mahina took a deep breath. Big things were happening, and after today, she knew that nothing would ever be the same for her and Tutu again.

Chapter Thirty-Five

When they got home, Mahina was dead tired, but not as exhausted as Tutu who agreed at her insistence to go up to bed and allow her to take care of unsaddling the horses.

By the time Mahina made it into the house seemingly hours later, she herself could hardly move. She gulped down another bowl of tomato soup without even heating it, fed Olina, and went upstairs to take a shower. She dearly just wanted to climb into bed, but the grime in her hair and on her skin was too much to bear. She was relieved that tomorrow was Sunday and no school. It helped, too, that Olina settled into her usual sleeping spot next to her on her pillow, even though the sun hadn't yet finished going down.

It was a dreamless night, much to her relief, but she woke up several times hearing Tutu's muffled voice from her bedroom down the hall. Who was she arguing with? Maybe herself, Mahina thought.

At breakfast, she mentioned to Tutu that she heard her crying out in the night.

"You might hear more of that, dear," Tutu said. "The curtain has been lifted on my dreams now. I have a lot to make up for."

Rather than looking rested, Tutu looked even more worn out than when she went to bed, and so did Mahina. They decided they both could use a quiet day in the garden, and after chores that's exactly what they did, working side by side, and stopping only to make fresh salads for lunch and to take frequent naps in the warm soil between the rows of tomatoes and taro.

The next day at school, Koa met Mahina by the bus and was ecstatic about the gardening project. "Your tutu is so cool!" he said.

"The kids can't wait to go back, and I heard you had a successful Saturday, too."

"How'd you hear that?" she said, knowing he meant flying with Slide and the mysterious oil executive, even though the biggest part of the day for her was what happened with Tutu.

"Ms. Reynolds called me on my cell on Sunday." Koa looked around at the others walking near them toward the trailers. "She said the folks you were with were *transformed.*

"By the way, I stopped by her place yesterday to pick up something she got for you. I'll give it to you at lunch."

Mahina took him aside by the arm where no one could hear them. "Just tell me. I hate surprises."

Koa smiled and reached into his pocket and pulled out a phone. "I'll have to call her to ask," he said. Then he laughed and gave it to her. "Or *you* can use *your* phone to call her."

"What? A cell phone? For me?! It looks just like yours!"

"Yep, my idea, her plan. She said it was almost free, some kind of teacher discount. Makes things easier, don't you think?"

"Definitely! No more sneaking into the kitchen. But you'll have to show me how to use it!" She turned the phone over in her hand, admiring the moon and stars on its cover.

"Right-o. See you at the tree for lunch!"

During English, suppressing her excitement, Mahina made a special effort to keep things looking normal with Ms. Reynolds and Koa. They worked on more birdhouses and shared each other's poems. The only time they almost slipped up was when Ms. Reynolds looked at the news feed on her phone and screamed out that Emperor Petro's CEO just announced that they were cutting back drastically on drilling for oil and were diverting their assets into developing technologies for carbon reduction and pollution-free engines that run on hydrogen. She looked right at Mahina and Koa and gave them a big thumbs-up. "Well, that's a start, I guess!" she said.

"Yay! I wonder what made them change their mind?" said Koa, winking at Mahina secretly.

"I can't believe it worked!" said Ms. Reynolds.

"What worked?" asked Jacob.

"Nothing, never mind," said Ms. Reynolds.

"He's been getting lobbied heavily for that," Koa explained, covering for her. "No one thought he would come around."

"Oh," said Jacob, going back to painting his birdhouse.

At the big tree at lunch, Koa took Mahina's phone and showed her how to program one-touch dialing for his and Ms. Reynold's number and how to use the flashlight. "For, you know, when you happen to be in dark places, or you need to contact one of us fast. Most of the time, though, you can just text."

"That, I know how to do," she replied.

Just then, her phone rang. It was a weird whining sound like aliens landing to take over the world.

She gave Koa a look and answered. "Hello?" she said. She put it on speakerphone.

"Hi, Mahina, Ms. Reynolds here. So, you got my present."

"Yes, thanks so much, Ms. Reynolds! I'm having lunch at the tree with Koa."

"I'm in the teacher's bathroom because it's easier for me to talk here without having to sneak off to the park, and yes, we have a lot to talk about. Slide never left the island. He's coming up from Kona on Saturday with more people jetting in from the mainland. He has enough people lined up to do Wednesday mornings as well, starting next week.

"I can meet him on Saturday like before, I think. But on Wednesday? I don't know."

"I know, it's a problem because we haven't figured out how to get you out of classes yet. I'm working on that. How do you feel about taking Mr. Kinkle up for a session?"

"Fine, I guess, but wouldn't he tell someone?"

"Not if Slide tells him not to. Here's what I'm thinking. Mr. Kinkle goes up Saturday with the next group, so we get him on board. Slide suggests to the group, and to everyone he brings to the island in the future, to make a courtesy donation to the school or the Hawaii Wildlife Center. Because of the concert, that will be a plausible cover for them to be on the island. Next, you get approved for an off-campus independent study project on Wednesday mornings and whenever you need time off, and I get permission to use school time to keep this all organized."

"That's a lot to take in, but it sounds like it would work. We'd still have you for English class, though, wouldn't we?" She looked at Koa, who smiled.

"Of course, always the best part of my day. And after Saturday I'll make sure Koa has flexibility with his schedule, too, beyond just Wednesday and Saturday mornings."

"This is amazing, Ms. Reynolds. I hope I can keep up."

"I hope so too, but the minute you need a break, just let me know. I'll understand, and so will Slide."

"Thanks, Ms. Reynolds."

"My goodness, Mahina. Who would have thought? You've already done what thousands of lobbyists have been unable to do. You've changed the direction of the biggest oil company in the world!"

"I'm not so sure it was me, Ms. Reynolds."

"I know what you're saying, Mahina. But your dreams are a dream we all have inside us. We just haven't recognized them yet. You're helping the world to do that. Oops, somebody is trying to get in here. Got to go!" She heard a toilet flush, then the line went dead.

Chapter Thirty-Six

Water Use Banned For Lawns in California, Other States Follow Suit

Leading Plastic Manufacturer To Make Biodegradable Products Only

Biggest Chemical Companies Cut Pesticide Production, Invest in Organic Alternatives

Large Agro-farm Corporation Goes Organic, Opens Mulch Production Facilities Nationwide

Hawaii Energy Company Pledges 100% Renewable In Two Years

Airline Pledges Use of Electric Planes For All Short Flights, Raise Prices for Carbon Offset

Tech Company Giants Band Together To Fund Carbon Removal Systems

Auto Giant Announces New Battery That Doesn't Require Mining of Rare Minerals

Gas Leaf Blowers and Weed Trimmers Banned By European Union, US to Follow

High-Rise Developer Funds Rooftop Gardens For Every Building in London and New York

"Wow," Mahina said. She, Koa, and Ms. Reynolds were looking at the printout of all the recent headlines and articles in Mr. Kinkle's office.

"It's nothing short of a revolution, and we can trace each one of these back to flying sessions with you, Mahina," said Mr. Kinkle.

"And for Mahina's Tutu's sake," said Koa, "we better hope nobody else traces them to us. Uh, oh. Speaking of which, here's something that just popped up on my Google alerts: 'Top executives now supporting climate change mitigation efforts all recently vacationed in Hawaii.'"

"That was a *headline* somewhere?" asked Ms. Reynolds, worried.

"A paparazzi page. Someone in London," said Koa, staring at his phone.

"That's worrisome," said Mr. Kinkle.

"I'm talking to Slide this afternoon," said Ms. Reynolds. "I'll emphasize again how careful we have to be."

"I agree," said Mr. Kinkle. "Mahina, that flight with you was the most incredible experience of my life, and I'll be grateful forever for it, but if the media gets wind of this, watch out. They'll sensationalize it for clicks and follows, and the fallout won't be pretty."

She groaned. The world finding out, it just couldn't happen! Tutu was going through a lot of changes right now, and the last thing she needed was her worst fear to come true—massive numbers of people clambering to enter the ranch before she was ready for them.

Mahina looked at the printout again. No doubt they were turning the tide, but as she snuck more and more executives into the cavern, Tutu's nightmares seemed to be getting worse, and Mahina's own health was declining to the point that she was losing weight and battling daily migraines that left her exhausted with dark circles under her eyes.

Although she was sure the garden was the only thing keeping her and Tutu going, even that was losing its effectiveness. If the paparazzi started stalking them and her "clients" at the ranch, the stress would be a disaster for both of them.

"Maybe we've done enough," she said. "Maybe I need a break. I feel horrible. The nurse says I'm anemic even though we've been having beef and beet greens practically every night." Mr. Kinkle nodded with concern and glanced at Ms. Reynolds.

"Anytime," said Ms. Reynolds. "We promised you that."

"But Slide is coming tomorrow with another batch of people, the ones he has been working on for so long," Mahina said.

"They're grownups. They'll deal with it if you can't do it," said Ms. Reynolds.

She nodded. But she knew the foundation executives coming from Seattle were among the richest and most influential people on earth, and her best chance to make her biggest impact yet. They may never decide to come again if she cancels. She looked out the window at the section of the beautiful sloping outline of Mauna Kea visible from the window of Mr. Kinkle's office and thought about the world and how much it needed her. A quote came into her mind, "With great responsibility comes great sacrifice." She didn't remember where she had read that, but it made a lot of sense to her.

She hesitated, then said, "I can do tomorrow, but then I really need to rest."

"Okay, if you're sure, because we need to be extra careful now," said Koa. "I've been looking at this celebrity website that follows Slide while we've been talking. Their reporters are ruthless at sniffing out a story."

"I'll contact Slide," said Ms. Reynolds, "and tell them I will pick them up at the back door of the resort myself tomorrow. Even the paparazzi won't expect him to tool around in an old Prius."

"Tell him to leave his hat at the condo—it's too recognizable," said Mr. Kinkle, who then rose. "Thank you. We're out of time. If you change your mind, Mahina, that's okay. You all need to get back to your classes, and remember, this meeting was to discuss the dedication celebration for the new classroom building when it gets finished. People are always curious about what goes on in here. I sometimes feel like I'm hounded by the paparazzi myself!"

"Got it, Chief. Thanks," said Ms. Reynolds. "Come on, you guys. Let's go finish those birdhouses."

The next morning rolled around with Mahina leaving on the bus after chores as usual, except this time Tutu was running a fever after a bout of horrible nightmares, so Mahina had to feed the pigs and the horses too, not just the chickens.

Despite three cups of coffee at breakfast, Mahina's head was splitting when she finally made it to the bus. When she left campus to meet Ms. Reynolds and the executives at the skateboard park, she could barely walk. *How am I ever going to do this today?* she wondered. Sacrifices were one thing, but she felt like she was *dying.* She leaned up against the tree and pulled out her cell phone. "I'm ready," she said.

The Prius pulled up silently, and she slipped into the back seat with Slide and an older man with droopy red eyes and a lot of wrinkles. His face looked familiar, but she had learned it wasn't helpful to be starstruck by the people she was meeting lately. After all, they would be stars to her only after they did the right thing for the environment and for the children's future.

It was a little squished in the Prius. This was the first time a woman was coming to fly, aside from Ms. Reynolds. On the way to the ranch, it became obvious that she was the wife of the wrinkled man, even though she looked much younger than him.

Slide and Ms. Reynolds kept up the usual banter about Hawaii, Mauna Kea, and the cattle industry. She was grateful that she could just rest and close her eyes as they drove back toward her ranch.

The day was sunny and only mildly windy, and the routine started off as usual. She thought she might have to help her "clients" float early in the lava tube as she did for Slide and Mr. Smith, but the husband and wife team were sprier than she expected.

In fact, she was the only one who stumbled a few times making her headlamp beam gyrate wildly against the lava tube walls. Each time she did, she had to take a few deep breaths to gather enough energy to go on.

Help me, Mother, with this one, she pleaded silently. *Give me the reserves to pay the price.*

Once they finally reached the cavern, the light streaming from above reenergized her as it always did. With glowing hands, she taught the couple to fly, and they soon emerged one at a time through the hole in the ceiling into the heart of the upcountry morning. The sky was clear, and the air was warm and fragrant.

Mahina checked extra carefully for trespassers on the ground, but there were none. She headed northeast as usual, with the couple following her and exalting in the experience of freedom and flight, as everyone always did. Gamboling flyers, one and all.

At the far end of the ranch just before turning back, a high-pitched buzzing sound reached her ears. Mosquitos?

"That's a drone!" shouted her client. He pointed. "Over there!"

She saw the white-bodied contraption. It was just like the ones obnoxious tourists liked to fly up and down the beaches even though they were strictly forbidden.

"Crap! We've got to go!" she said. "Follow me!" She headed back, hoping the thing hadn't spotted them yet, but it was too late. The drone's buzzing got louder, and soon it circled them, obviously very interested in what they were doing and undoubtedly recording everything.

It was too late to land and pretend they were on a hike. She turned and tried to chase the drone and maybe kick it out of the sky, but it was nimble and avoided her foot easily. No doubt the jerk controlling the thing was an expert hiding somewhere nearby, working the controls with sweaty hands.

"Stick near me, be quiet, and lower yourself to the ground when I do!" she said when they got close to the road. She landed them just on the other side of the eucalyptus hill, where Slide was waiting for them. Mahina was the only one to stumble and fall over. She looked up from the ground to see the drone hovering twenty feet above them.

"Slide! Get us out of here!" she yelled, and Slide, seeing the drone, pulled out his cell phone and gestured to the couple. She jumped up quickly and, feeling faint, followed them around the trees and onto the path leading to the fence.

Just when they were all under the wire, and Ms. Reynolds was speeding toward them with the Prius, a young man with a neatly cropped beard popped up from the grass in the ditch and ran at them, snapping photos with a professional-looking camera. A control box with a joystick swung wildly from his neck. "My, my, and who do we have here?" he said, stopping about ten feet away.

"Get your snooping paparazzo ass away from me!" growled Slide. The clients were covering their faces with their hands.

"Now, now, Slide, nothing wrong with me taking a little walk on this beautiful road, is there? It's a free country, right? You like it here, and it seems a lot of your friends do too lately, and now I know why!"

"You don't know anything. Go home, you idiot!" said Slide. "Leave us alone."

"Oh, I will, Slide, just as you ask, you and your shy friends. But you're wrong that I don't know anything. In fact, I know who *all* of you are, and I know what you've been doing, and it's truly remarkable, I must say" he said, patting his drone controller.

The Prius pulled up and Ms. Reynolds jumped out with a worried frown on her face. "Oh, I see you have to *fly*. Your ride's here. Don't let me keep you. Wonderful to see you again, Slide. Ta-ta!"

Mahina watched the man run away, then black dizziness overwhelmed her. She sank to her knees and crumpled flat onto the ground.

Chapter Thirty-Seven

Mahina opened her eyes and saw the afternoon sky through the tomato vines. She remembered being carried into the Prius then arguing with Slide and Ms. Reynolds at the gate before convincing them she could walk by herself down the driveway. Blacking out like that was scary. Would doing any more of this make her black out forever? She headed straight for the garden.

As usual, digging her hands into the soil made her feel better, but not very much this time. She fell asleep in the taro. When she awoke, she forced herself to sit up, and she recalled with cold dread the disastrous run-in with the paparazzo.

She knew she needed to go inside and open her computer to try to do something before their gate was mobbed by curious people. "Tutu, I am so sorry," she said to the soil. Her whole body felt chilled, but at least she had gained enough mana now to drag herself across the yard and into the house.

Tutu was in the kitchen and stared at her in dismay. "Look at you! I don't know what you do these mornings when the kids come to the garden, but it can't be anything good. You always come back looking like something Olina dragged in."

Mahina staggered to the kitchen table and leaned over it with her hands holding her up. "Tutu, I don't feel very well. I'm really chilled. I think I have a fever."

Tutu came and put her hand on her forehead. "Goodness, child. You're burning up!"

"I did something bad, Tutu. Something even the garden can't make me feel better about."

"I saw you lie down hours ago. I got all the kids to lie down there today, so I left you alone to catch their mana. I should have checked on you earlier. What bad thing? Sit down, dear, before you fall over!"

You can tell her now. It's her time.

She slumped in a chair. "People, Tutu. I've been bringing people to the ranch."

"Oh, child, I told you Ms. Reynolds meant nothing bad. She can come back anytime, although ..."

Mahina stared at Tutu and then lowered her eyes.

"Oh, you mean *other* people." Tutu sat down next to her.

"Lots of other people. Important people. The biggest people in the world. To the cave, to the sacred cavern, Tutu, to meet Mom, to ... fly."

Tutu put her hands on her face and dropped her head for a long moment. Then Tutu looked at her and said, "Like in your dreams. This has been going on for a while, hasn't it?"

"Almost two months." Mahina felt like she might pass out again.

"Ever since my nightmares started up again. I should have known. You're trying to do something all on your own, like Hana." She reached out to touch Mahina's forehead.

"I'm sorry, Tutu."

"No, Mahina, *I'm* the one who should be sorry, but now's not the time to explain. You're burning up. Best you get up to bed. I feel so ashamed. I'll bring you a pitcher of ice-cold water."

"Tutu, someone saw us, someone bad."

"I see."

"I have a cell phone that Koa gave me. It connects to my computer. I need to get on it and call him when I get upstairs. He might know what to do."

"I don't know how you can do anything right now in the condition you're in, Koa's help or not, but I guess you must do what you must do. It's too late to stop you, and maybe I shouldn't. Do you need help up the stairs?"

"No, Tutu. Sorry, but I think you should go and lock the gate."

Tutu left, and Mahina struggled up the stairs, leaning heavily on the banister. Her head felt like it was in a vice, and painful shivers were racking her body with every step. In her room, she fished out her laptop from her backpack and turned it on, then took out her cell phone to call Koa.

There were three texts from him: "What happened? Uh oh, bad video! Call me!!!"

She opened her computer and dialed Koa on her cell phone.

He picked up on the first ring. "Hey, Mahina, what happened? Ms. Reynolds texted there was paparazzi!"

"Yes," she said. "It was a disaster, a drone. It got footage of us in the air, I think."

"It sure did. It's all over the internet."

Mahina punched in 'Slide Pickens, Hawaii Island,' and it came right up, along with old videos from the concert. There they were, shots of them next to the fence, a bouncy sequence of her and the rich philanthropists from Seattle flying urgently through the air with Mauna Kea looming in the background.

"Ugh," she said, "I see it." Her heart sunk in her chest. "What are we going to do?"

"I'm working on that with Slide and Mr. Kinkle. They said we could publish a statement saying the video is a fake generated by AI, but they think it's best to just wait for now and see what happens. Slide says things like this fizzle out in a few days as people move on to other gossip."

"Meanwhile, the ranch is a target," she said, with deep regret.

He sighed. "Yeah, I'm afraid that's probably true. I could get Dad to bring me out there to watch the gate and patrol the fence line if you want, but that would mean telling him."

"Go ahead. That would be great. He's going to see it online soon anyway, or someone is sure to tell him. Same with Tutu, so I had to tell her this morning."

"That sucks. Sorry, Mahina. This is just what you didn't want to happen! Wait, I'm getting a new alert. Listen to this: '*The Star* has learned that a thirteen-year-old student at Po'okela Academy, the same precocious minor who organized a concert fundraiser for the school after last year's Hurricane Byron, might be behind recent celebrity donations all over the island.'"

"They probably know my name but can't publish it because I'm underage. That happened during the concert too, although a lot of reporters did anyway."

"Probably. Wait, here's another one: 'This "I can fly" video is clearly a fake and a scam to somehow attract more donors to the school, or else a cheap promotional stunt to bolster Slide's stagnating career. The Slide-n-Rider himself actually flying? Give me a break!' That was a post from a guy named 'Zippy Fraud Finder.'"

"I see it," she said, typing in his name. "Here's someone's response: 'Not a fraud. My boss went to Hawaii recently, and now our company is going 100% carbon neutral.'" She scanned her feed as fast as her splitting headache would allow her to.

"Found another one," Koa said. "'*Top Dog Watch* reports every executive now implementing major climate change reforms visited the Hawaii Island within the last two months. What's the connection?'"

"How did they find *that* out?"

"I don't know, Mahina. These paparazzi have informants in all the high places, I guess."

"I better go, Koa. I feel sick, and I don't think Tutu is going to feel any better if a crowd of people starts pounding on the door."

"I hear you. I'll be out with Dad as soon as I can. Keep your cell phone handy."

"Will do," she said.

As soon as she hung up, Tutu knocked and came in, holding Olina in her arms. Olina struggled to get loose and ran under her bed. "Olina's upset with all the people out by the gate. I locked it just in time."

"I'm upset, too, Tutu. Sorry."

"They were shouting at me about some video."

"Flying, I told you. It's a video of me flying, Tutu. That's my power, just like Mom's power was to change the weather, and yours is to find the truth and be strong. I didn't want to tell you about it because I can only fly when I go into Mom's cavern." Her head was spinning.

Tutu sat down next to her on the bed. She reached out and touched Mahina's laptop. "My power *would* have been strength, had I not been a coward and chosen a path of weakness. Show me."

Tutu watched the whole video silently, inhaling sharply when Mahina's foot tried to kick the camera, and then shaking her head when it ended with a series of still photos of Slide's angry face.

"Why, Mahina? What's your hurricane? Why are you doing this?"

"To change people, Tutu, to save the environment before it's too late. Mom was wrong, It's not the earth that has to change. It's the people. The earth is sick, just like I'm feeling, and the world is not going to be a place any of us can live in anymore if people don't do something about it *right now*."

"And this is what you're doing? Big eyes? Showing off your power to famous people to get famous?" Tutu shook her hands in front of her face. "No, I'm sorry I said that. I didn't mean it."

"I'm not showing off, Tutu. I told you, flying *changes* people. It makes them appreciate things *the way they are*. They become friends of the earth, not selfish people exploiting the earth for money and power."

"Amazing. Your dreams showed you this?" asked Tutu quietly. Olina crawled out from under the bed and jumped up next to them. Mahina petted her gratefully.

"Tutu, we never talked about it very much, but you know that I have been flying in my dreams for years, and the flying mostly happens inside the cavern—when my dreams let me into the lava tube, that is. I was there when my feet got all bloody. It was a dream that dropped me alone in the cavern. I had to feel the way out with my pajamas on my feet. That's how I found out where the cavern is, and that's when it started."

"You could have been lost forever! *I* should have been the one taking you in there. *I* should have known the way. I should have taken Hana in there, too. It was my *duty*, and instead of using my strength to help, I used my strength to avoid learning and helping. How could I have been so stupid? How could I have ignored the truth? One can't turn back a lava flow. It's in our very blood! I should have known there was no stopping the divine Moemoea destiny, in myself or in my offspring." Tutu looked devastated.

A wave of nausea came over Mahina, and she had to lie back on her pillow, holding Olina. Finally, after a few deep breaths, it passed. "I don't understand, Tutu," she murmured.

"You're right about the cavern. Mama went into the cavern, as did my tutu. I knew it was the source of all their powers of vision. They closed the gates to the ranch and entered the cavern when they needed help or inspiration. I always stayed behind."

"You were scared, Tutu. I understand."

"No, you don't, Mahina. It was not just being afraid of going in there with them. Mama and Tutu would have protected me. I was scared of what the cavern might teach me."

"You mean about your strength?"

"No, that power came later. Dreaming about reality was my first power, girl. I foolishly tamped it down and turned it into merely physical strength, but I was the first to use dreams to be strong, not just visions and intuition. Tutu's waking visions gave her a sense of the future, and Mama's were even clearer and more dreamlike, but *my* actual dreams could reveal the *truth* about all things, and the power of that scared the living wits out of me. My mother urged me to visit the cave to develop my gift so that it wouldn't feel so unpredictable, so that I could help the world and pass down my wisdom, but as you know, I didn't. Instead, I used my dreaming power to dream myself out of dreaming."

"And you focused on the garden."

"Yes, being physically tough and working hard. But that was a waste. It was a step backward for our family, a diversion no one could argue with because growing food was important. I fooled myself into thinking communing with plants and dirt was special enough, but there are plenty of people who can sense mana in the soil and share that knowledge. I squashed in me what was truly special, a destiny of dreaming, just like yours and Hana's. So, because I didn't follow that destiny, I wasted the nurturing mana of Tutu and Mama. And then Hana on her own tried to follow her dreaming destiny and weakened and perished because of what I had not passed down to her, and now, because of Hana's weakness, you are getting sick trying to follow *your* destiny."

Tutu looked as sad as Mahina had ever seen her look. She made room for her on the bed to lie down. Olina snuggled between them, purring.

"They are saying online that the video is a fake, but it isn't, Tutu," she whispered. "When I take people into the cavern to fly, the world gets better."

"I believe you, Mahina. Unlike me, you are a true Moemoea, helping humanity and following in the footsteps of the goddess who is your mother. But each time you help someone, you get sicker, and that's my fault. You are carrying too great a burden, child, the burden of all your mother couldn't accomplish because she tried too hard, plus all I didn't accomplish because I was too afraid to try at all.

"Failure. I am the missing link. I fought Hana instead of trying to help her. Your school and that radical teacher, who I swear has part of Hana's spirit in her, have done more to support you than I have. Those people out there at the gate are my punishment and your salvation. Let them in. I deserve to lose my hiding place on this ranch. Everyone in the family but me knew the ranch loved *everyone*, not just us. I've been weak. I am so *ashamed*, so stupid ..."

"Oh, Tutu! It's not your fault. You did the best you could, what you felt was right."

Mahina reached over to hold Tutu close to her. Together they rested and listened sadly to the crowd chattering loudly out by the gate and to the occasional raised voices of Koa and Mr. Kahalc holding them back and protecting them.

Chapter Thirty-Eight

The next morning, Mahina awoke well past breakfast and chore time, but there was not one cell in her body capable of getting out of bed. Only the desperate need for a drink of water and to use the toilet gave her the motivation to swing her legs over the side and stand up for the groggy journey down the hallway.

She shivered with chills and used her hands on the walls to keep her upright. Why was it so *cold* in the house? Olina appeared under her feet and meowed for food, but it was all Mahina could do to use the bathroom and make it back to bed.

Hours passed before Tutu appeared to check her forehead. She opened her eyes to the afternoon light streaming through the window and was horrified by how Tutu looked.

Then she knew. "You had another nightmare, didn't you?" she said.

"Not a nightmare, dear. A catch-up dream, a jumble of dreams together I should have been dreaming my whole life. I've ignored the world's truths for too long. It's a terrible mess, and your fever is worse."

"The chores? Olina ...?"

"I did them, I don't know how or when, maybe in my dream, but anyway, they're done, and Olina's fed. There are still people milling out by the gate, though."

"Is it beautiful out?"

"Yes, Mahina. It's always beautiful out."

"Tutu, I feel like I am dying. Take me to the garden."

She saw Tutu's face sadden. "You should stay in bed until you feel better. I'll bring you some coffee, or some mamaki tea."

"No, Tutu, this isn't something a bed can heal. It's my head that's dying. I'm so drained. I need the earth. I need the sunshine."

I need my mom.

Frowning, Tutu helped her get into a pair of jeans and a flannel shirt. Together they hobbled down the stairs, pulled on boots, and went out to the garden. The warmth of the sun felt good on her chilled face, but this was the worst she had ever felt in her life.

Ignoring the sounds of the crowd up at the road, she found her place in the garden and lay down, exhausted from the short walk from the house. Tutu lay down next to her. Together, they buried their hands in the soil and closed their eyes, but even many minutes later, she didn't feel any better.

All she could sense from her hands was a far-off tingle, like whispered calls from a ship she really needed to be on that was sailing off into the horizon without her.

Tutu was sleeping next to her, restlessly kicking the taro plants. Suddenly she shot up and stared at Mahina. "You're right, Granddaughter. Oh, my power! I have dreamed the truth just now. It's not just a feeling. You *are* dying. You are not strong enough to do what you must do to save the world because *I* have failed you. I wanted to limit the vision of your love and the love of your mother to *my* vision. That was wrong. I must do now what I should have done long ago, instead of hiding away, blaming others for ruining everything, and condemning people who are not like us. The garden is not enough for us right now. Take me to the cavern so I can learn to fully love again. Oh, and I hope it's not too late!"

"To the cavern? Tutu, I can barely walk!"

"Too bad. Be strong! Stay there while I get Ikaika," said Tutu. "Ask Hana for help. Tell her I'm coming!" Tutu pushed herself up and disappeared into the barn.

"Help me, Mom," Mahina said to the soil, "and help your mother!"

Tutu came back with Ikaika on a bridle but no saddle. "I couldn't manage the saddle, but we can climb on her back by the lanai. Come on, Mahina. mana, now. You need to take me to her, to the real garden I should have been tending all along."

Mahina forced herself to climb the railing surrounding their lanai and slipped her leg over Ikaika's gentle back. She held the reins while Tutu climbed on behind her.

They moved slowly through the back gate, with Ikaika somehow knowing not to make a fuss this time about leaving Costco behind. Gently the horse carried them northeast toward the hill and the entrance to the lava tube.

When they got to the cement blocks, Tutu slid off the back of the horse, helped Mahina to the ground, and then removed the bridle from Ikaika's head. They watched her trot gratefully back toward the barn.

"Best horse ever," said Tutu. Mahina didn't question Tutu about setting her free.

Just being this close to the cavern already made Mahina's head feel slightly less painful, but she couldn't believe Tutu wanted to go into the lava tube with her. They didn't even have a headlamp. Only if her strength returned inside could she do this. Out here, she could hardly stand on her feet.

"Come on, Mahina, there's not much time," said Tutu.

"Why?" she said.

"Hurry! No time to explain. Because I should have been in there years ago," said Tutu, walking straight to the opening in the cement blocks and crawling inside.

As Mahina followed, she was relieved to feel a warm glow of deep-earth mana dispelling the fatigue in her body. There was Tutu, already twenty feet into the lava tube, glowing brightly enough to illuminate their way.

"I was in here last night, in my dream," Tutu shouted back over her shoulder, "following you to the cavern. It should have been the other way around."

Mahina almost had to run to keep up with her. Tutu, clearly as worn out as she was, was also moving like a person newly recharged.

But at the narrow passageway, Tutu tripped and fell. Mahina rushed to her side. "Tutu, are you okay?"

"It's my heart, Mahina. It's breaking."

"No, Tutu! We're so close. You can't give up now!"

"I'm not giving up, Granddaughter. It's just broken, and I need you to teach me to fly so I can mend it, mend my connection with you, with your power, with our purpose. Help me know your heart, so I can know mine better and help you."

Mahina took Tutu's hand and closed her eyes in concentration. "Give me strength. Help me heal this family, so we can heal the world," she whispered to her mom.

Slowly, when the time was right, and both her and Tutu's skin were glowing as brightly as they ever had before, she bent her knees beneath her and raised her feet.

Then Tutu rose with her, and Mahina gently pulled her through the narrow passageway into the cavern.

"Thank you, Mahina. I feel it now. You can let me go." Tutu looked up at the opening and gently spoke. "Oh, Hana, my sweet, sweet daughter. With the spirit and gifts of Mama and my tutu, I am finally here to apologize to you and to do what must be done."

Tutu floated toward the last of the evening light softly illuminating her upturned face.

With her voice filling the cavern and echoing off its walls, she said, "Yes, I am ready. It is my time to give what should have been given long ago to this sanctuary. I know my purpose now, my destiny.

Thank you, Hana, for calling me in my dream, for not giving up on me, for forgiving me. Oh, the power of this cavern! Oh, the light of the opening! Oh, the love! Tutu, Mom, Daughter, Granddaughter, I'm so sorry I was afraid! I went down the easy path, the wrong path, but I am ready to take my rightful place. To learn from my mistakes. To pass on the strength of truth. Take from my humbled spirit what I now freely pass along to you, our family's accumulated power, our love, our strength, our divine gift of dreaming!"

Go to her, Daughter. Hug her for me. Be happy. The circle of love is complete. The cavern is whole again. She has given us everything we need to destroy what must be destroyed and create what must be created.

Tutu slumped in the air, and Mahina willed herself upward and took her gently in her arms. Tutu's eyes were closed, but a smile was on her face. "I'm done here, Granddaughter," she whispered. "My heart is healed. Deliver me upward. Fly me through the beautiful air to the garden now. I want to feel it one last time."

Upward with a burst of light Mahina rose, holding Tutu in her arms. Would anybody from the road see them erupting from the hilltop? Maybe, but it didn't matter. Theirs was the ultimate power of creation and joy. The ranch was everyone's now. Understanding was on the horizon. The clouds were lava-red with the setting sun.

The wind blew Tutu's hair into Mahina's eyes as she flew over the cow path until they passed over Ikaika grazing peacefully by the back gate. Circling low around the house, Mahina headed toward the garden that spread majestically below her in a crimson glow.

Gently, oh so gently, she descended to the ground and laid Tutu once again on her favorite napping spot.

"Oh, look, Mahina! It's more beautiful than ever!" whispered Tutu, hugging the ground.

Those were the last words Mahina ever heard her speak.

Chapter Thirty-Nine

Mahina decided to hold Tutu's memorial service in the garden, of course, on a Sunday morning with the barn in the background and Olina inside under the couch hiding from the parade of neighbors bringing food into the kitchen and living room.

The Oahu Moemoeas—a large contingent of aunts, uncles, and cousins she had never met—came mostly because they wanted to see for themselves what the fuss on the internet was all about and to rub elbows with Slide. Mahina enjoyed their loving stories about Tutu's mother and Tutu, both of whom had influenced their lives greatly despite the distance between the islands. But none of them would go so far as to move to the ranch to finish raising Mahina.

There were songs and chants, prayers and speeches. Mr. Kealoha spoke tearfully about being their neighbor and about how much Tutu loved the ranch and helped others as much as they helped her despite all her responsibilities. They promised Mahina that they would take care of the cattle for her until she was old enough to do it herself. She was grateful for that but insisted on still doing the chores and feeding Ikaika and Costco.

Ms. Reynolds, though, was the real hero, arranging to take custody of Mahina and moving into the guest bedroom downstairs so Mahina would never have to move away from the ranch.

When the service was over, and people who had driven from the airport and from all over the island walked back to their vehicles parked up and down the road, Mahina asked the Kahales, the Kealohas, Mr. Kinkle, and Slide, to help her scatter Tutu's ashes in the garden.

"There's no better resting place for her than here," she said, passing the urn to each of them. "Every piece of food from this garden, nourished by her even in death, will carry her love to the world."

The ashes were watered into the ground by their tears, none more than Mahina's, who knew the depth of the sacrifice and compromise the garden had been for Tutu.

When the ashes were scattered, and the urn was buried in the corner of the garden closest to the cavern, she led them on the short hike to the entrance of the lava tube.

As Koa passed out headlamps for all of them, she said, "This is how I want you to remember her. Her heart was in the garden, but her soul had its home here with her daughter, Hana, my mother, and Kiawe, my father.

When you fly from the sacred cavern today, you will be flying with their spirits and with Tutu's. You will feel their love for you and for the earth that is our real mother."

Mahina turned to walk into the lava tube, her home.

Koa quickly followed and caught up to her inside as she waited for everyone to gather and test their headlamps.

"Mahina, are you sure you have the energy for this?" he asked. "You've never done this before for so many people at once."

"I will never tire again, Koa. That was the gift Tutu passed down to me and what I eventually will pass down to my daughter. I will *grow* in mana from this because Tutu finally learned that she is a true Moemoea, a person who gives to others."

"I love you, Mahina," said Koa.

"If I jokingly answer you 'in your dreams,' you'll know just how much that means I love you, too, Koa."

It was a bit crowded, but Koa's younger sister and the Kealoha children kept things upbeat by oohing and aahing at each turn on the way through the passageway to the cavern. Mahina could feel her mom's spirit feeding on the mana of the children and on the hope everyone held in their hearts for the manifesting purpose of the cavern.

When they all emerged from the narrows, they gathered in a circle under the afternoon light still strong enough to make the walls of the cavern glow.

Mahina asked for a moment of quiet, then she concentrated and lifted each person, one at a time, into the air with her glowing hand. Joyful chattering of children and appropriate expressions of awe echoed off the walls.

When they floated out into the beauty of the fading day, she was certain there would be photographers on the road training their powerful lenses on them and sending drones to record their flight.

She didn't care anymore. She was glad they were there. There would be plenty of time now to turn the extraordinary into the ordinary for them and for uncovering once more the magnificence of the everyday.

Slide laughed and shouted, "This is more fun than any song I have ever written! Or maybe it's the same, I guess!"

"Yes, Slide. It's the same. It's *all* the same!" Mahina shouted. "Come on, kids! Follow me!"

This time, she led them across the road toward Mauna Kea. They passed over hundreds of cattle and cowboys on horses, who stopped to wave at them. They flew over and around ohia trees in small groves that were spared from the clear-cutting long ago, and then up the flank of the mountain until they were high enough to see all of Mahina's ranch and all of the land stretching west to the Kohala coast and northwest to the magnificent valleys of Waipio and Waimanu.

"It's the most beautiful experience of my life!" said Mr. Kahale.

"I told you it was, Dad," said Koa.

She smiled. *Family ties are the strongest ties there are, except maybe to the earth,* she thought.

As the sun set spectacularly over the ocean, she led her flying flock of happy humans back to the ranch for a soft landing in the garden in honor, once again, of Tutu.

Knowing her ashes were there and not having Tutu with her on the flight with her beautiful friends made Mahina sad. But it made her happy at the same time, as life, with all its problems and complexities, should always do. “I like problems and complexities. Let’s solve them!” she said out loud to the garden. Koa looked at her strangely but seemed to understand.

The morning after the ceremony, it was different to get up to do the chores and make coffee and breakfast for Ms. Reynolds, instead of eating breakfast by herself or with Tutu, but feeding Olina when she meowed impatiently was the same. Olina had slept right up against her head all night long, as if she couldn’t get close enough no matter how hard she tried.

“I should be making your breakfast, Mahina,” said Ms. Reynolds, “but I’m not a morning person. Maybe with time, I will be.”

“Chores help. Maybe you can take over feeding the chickens?”

“I’ll do that. I’d like to. But I must tell you, if I keep having the dreams I had last night, I may never get out of bed again!”

Ms. Reynolds found a mug to fill with coffee. Mahina was happy it wasn’t Tutu’s favorite one. Maybe she would bury Tutu’s mug under the mamaki bush.

As was usually the case now, Mahina didn’t dream after taking people into the cavern, and she also didn’t feel tired from the long flight to Mauna Kea and back. Her heart filled with gratitude and love for Tutu’s gift of knowledge and strength to her.

“It was a flying dream,” continued Ms. Reynolds, after a long yawn. “I went to bed thinking how great the service was for your grandmother and how cool our flight was, and then all night long I dreamed of flying. I could fly wherever I wanted to!”

“That’s very cool,” Mahina said.

The day passed with cleaning up from the memorial service and helping Ms. Reynolds move stuff from her old house.

Koa texted shortly after breakfast: "Hey Mahina. Great service yesterday. Dreamed I was flying all night long. So did Mom, Dad, and my sister. So much fun! Call me later."

Slide texted mid-morning: "Amazing flight yesterday. Great way to remember your grandmother. Dreamed of flying last night. Even better than the real thing!"

Mr. Kealoha in the afternoon: "Hi neighbor. Will be over to help clean up and check the fences today. Dreamed I flew over them last night! I hope you are doing okay this morning."

Mr. Kinkle at dinnertime: "Wonderful service. Went to sleep and dreamed I was flying. Thank you for being you, Mahina! Aloha, Mr. Kinkle."

At the end of the day, she rode Ikaika to the top of the cavern.

"Oh, Mom," she said, kneeling by the opening as Tutu had done, "I understand now the other gift Tutu passed on to me for the world besides her mana. I may be the master of flying, but she was truly the master of dreaming. Thank you for forgiving her."

Chapter Forty

That night, Mahina snuggled closely to Olina and dreamed ...

I WALK, AS I ALWAYS do in the early morning, to the gate to open it for the people. I won't let anyone else do that chore. It is mine to welcome all the people of this island that is the earth. The crowd, with faces of all colors, streams down the driveway, chattering and excited, as they should be. They register in the barn museum, where Koa and our teenage daughter give them headlamps and take them on a tour of the displays of all the projects inspired by the cavern to help the planet over the years. A huge portrait of Tutu hangs over the main door, as well as ones of Slide Pickens, Ms. Reynolds, Koa, Ikaika, Costco, and Olina.

The cow path is paved to ease the walk from the barn to the entrance to the lava tube. Inside there are steps and railings, and a string of solar-powered lights along the handicapped-accessible walkway. Only at the wet narrows do the people need to travel single file.

I lead them with the same enthusiasm and awe as the first time Koa and I explored here so many years ago. Would it matter what I do for a career, this or some other thing? No, life is always the way it is now: amazing. But *this* is my Moemoea destiny, my adventure—to connect with people and help them connect with life and the earth. I will never be lonely again.

Each flight is different but also the same. Each person is different and has their own way to discover how to help, how to grow, and what to leave behind. Yet we are all earth's children, and she feeds us and takes care of us because she loves us.

Here, people learn to love her back.

That's the magic of the sacred cavern, the legacy of my family's destiny and duty. They leave here knowing how to fly while they live—and whenever they close their eyes, to dream of flying as the earth dreams of paradise for all its living creatures.

On my flight to the mountain, I look down at my magnificent daughter, laughing with her friends in the garden. What power will she have when she grows up? I don't know, but it will probably be greater than mine, and I'm okay with that.

More importantly, I know that she will need my courage and support on this earth to discover the fire in her Moemoea heart with clarity, purpose, and love.

Glossary

Names:

Hana—work

Ikaika—strong

Kiawe—mesquite tree, common in Hawaii

Koa—a strong tree native to Hawaii

Moemoeā—dreamer

Mahina—moon

'Olina—joyous

Pele—the goddess of fire and volcanoes, both destroying and creating land

Tūtū—grandmother

PLACES:

Ahupua'a—a district shaped like a pizza slice from the mountains to the ocean

'Āina—land

Haleakalā—volcano on Maui, visible from the west coast of the Hawai'i Island

Heiau—ancient Hawaiian monument

Hilo—a small city on the southeastern side of Hawai'i Island

Kīholo—a secluded lagoon on the Kohala Coast

Kohala Mountain—the northernmost extinct volcano on Hawai'i Island

Makai—on the ocean side

Mauka—on the mountain side

Mauna Kea—an extinct 13,803-foot volcano on Hawai'i Island

Pelekane Bay—sacred bay at the foot of Pu'ukoholā Heiea

Pololū—another deep valley on the north side of Kohala volcano

Puakō—a coastal community famous for scuba diving

Pu'ukoholā—a heiau on Kohala Coast built by King Kamehameha to unite the islands

Waimanu—yet another deep valley on the north side of Kohala volcano

Waimea—a small town between Mauna Kea and Kohala volcanoes

Waipi'o—a deep valley on Hawai'i Island's north side, part of Kohala volcano

TERMS AND EXPRESSIONS:

francolins—a type of grouse found in Hawaii

imu—fire pit for cooking meats

lānai—porch or deck

māmaki—a native Hawaiian bush with medicinal leaves used as tea

musubi—a type of rice roll made with Spam, seaweed, and sometimes egg

'ōhi'a—('ōhi'a lehua) a strong tree native to Hawaii

a hui hou—until we meet again

'aumakua—ancestors who can assume the form of animals and plants occurring in nature

chicken skin—goosebump feeling from something cool or significant happening

dakine—that kind

hamajang—all mixed up; crazy

haole—a person who is not Hawaiian, especially a white person
kupuna—elder (often associated with wisdom)
lōlō—crazy
mahalo—thank you
mana—spiritual energy and power
ohana—family
'ono—good
paniolo—Hawaiian cowboy
po'okela—excellence
talk story—having a friendly chat, usually of long duration
wahine—woman or women

Acknowledgements

There are many people to thank for giving this story wings. John Sucke, Kim Giffin, Nicole Anakalea, Eunice Saito, Christopher Sammond, Sally Lefeber, Pearl Tulay, Kolby Moser, Britt Bailey, Duncan Dempster, and Jerry Bleckel, your insightful edits and comments have made this novel so much better, and I could never have accomplished this without your encouragement and support. Thanks to the multi-talented photographer, Kolby Akamu Moser, for the cover photo of her daughter viewing the November 2022 Mauna Loa eruption. Many thanks also to my editor, Kahina Necaise of The Fabled Planet for both developmental and line editing of a quality far beyond my ability to express. Finally, this novel would have crashed and burned without the consistent and amazing support of my partner, Kate Mulligan. Thank you, Kate, for a lifetime of insights and for helping this crazy writing dream of mine to fly.

As we heal ourselves, so will we heal our planet.

Other Books By John Blossom:

.

Horse Boys
Trespassing
The Tunes of Lenore
Lenore and the Problem With Love
The Last Football Player

.

.

(If you enjoyed these works, please rate and review them on Amazon or wherever you purchase your favorite books! It *really* helps. Mahalo!)

About the Author

Mr. Blossom holds a BA degree in English from Carleton College and an MAT degree from Colorado College. Teacher and artist, Mr. Blossom concerns himself deeply with technology and environmental issues and feels there is hope to create a better world through the power of stories to change hearts and minds. He presently lives on an organic farm on the Big Island of Hawaii where he gives away fruits and vegetables and maintains an active free library at the end of his driveway. http://www.jtblossom.com

Read more at https://www.jtblossom.com.

Made in the USA
Monee, IL
15 June 2025

19326622R00152